The Covington Heights Crew

FORCE

DEANA BIRCH

Force

ISBN # 978-1-83943-755-7

©Copyright Deana Birch 2021

Cover Art by Louisa Maggio ©Copyright November 2021

Interior text design by Claire Siemaszkiewicz

Totally Bound Publishing

FORCE

Dedication

For Cora, Meka and Lily.
Your support means the world.

Chapter One

Frankie

I parked my baby-blue Porsche in my brother Leo's cobblestone driveway. He'd bought one of those huge historic homes and made everything inside modern. I thought it was flashy and a bit of a way to gloat about how much money we were making, but he'd done it to make his girls happy. Besides, who was I to judge? My apartment overlooking the East River was just as over the top.

In truth, I loved that Fiona and Violet had given Leo the shove back to putting his family first. His friend Anton had taken too much of his loyalty over the years. I was glad it was focused back where it belonged. I rang the bell for Sunday dinner with my favorite bottle of Tignanello cradled in my arms like the treasure that she was.

The door swung open, and Leo rolled his eyes. "Thank God you're here. Can you please explain to my very pregnant and very stubborn wife that she can't just hire a nanny after one Facetime because they 'bonded'." He air-quoted the last word, which was a mistake, because Fiona noticed it right away and stomped over. I had no idea how she moved so gracefully with her massive belly.

"I like her. She has a degree in early education. She'll be great for Vi and the twins. Plus, I'm the one who will be spending time with her. It's my opinion that matters."

I scanned the entryway for any signs of my Aunt Chezzie, the dog or any damn neutral ally, but found none.

Leo made way for me to enter then turned to his wife. "Fi, I'm just saying let me do a background check. It will take twenty-four hours." Calmer, and with a smile, he continued, "Then—if everything checks out—we can offer her the position."

I leaned over and gave Fiona a kiss on the cheek. "You look great. How you feeling?"

She narrowed her eyes. "Don't do that, Francis Ricci. Don't change the topic for his sake. But thank you…and I'm exhausted. Chezzie came early and took Violet to the beach, so I napped then hired a nanny." She grinned at Leo, whose nostrils flared as he reached for the bottle.

"Nice," he said as he read the label. Then, to his wife, "You gotta give me twenty-four hours. I can't let a stranger into our house—our life—without at least running her social security number. Come on." With his free hand he tucked a strand of her long, brown hair behind her ear. "It's just to keep you safe. You know that."

Fiona frowned, but Leo's soft tone had worked its charm. "Fine. But you have to promise not to be biased against something stupid like bad credit. That was me three years ago. There are people out there who just need a break." The little lift of her eyebrows and tilt of her head emphasized that she wouldn't budge on her final point. My sister-in-law was clear on many things. One, her house had to be immaculate at all times. It was how she respected the wealth she was experiencing. Two, Sunday dinners were mandatory. And three, she always remembered where she came from.

Leo cut his eyes over to me in a 'see what I'm dealing with here' glance. And I did—not that I would admit it in front of her. But we had to at least run a credit check on the new nanny.

I pointed my thumb to the door. "I have my laptop in the car. I can run her details while we eat then have a look after. You'll get your answer tonight like that."

Fiona smiled but Leo scrunched his face like he'd smelled something foul.

He shook his head down the hall to the kitchen and mumbled, "Always gotta be the hero."

It wasn't far from the truth. Since Leo and I had changed the direction of our lives, I'd gotten a lot of satisfaction from doing the right thing. But it was odd to let a talent go to waste. Not that I'd enjoyed killing people, but I was just so damn good at it. Our father had been an outstanding teacher. It was fucked up—*we* were fucked up—but there had been a perverse pride in a job well done, another unsolved murder. With our new roles of keeping people safe, the feeling wasn't the same. It was somehow status quo.

Fiona mouthed a 'thank you' and reminded me that I had work to do then quietly clapped her hands to the kitchen where she kissed her husband. His annoyed stance from before melted like chocolate on a hot day. It was pretty fucking disgusting how happy they were, especially since I'd failed—yet again—to find a spark with the last woman I'd gone on a date with. Chezzie had told me I was 'emotionally unavailable'. To me, that sounded like a bullshit label to make a man feel guilty about not wanting to talk about stupid shit. Maybe my standards were too high. I'd seen what Leo had. I wasn't sure I deserved the same thing, but I wouldn't take any less.

I let myself out and grabbed my laptop from the small trunk then settled into Leo's study. Fiona bounced in with a sheet of paper and handed it to me. "Here's everything I know about her."

There was no date of birth or social security number, just a small photo, a list of odd jobs and her education. *Yeah, little brother, I see what you're dealing with.*

But there was contact information, a current employer and an address, so at least I had something.

I faked a smile to Fiona. "I'll get started. Call me when it's time to eat."

"You're the best. I appreciate this so much." She rubbed her hand over her belly, smoothing the white sundress, then was gone in a whoosh.

Okay, Megan Walsh of small-town Iowa, let's find your secrets.

I started with social media. If she were a drunken party girl, there would be proof. But none of the Megan Walshes matched her photo or location. What twenty-something didn't want her face plastered everywhere so her friends could tell her how pretty she was?

Without a social security number, I couldn't run her credit, and finding her date of birth without some kind of hint from a public profile would require me guessing what county she'd been born in and hacking into their records—something I would have hired an expert to do. I did manage to find a picture of her apartment building, which was small and ugly. That only made her poor, but what person trying to be a nanny would be wealthy, anyway?

After about an hour, I didn't have much.

"Hey." Leo leaned into the study. "Please tell me she's a serial killer so I can be right just one damn time."

"She's not anything for the moment." I held up the piece of paper Fiona had given me and waved it. "There's not a lot here to go by."

Leo scrubbed his face. "What am I gonna do? I can't bring a stranger into our house. Shit. But dinner's ready. Let's eat."

I closed my laptop and followed him down the hall to where Chezzie and Violet were already at the table with Fiona. Leo had grilled some sausages and a massive steak. Three of Chezzie's best salads were in the middle of the table. I kissed my aunt and niece then sat opposite them.

"Uncle Frankie? Did you know that Nana's secret to making salad was to rub the bowl with garlic first?"

"I did." I winked and unfolded my napkin. I loved how Violet had blended perfectly into our family and made it her own. Chezzie had a way of highlighting all the positive sides of our past and keeping the dark secrets dead and buried where they belonged. I also appreciated the bond that my aunt had with Fiona's little sister. She'd never been able to have children, and my father had made her boyfriends uncomfortable, at best. No one had been good enough for his little sister. Leo and I hadn't been the only ones who'd suffered from his need to keep his family under his insistent thumb.

Fiona waited until everyone was served and we'd started eating before looking at me and saying, "So?"

"Sorry. Big nada for the moment. But the agency must have run a check on her, right?" I wiped my mouth and short beard with the cloth napkin.

"I think so." Fiona cringed a little and Leo pounced. "Fi, seriously?"

"I know. I'm sorry. But I liked her so much. She's young and her dream is to live in New York." Fiona's whine was chipping away at my brother before our eyes. She continued, "And I need someone. Chezzie has a business to run. Those beautiful babies we made could come any day. I don't want a snooty old lady looking down on me for how I change a diaper or swear in front of Violet. I want Megan."

Leo closed his eyes and Chezzie shot me a glance to fix it, probably because she knew I could.

"I'll fly out tomorrow. Leo, you stay close to home, and Jackson can handle the security detail solo for forty-eight hours. I will check out this Megan Walsh and report back. Happy?" I turned to Fiona and offered a small smile.

"Yes. Thank you." Fiona beamed, Chezzie changed the subject and Leo discreetly flipped me off while pretending to scratch his ear.

As soon as dinner was finished, I excused myself to go home to prepare. I booked my plane ticket for the next day. For some ridiculous reason known only to the airline gods and their intelligent fuckery of how to make air travel the least enjoyable experience possible, I had to fly south to Charlotte in order to fly west to Iowa. That meant that my entire day would be wasted. But what was I going to do? Fiona had probably the closest thing to kids in her belly that I would ever have and was doing a stellar job of raising the little girl who had captured all our hearts. That bit of family, those Sunday dinners, they were the only things keeping me affixed to happy and normal. They were my reminder that my life had changed and needed to stay on its current path. There was no way I would lose them.

* * * *

When I woke up early and took a car to the airport, I was sure I was a sucker. And yet, somehow, I was glad to do it. During my three-hour layover in Charlotte, a place that couldn't have been more random of a stop, I booked a cheap motel not far from Megan's apartment. I'd decided to be business casual, but as soon as I got off the plane in Iowa, I knew I was still too conspicuous. It was a different world.

Cargo shorts and sports T-shirts accosted my eyes. *Jesus, I'll never fit in.* I'd blended into dozens of cities around the globe over the years, but the Midwest was an entirely different playing field. I called Leo to let him know I'd landed but mostly to complain and make him feel guilty. *What else are big brothers for?* At the one open kiosk in the airport, I bought a yellow and black baseball hat and promptly planted it on my previously well-groomed head.

I got my rental car — a four-door sedan in a shade of gold that I was sure didn't belong on an automobile — or anywhere, for that matter. I had about an hour's drive north to Megan's town. The sides of the highway were peppered with massive water towers and occasional farms backlit by the setting sun. The little towns I passed through were just that — little and gone in a blink. It was a completely different world, and I'd never felt so out of place.

At the motel, a middle-aged woman greeted me with a massive smile from behind the counter. Right... People were genuinely friendly — also new and foreign. I gave her my reservation number and she pulled it up on her screen as I got out my wallet.

"What brings you out to these parts, Mr. Ferris?" She glanced at my fake ID from Florida without suspicion.

"Work." I tucked the ID back into its spot then waited with a tight smile that begged her not to pry further.

After a good night's sleep with the occasional disturbance of an animal sound and not the restful hum of city traffic, I drove over to Megan's apartment complex and parked on the street. The address said she was number one, which meant she had the corner unit. I rolled down the windows of the sedan, and the oppressive Midwest humidity settled in like a swamp. I brought my phone to my ear and pretended to be making a call while a sheriff's cruiser pulled into the parking lot.

A petite brunette came out of the unit and locked her front door, checking the handle twice. That meant either OCD or nerves. *Noted.* She spun around and took a long blink when she spotted the cop. From inside his car, he pointed to his wristwatch and tapped twice before driving off.

What the hell?

The woman, who I was pretty sure was Megan, hurried to her car and climbed in. It made a horrible noise when she cranked the engine. I followed her to a mall, which was where she worked at a shoe store, and she rushed in.

It was exactly ten a.m. — interesting that she would wait until the last minute. I would have been fifteen minutes early. Then again, how many people are waiting to buy shoes first thing in the morning?

There was a huge department store attached to the mall and I went in to get a new wardrobe. In the public bathroom, I changed into khaki shorts, a plain cotton white V-neck and flip-flops. I stored my old clothes in the car and put on my new baseball hat for good measure.

I grabbed a soda from a pizza place—because I noticed everyone else was shopping with them—and headed to Burt's Shoe Showroom. Megan was at the register checking her phone, and her dark hair covered her face. I meandered by the running shoes, sipping on my drink and examining random models.

Megan whimpered then tucked her phone into her back pocket before heading in my direction. I kept my eyes forward on the display until she said, "Anything I can help you with?" Her voice was sweet. *Lord...* It was so genuine that it took me off guard.

I looked over and was met with two beautiful green sparkling eyes. In the small picture, it was obvious that she was pretty, but up close? She was fucking beautiful—light skin with a little powdering of freckles, zero makeup and high cheekbones. I didn't even know how to take her in. Her lips were the perfect shade of pink and had a slight pout. *Damn.*

"Sir?"

"I—" How was I at a loss for words? I was a grown man—a grown man staring at his brother's potential nanny. I blinked hard. It was apparently the only thing I could do.

"Are you a runner?" she tried.

I managed to find a story somewhere. "Thinking of taking it up. What about you? You run?"

She let out a nervous laugh then blinked. "Is that an East Coast accent?"

"Yeah. In town for work."

"Buying running shoes?" She lifted her eyebrows. *Fuck.*

Chapter Two

Megan

Heat crawled up my back and spread over my neck while my heart sank to my stomach. Fiona Ricci had said she would offer me the job through the agency two days prior, and I still hadn't heard a peep. An aching in my gut had told me something was wrong, and I was pretty sure the proof was standing in front of me. It was too much of a coincidence that a random customer would have that accent. And kudos to Fiona — her husband was the kind of man who belonged in one of those cologne ads with his shirt halfway open.

He narrowed his deep, dark eyes.

Shit. If he'd come all this way, he would find out all about me, and I would never get the nanny job. I'd had my posting on the job site for three months, and Fiona had been the first to bite. My contact at the agency said it was my lack of experience, but I was sure it was my shit luck and ill-fated destiny. I would be selling shoes until I died. And, if I didn't get out of the small town where I had no power and zero resources, my death would be sooner than later. My lips quivered and he clocked it.

I closed my eyes and cursed hope. What a fool I'd been to think I could just relocate and get a job without exposing my stupid life. But if this man were here to check me out, I would need to make the most of the opportunity I had. Maybe, just maybe there was a chance. Best to make a good impression... *It may be my only shot.*

With a cheery smile, I said, "Sorry. None of my business. What are you? An eleven?" I glanced down. His toenails were clipped, and the cuticles were pushed back. For someone who'd been wearing flip-flops in the country, there was no hint of dirt. Everything was normal and clean. A wave of relief flushed over me. I'd seen a lot of mangled feet, and having them in my face all day had given me a certain respect for when things were all in place and tidy.

"Exactly." The little worry lines around his eyes crinkled, then he chose a shoe from the display wall. "I'll try this one."

"Sure." I hurried to the storeroom and, in the small bathroom off to the side, I splashed cold water on my face. Maybe I was imagining the entire thing. Maybe it was just a dude with an accent. I had been so obsessed about getting the job with Fiona and her family that I was making mountains out of mole hills. I found the shoes and plastered a smile across my face then went back to where he was seated on the orange leather circle in the middle of the store.

I knelt in front of him and started lacing the shoes. He pulled his lips inward, his gaze steady. *Is he checking me out?* Oh, this could be horrible or wonderful, depending on who he really was. I shook off the shiver that threatened at the base of my spine then reached for the disposable nylon socks from the box under his seat and offered him two.

He turned up his nose. "Do you have regular socks?"

"To borrow?" *Gross.*

"No, just get me a pack and I'll buy them after. I'm not putting those on my feet." He added a small snarl to the nylons, and I'd never imagined something so small could be so offensive.

I pushed on my knees and walked over to the counter, where I grabbed a packet of sport socks then went back. "These better?"

"Perfect." He took the package, and while he opened it, I studied him. Surely, he had to be related to Fiona Ricci somehow. Men like him—composed, sophisticated—didn't buy running shoes first thing in the morning. And they certainly didn't come to do so in the crappy mall where I worked.

New approach.

"How long you in town for?"

Mr. Tall, Dark and Out-of-Place slid his socked foot into the running shoe. His arms were defined but not bulky and his back stretched the T-shirt exposing small mounds of muscles. His dark hair had small hints of gray and he had a short, well-groomed beard. In fact, every inch of him was perfectly in place. He even smelled fantastic—like some kind of citrus with a light spice, nothing like the supermarket body spray the guys I knew bathed in. His confident energy was slightly off-putting but drawing me in with curiosity.

He stood, rocked back and forth in the shoe, ignoring my question until he said, "Just long enough to figure out what that sheriff car was doing in your driveway this morning."

I let out a small gasp.

He held out his hand. "Frank Ricci. I believe you had a Facetime with my sister-in-law." My face fell. Although I'd been right about his identity, I hadn't counted on him being my second stalker.

A flush of heat burned on my neck. Good news — he wasn't my new boss. Bad news — once he found out about Billy Johnston and my measly life, I wasn't going to get a new boss. Still, I had to try.

"You flew all the way to Iowa to check me out? I passed all the security questions on the agency's website. They obviously feel I'm well-qualified." I put my hands on my hips, but the little squeak in my voice didn't help my show of confidence.

"That agency runs a standard background check that only shows if you have any felonies. Then they take their cut and wipe their hands of you. I know, I read the fine print on my flight."

And that had been precisely why I'd chosen that agency. They didn't have a bad reputation. They were just less thorough than others. Also, they came up first on the Internet when someone searched for a live-in nanny.

I bit my thumbnail then quickly stuffed my hands into my back pockets and let out a long breath. "Billy Johnston is the sheriff's son. He likes to keep tabs on me."

After a slight blink of the eye — maybe he appreciated my honesty — he asked, "And why is that?"

"Beats me." I shrugged and pointed to his feet. "Are you going to buy those? I'm on the clock here."

He raked his gaze over me, not impressed either with my answer or by me. *Probably both.* "I'll take them, and I'll leave you to your job. Can you meet me for dinner? I'd like to wrap this up and fly back tomorrow." Frank raised his thick eyebrows.

"Um…" My pulse raced. There was no way I could have dinner with him. Someone would tell Billy then he would figure out a way to get to the bottom of it. I couldn't risk him knowing I was going to leave town.

A young woman walked into the store pushing a stroller, and her presence meant all personal conversation would end. *Phew.*

I went back to my cheery salesperson tone. "You going to wear those out? If so, there's no refund."

He rubbed his lips back and forth, obviously in no hurry to answer. There was a whole lot of intensity in him that had been hidden until that moment. "Sorry. I should be clear. It wouldn't be a date. Consider it an in-person interview."

"Why would I think it was a date?" I swiped the box and the sock package and headed for the counter while he put on the other shoe. A cold sweat dripped down my spine underneath the beige polo shirt that was my work uniform. *Chill.* I needed to chill. It was just an interview. He hadn't gotten one glimpse of me and reported back with a no. Also, small round of applause for my instincts—they'd been right about him.

When I looked up, he was opposite me. *How did he get here so fast?* "Cash or credit?"

"Cash."

I scanned the bar code. "Do you want this?" I pointed to the box.

"Can we meet or not?"

"Uhh-h…" *No.* But I had to.

He studied me for a beat, glanced away then back. After a mumbled curse and something about Fiona, he said, "Where can you meet me that's safe?"

The intensity in his eyes had switched to kindness, and it occurred to me that he might want to help me.

"There's Mass at the Catholic church two towns over tomorrow night. The priest will let me use his office. I go every Sunday and Wednesday. It's part of my schedule."

Frank reached for a pen and took a random business card from the little stand next to the register where people were allowed to advertise their services of coaching or personal training. He wrote something on the back then returned the pen to the round container.

"This is my number. Call me if you can't make it." I stared at the card while he counted out the two-hundred dollars he owed for the socks and shoes. He'd written his name as 'Frankie' not 'Frank'. I didn't know what it meant but wanted to imagine that it signified something.

"His dad is the sheriff," I whispered.

"You mentioned that." It was almost as if he'd shrugged.

I took the money and put it in the register. "That doesn't scare you?"

He closed his eyes and shook his head. When he opened them again, there was a warm smile on his tanned cheeks. "No, Megan, that does not scare me." He tapped his hand on the card before walking out.

"You forgot your flops!"

He waved over his shoulder. "Trash them."

I stood behind the counter, stunned, for what must have been fifteen minutes until I realized his flip-flops were still on the floor and the woman with the stroller had long left.

One thing was sure. I wouldn't let hope creep back up and get a hold of my heart again. If it happened, once I was safe and in a new location, only then I would let my guard down just for a minute to be thankful. Nothing was set in stone. There wasn't even a plan of action. But for someone who had been wary of strangers for years, I had faith that at the very least Frankie would meet me at the church. Maybe I was too much of a risk and I wouldn't get the job, but at least I would have the sympathetic ear of an outsider for an hour or so.

I ate dinner at the mall with Frankie's number hidden between my phone and its case. So many times I was tempted to write a message either to thank him or make sure it was real. But the short-lived reward never suited the long game. I had to keep my eye on the ultimate prize.

At home, Billy's truck was parked on my street, and he got out of it the minute he saw me pull into the parking lot. The secret business card had somehow given me a boost of confidence that I needed to suppress. Billy would smell that out like a gun dog retrieving pheasants.

"Where you been?" He charged at me, and his sour beer breath hit me like a putrid slap.

I smiled anyway, always ready to deflect. "I couldn't take it. I smelled that pepperoni deep dish all dang day. I broke down and bought myself a slice for dinner."

"Whatever. You gonna tell me today?"

No. I wasn't going to tell him any day, ever.

"I have no idea what you're talking about."

He raised his hand and my heart stopped. He was going to hit me right there for everyone to see? A screen door whacked shut and startled us both.

"Meg! Is that you?"

A neighbor I had only said hello to a few times waddled over waving a small piece of paper. Janet had on a light-blue house dress with huge sunflowers all over it. When she was in front of us, she nodded her greeting to Billy then turned to me. "I missed the delivery of my medication, and now I need to get it at the post office. You know I don't drive."

Billy's stomach rumbled and my neighbor glanced over to him. "You need to eat, boy. Go on. Skedaddle." Back to me, she said, "Now if you just come inside, I can give you my ID and they should let you pick it up since we have the same address. I hate to impose, but it's urgent. You'll need to go first thing in the morning..." She put her arm around me and guided me back to her door. I shrugged my apology to Billy, who stared at me, probably wondering if I'd set the whole thing up. He knew I didn't talk to my neighbors very often. In the two months since I'd been living in the small apartment, he'd watched me go in and out almost every day.

Billy walked over to his truck in a huff, and once I was inside Janet's place, his tires squealed as he pulled away. *Crisis avoided.*

She braced herself on her dining table, which was half covered with shoe boxes containing various prescription bottles. The little exchange had been more effort than I'd seen her make in our brief interactions.

"I don't really have a delivery to pick up. But you, my dear, have a stalker. That boy's been sitting in his truck for two hours drinking beer. I see him almost every time I go out. You need to talk to his daddy and get his head straight."

My mouth went dry. It was there. That rare moment where I could have opened up, could have poured my heart out, told my story—but that wouldn't happen.

Instead, I shot my eyes to the floor and said, "He's just a concerned friend." I left and went home to crawl into bed. I took out Frankie's card and held it tight.

Chapter Three

Frankie

"You can't hire that woman." My phone sat on the floor in front of me as I did my morning push-ups. I had it on speaker and prayed that my brother hadn't done the same. His wife wouldn't like the news.

"Fuck." Leo's airy curse was more of a sigh than a word. Yeah, Fiona was going to be pissed. If she'd proven one thing since he'd put those babies in her belly, it was that she knew how to get her way, despite the consequences.

I continued to push up and down and wondered who designed carpet for hotels. I'd checked out of the original one and moved three towns over, but the décor was equally atrocious. Orange and brown should really only have been mixed in autumn leaves.

"She has a stalker. He's a deputy sheriff. Tell your wife to find a different nanny. This one is a security risk."

"What's he saying? Put him on speaker." Fiona's voice echoed through my phone. Poor Leo was toast. Although, I did take small pleasure in the fact that his wife tortured him.

"Are you sure?" Leo asked, his voice now farther away.

I held my body in a high plank position and wrinkled my nose. "What am I? New? Yes, I'm sure."

"What is he sure of? What are you sure of, Frankie? And you better be honest. No hiding shit from me." God bless Fiona and all her spite.

"She has a stalker. We can't bring that into our house. Apparently, he's a cop. Listen—"

"She has a *what*? Oh my God. That poor girl. Frankie, you have to get her out of there." My sister-in-law's plea sounded exactly like I'd expected it to.

"Fiona, I have to get *me* out of here. I need to go back to work. I need to eat food that hasn't been processed or fried." I was lying. I'd found some healthy restaurants that boasted of local produce, but I didn't mind throwing on a layer of drama.

There was a long silence on the other end of the phone, and I could only image that Fiona was giving my baby brother the ultimate stare-down. It also meant that I wasn't going to be on a plane back to my own life the next day as I'd hoped. I flipped to my side and started my side plank crunches. Just because I was missing my morning sparing sessions didn't mean I was going to take the days off. Besides, I was slightly vain and liked my washboard stomach.

"No." There was too much defeat in my brother's voice. He'd already lost, and we all knew it.

Fiona huffed. She probably had her arms crossed in a pout. "We can't leave her in the hands of a stalker."

No, we couldn't. And although I was recommending washing our hands of Megan Walsh and all her problems, from the moment I'd laid my eyes on her and had felt that little zing, I was sure I would help her. I didn't even know how.

Because the problem was, I had serious mommy issues. I'd watched my father crush the spirit of the helpless woman he'd married until the point of no return. She'd left when I was five, Leo had barely been out of diapers and she'd never come back. Over the years, I'd searched and searched, but it was as if Angelina Ricci had never existed. And so, much like how my brother had subconsciously wanted to rescue Fiona, I was sure I was about to do the same with Megan. It was like my mind and body were being propelled by a force greater than my reasoning, like I was attempting to repay a debt I'd never incurred.

I wasn't sure if Megan would end up being their nanny, but she wasn't going to finish in the hands of that blond prick who'd driven past her car in the parking lot of the mall four times the day before. The fact that he was a cop was complicating matters. If she dropped off the face of the earth, he could file a missing person's report then start digging. I would need to be smart.

"I'll handle it." I shook my head, knowing better.

"See? Frankie's gonna handle it. Thank you, Frankie. You can be the godfather of one of the twins."

Who else would be godfather? Fucking Anton? "Both of the twins." I had to make it a little hard, for Christ's sake.

"Deal." The victory in Fiona's voice was probably killing Leo. It made me smile.

The truth was that it didn't matter who Megan was. Leo and I were capable of protecting our family, no matter what. That truck-driving hick? He didn't scare me. My brother could take him out while yawning and never give it a second thought. We were cold-blooded killers. Me flying to Iowa was part of the façade that we would never slip back to our former selves, keeping up with the fantasy that we led ordinary lives.

All Leo's objections were part of a dance. We both knew it didn't matter who Megan was or wasn't. The minute Fiona had decided that was who she wanted as her nanny, the deal had been sealed. The formality of us objecting covered the underlying truths we all knew were there. Leo would give Fiona anything she wanted, and at the same time, he would stop at nothing to keep her safe. They weren't exclusive.

We liked to pretend we were normal, go through the motions—but we weren't. I alone had killed twenty-seven people, and none of them had seen me coming. Hell, I'd daydreamed about putting a knife in that cop's throat and watching him choke on his own blood, and I'd only seen him a handful of times. I liked to force myself to think that was 'old Frankie'. But Frankie was Frankie and Leo was Leo. Ricci was Ricci.

"I'll keep you posted." I reached down and disconnected the call with a small swipe of my index finger then went back to the crunches.

I showered, dressed as casually as I could, then found a drive-thru for my breakfast. In the parking lot of the mall where Megan worked, I ate while she jogged to the double doors and her stalker cruised past. She gave him a friendly wave, which was probably her way of playing nice. Once they were both gone, I made my way to the church we were meeting at later and noted all the entrances and nearby stop lights. The small-town bonus meant there weren't any cameras. I'd already decided that we would make our break for it the following Sunday during mass. A plan had formulated in my head all by itself.

From the parking lot, I called a guy I sometimes used in Northern California and asked him to set up a post office box and get me the information later that day. It would be tedious to get her mail forwarded from there to the box I used in New Jersey, but that one extra step might buy us some time if we ever needed it, because that cop was going to be pissed when the object of his obsession was gone. He wouldn't just let her fade away like a memory, especially if he was checking in on her night and day. The mystery was, why her?

After lunch, I parked my rental car eight blocks away from the church then walked through the surrounding neighborhood, pretending to be on my phone the entire time I staked it out. Every now and again I would snap a photo, never letting the phone drop from my ear. The area was mostly residential, and I didn't see any homes boasting of a security company. There were occasional 'beware of dog' signs, but no dogs barked. The summer heat must have kept them inside.

I went back to my car and planned my drive back to New York. If we stopped at major airports along the way and rented new cars from different companies — all the while using different identities — it would be pretty damn hard to track us. To be done right, it would require patience and a whole lot of being inside a car. The food would suck.

About an hour before Mass was set to begin, I entered the church. The stone building offered a nice relief from the humidity and the faint smell of rituals brought an unexpected peace.

I sat in the last pew and bowed my head. My former dirty, sinful acts replayed in my memory as a stark reminder that I didn't belong in my surroundings. There was no good deed that would justify the wickedness of my past. But damn it if the thought of getting Megan out of her current situation didn't make me at least feel like I was on a better path. I was a far cry from a hero and my motives were plainly selfish, but maybe doing good would feel a hell of a lot better than taking pride in a precise bullet hole between the eyes of a criminal. At the very least, it wouldn't be status quo.

"Need someone to talk to? I'm a pretty decent listener." A tall, middle-aged priest sat in the pew in front of me. He had warm eyes and a kind smile. I envied his ability to display both so easily.

I shook my head, there would be no true salvation for me. "I'm meeting someone in an hour. Megan Walsh? She said we could use your office."

"I'll help that girl however I can. She's had quite the go of things." His level of gravity made me wonder how bad. "Let me show you to my office. You can wait there." Maybe he sensed the unholiness of my presence in a sacred place.

I followed the priest through the vestibule and into a small office. When he gestured for me to take a seat opposite his desk, I obliged. The central air conditioning was a bit stronger in the smaller room, and it was the first time I was grateful for my suit. And even though it was light beige and I wore a white collarless shirt underneath, I still stuck out in the more casual Midwest.

The priest offered a tight smile and the wrinkles creased around his eyes. They weren't quite as deep as mine, and I wondered if it was because I'd lived a darker life. He seemed to be waiting for me to start a conversation, but I was more of an anti-education advocate. The less he knew, the better.

My phone vibrated from my inner pocket, and I excused myself while I checked the message. My contact in California had sent me the post office box where we would be transferring all Megan's mail. That was, if she would be ready to go along with my plan.

"I don't think I've seen you here before." The priest tilted his head, his tone casual. He was good at small talk.

"No, you haven't." I checked my watch. Mass was starting in thirty minutes. He must have preparations to do.

He stood and let out a long breath. "I've been praying long and hard for the Lord to deliver that girl from the sorrow around her. I don't know if that's what you are, but I can guarantee that if I can be of service, I will." With that, he nodded and exited through the door behind his desk.

"Where does that lead to?"

He stopped and tightened his eyes. "My residence. It's always open during Mass because I lock that one." He pointed to the door we'd entered from the vestibule.

"Good to know."

Fifteen minutes later there was a light knock before Megan stepped into the office and closed it quietly behind her. She wore a simple brown skirt and a white T-shirt with tan canvas tennis shoes.

She gazed over me, and a small hint of wonder danced in her stunning eyes.

"Hi." A warmth blanketed my chest. It struck me as odd but not unwelcome.

"I didn't think you would come. Actually, after twenty-four hours, I'd convinced myself you were a dream." Megan shook her head and her dark locks tumbled behind her shoulders. "I haven't heard from Fiona or the agency…"

"It's on purpose, in case you decide to…" I stopped myself and changed my matter-of-fact tone. I was getting ahead of myself. "Do you want to sit?" I stood and gestured to the chair next to me then took off my jacket and rolled up my sleeves.

Megan crossed the room, and I maneuvered the two chairs so they were facing one another instead of the priest's desk. Once she'd sat with her foot wrapped behind the opposite calf, she started nibbling at her thumbnail.

I settled opposite her then leaned forward with my hands in prayer in front of my face. I closed my eyes and let out a long exhale, hoping the release would calm us both. On the inhale, I turned my gaze to her and wet my lips.

"First of all, I want you to know you don't have to tell me anything. I'm not interested in forcing you to divulge information that you've probably become a master at bottling up and trying to forget."

Her gaze fluttered away to the floor but then came back to me. Maybe no one had ever been that direct about how obvious it was that she was in a bad situation. Also, people tended to like gory details. I would have bet my Porsche that she'd had her share of conversations where people had tried to convince her that talking would help. Talking was overrated, as far as I was concerned.

It took her a beat to come to terms with the fact that we weren't going to pussy-foot around. She was in danger. There was no need for her to confess the obvious. And I didn't need to know more.

"Thank you for saying that."

"I know I've only been in town for a couple of days, but this is how I see the broad strokes of what's going on here. Correct me if I'm wrong." I rubbed my beard, being gentle made me itch. "You're interested in leaving this small town, otherwise why would you have contacted Fiona to begin with, right?"

"Yes."

A small hum escaped my throat. Leo said it was my tell of how I was about to show him the hole in his plans. He wasn't wrong. "But have you thought about how you're going to leave, Megan?"

She stopped biting the nail, fiddled a little with her hands then placed them in her lap. "What do you mean?"

"He's a deputy sheriff. You try to disappear without a trace and all the sudden you're a missing person. That gives him a whole lot of resources to find you."

Her face fell, and I was sorry for my honesty. But it also confirmed that her exit strategy needed help.

An unfamiliar part of me wanted to reach out and touch her leg, but that would have been wildly inappropriate on numerous levels. My fingers twitched in objection.

I continued in the softest voice I'd ever heard come out of me. "Answer me this. Are you really, truly ready to leave your entire life behind?"

She stared at her hands and bright pink patches appeared on her neck. When she looked up, her eyes were bloodshot. Megan Walsh had found the three remaining heartstrings I had and yanked—hard. Jesus, I hoped she'd say yes. She held my gaze and there was so much fear and entirely too much sadness mixed in a horrific blend.

Finally, as quiet as a mouse, she said, "I have to."

"Okay." I reached over and ripped a piece of paper from the small, lined tablet on the priest's organized desk then grabbed a pen. I took out my phone and copied down the post office box I'd just set up on the West Coast.

"Okay? What do you mean 'okay'?" There was confusion and a bit of panic in her voice, which was normal. Shit had just gotten real.

"We leave Sunday during Mass. Come here like normal. Only bring what you can fit into one inconspicuous bag. We'll buy clothes on the way or once we get to New York."

Her green eyes bugged out, and she gave her head a slight shake. "Sunday?" There was a small crack in her voice.

"I'll be waiting in here. In the meantime, forward all your bills to this address." I handed her the piece of paper.

She took it and read. "This is in California. I thought we were going to New York."

"We are. What about your apartment? If you give notice, will the cop find out?"

Megan held up her hands, the sheet of paper between her thumb and index hid half her pretty face. "Just…just a second. Can we slow down?"

This time my brain didn't stop my hand from reaching out. I touched her knee, and her eyes followed the movement.

"Megan. I'm going to get you out of here. If we do it too hastily, there will be mistakes, but if we wait too long, he'll find out. The decision is yours, but the method is mine."

Our eyes met, mine pleading for her to say yes and hers so full of anguish that a gentler soul might have wept for her pain.

"But… Does this mean I got the job?"

"If you want it. If not, I'll still help you."

She closed her eyes and shook her head. "But why? You don't even know me. You don't know anything."

For the first time in a long as time, I was going to be honest with a woman other than Chezzie. Megan Walsh somehow deserved it. I let out a deep sigh. "Because I've known women like you, and the only way to freedom is to walk away and never look back. I can help. I can cover your tracks. You can be safe. I promise."

I should have told her not to make me out to be some kind of knight in shining armor. But all that hope in her lovely eyes had me hypnotized.

I tapped her knee. "Three days. You just need to get through three days."

She looked at the piece of paper, scoffed, then back to me. "It's insane that I'm trusting a total stranger."

"I agree."

Chapter Four

Megan

Frankie stood and folded his beige jacket over his forearm. My body was glued to the chair, the weight of the following days too lumbering to permit movement. I wanted to think that there was kindness in his stormy eyes, but that was for my own self-assurance. In truth, there was a coldness to him—and in a suit, a level of seriousness that punctuated the gravity of the moment.

"You have my number, and you know what to do. I'll be here Sunday." As Frankie walked away, I desperately wanted to tell him that he may have gotten the wrong impression. But what did it matter? He was offering me the golden ticket out, something I'd been craving for months, possibly years, and I needed to take it.

He had his hand on the doorknob when I said, "Frankie?" The confident look he shot back made it impossible to say anything besides, "Thank you."

After a long blink, he nodded once and left.

Once he'd gone, a million thoughts flooded my head. *Three days. How will I leave my apartment?* I didn't want to disappoint my employer and not show up for work Monday morning. *What if Billy senses something is off and he follows me to church on Sunday? If I change my address to the one in California, will my bills be late? What about my bank account? How sophisticated is the sheriff's office to track my payments or email?*

The shuffling outside in the vestibule meant that Mass was over. If I told Father Peter my plans, he would keep quiet, and he could tell my boss that I wasn't coming in on Monday — or ever, for that matter. I could cancel my car insurance and my phone. That would be no problem. The only other bills I had were my student loans, and I could pay them electronically. My rent was month-to-month, so a letter and a final payment would suffice.

Father Peter came into the office and closed the door.

"Sorry I missed service."

"I'm not," he said while he shook his head. "I'm hoping our prayers have been answered. Does that man mean what I think?"

"Should I trust him? He's kinda…"

"Serious and looks like he doesn't laugh at jokes?"

I was thankful for the small amount of levity that Father Peter added. But it was true that the only thing light about Frankie was his suit.

Father Peter sat behind his desk, and I moved my chair to face him. "You know, kiddo, this may be your only shot to get away from this place. I say you take it. What do the teens say these days? YOLO? Your friend certainly comes across like a dark angel, but we don't get to choose how the Lord blesses us."

I picked at a broken nail with my hands in my lap. "It's going to be soon. Can you tell Burt that I won't be in on Monday? I'd hate for him to be in a bind."

His easy nod reassured me. "I'll talk to him. He can say you took a vacation to anyone who asks. That should buy you a week."

My pulse throbbed in my neck. *Is it really happening? Am I three days away from leaving my crappy life as I know it?*

"Can I really do this?"

"It may be your only chance. Take the blessing. You deserve it. You know you do."

After all the wicked thoughts I'd had against Billy, I wasn't sure I deserved anything. But a small voice inside me said that Father Peter was right about one thing. It might be my only chance.

Before I left the church, I went to the nave and knelt in the last pew. I prayed for Frankie and Fiona to be real. I prayed for forgiveness for leaving without saying goodbye to many trusted friends. I prayed for the strength to get to Sunday and the courage to start a new life.

The next day on my lunch break, I changed my address on my two loans and hand wrote my termination of the lease to my apartment. I would still have to pay the following month, but it would be worth it.

Billy wasn't outside my apartment when I got home, but I knew better than to take it as a good sign. There was no doubt in my mind that I would see him before I left. I locked the three bolts behind me. I'd already scaled back most of my belongings when I'd moved into the apartment two months prior. The urge to pack right away poked at me like an angry chicken. But what would happen if Billy saw that somehow? I hated the rent-free space he had in my head.

Instead, I went to my closet and scanned the contents. There was a depressing story for each outfit — a yellow sundress with a barely visible bloodstain, the black turtleneck worn to hide the marks on a neck, the jeans I'd cut-off into shorts after the knees had been ruined. In honesty, I didn't want to take any reminder of the past. Maybe I wouldn't need to pack at all.

I heated some plain pasta in my microwave and watched funny dog videos on my phone. When it was time for bed, I took out the personal trainer's business card with Frankie's phone number on it, cradled it in my hand and tried to sleep. Two more days seemed like forever and a flash.

The next day, as I sat with my back facing the entry to the food court where I was eating my lunch, it hit me — that jolt of energy that could only mean Billy was near. His tangy aftershave stung my nose before his thick frame was in view. He was in uniform, brown pants and a short, crisp white shirt. His gun sat on his hip like a taunting reminder that he had power, while I had nothing. Except, I had knowledge.

"Hey!" I was determined to play nice until the end.

He smiled at my warm greeting and sat opposite me before taking my fries for his own and eating a few. "There's a fish fry at the lake tonight. You going?"

I lifted a shoulder. "Maybe. You?"

"Probably not." It might not have been a lie. Billy's high school buddies who were still in the area had mostly cut ties with him unless they got pulled over for drunk driving and needed a favor. Over the previous year, he'd become quite the loner. Rumors flew fast in small towns, and he was at the center of most of them in ours.

Me? I had my eyes on freedom. But I was going to play as normal as possible until I met Frankie on Sunday. I stood and collected my trash on the tray. "See ya."

Billy narrowed his blue eyes. He never could understand how I remained so cool, so even. It threw him off his game and robbed him of his power to instill fear.

The rest of the afternoon, the fish fry ate away at me. It would be my last chance to see some of my friends. Even if I wasn't close to that many of them, they were a part of my life I would be leaving behind for good.

On the way home from work, I stopped for a cold six-pack at the gas station and left it in my car while I went in to change. To my surprise, neither of my stalkers were around. Maybe Billy'd had his fill at lunch and Frankie was doing whatever sophisticated, handsome men did on Friday nights. I wouldn't know, however. He was the only one I'd ever really met.

With my bug spray in my bag and my hoodie tied around my waist, I headed out to the lake. I parked at the end of a long line of cars and walked over to the campsite. The sun was just starting to set, and the orange in the sky had turned the water a unique shade of purple. Country music played from big speakers propped in the back of a white pickup, and I added my six-pack to the community cooler.

I said hello to a few friends from high school then walked over to the water's edge. A giggle from behind me set off a memory of me and my sister Ruby as kids, muddy as hell and failing miserably at catching bullfrogs. *The good ol' days…*

"Meg?"

I turned around and smiled. Chad Flint, with a much bigger stomach than when he'd played baseball in high school, stood in front of me offering me a beer.

"I haven't seen you at a fish fry since…"

Two summers ago.

"I know! I forgot what I was missing. How are you?"

He rubbed his belly. "I'm fat. I work at the Dodge dealership in Fairfield. I still live at home, but you know, it keeps my mama happy."

I hooked my arm into his and walked us toward the table of food. "I bet it does. How is she, anyway? I can still taste her apple crisp. You need to smuggle me that recipe somehow."

The night went on, and Chad plus a few other old friends were the exact goodbye to my hometown I needed. The group had thinned out a bit and we were all comfortable around a fire with are hands tucked into our hoodies and sipping the last of our beers when Billy pulled up.

I didn't need to look to confirm his truck. The sound of his engine had a distinct purr that had taunted me for too long.

Quiet curses married with the crackling fire and the chirping of crickets as he walked up. When he arrived at the circle, an unenthusiastic chorus of, 'heys' rang out. I stared at the ground and debated his level of intoxication.

I'd seen many sides of Billy Johnston and there wasn't one I liked. I flashed a quick glance to Chad, who blinked—a small confirmation that he had my back. After all, I was more among friends than Billy was. It was just that Billy had the badge.

I stood and wiped the dirt from my behind then took a step to leave.

"Where you goin'?" Alcohol had always given Billy more courage than he could control.

I ignored him and kept walking to my car. But booze also had a way of making Billy both mean *and* stupid. When I got to the parking lot, he was right behind me. Over the months, he'd threatened me, but in the previous weeks he'd gotten closer and closer to actual violence.

He stalked behind me. "I want to know where she is. What did you do with Ruby?"

"I don't know what you're talking about." I always gave him the same answer. Messing with his head was the only pleasure I got from the otherwise-horrid situation.

"Your fucking sister! Do you not remember you have one?" He spun me around and pushed me into the side of a truck. His eyes were wide with crazy, and he could beat me senseless like he used to do to Ruby, but I would never budge. I would never give in.

I stared him down with a small, wry smile. "I don't know what you're talking about."

"Stop fucking saying that!" He grabbed my ponytail and yanked hard. My scalp burned but I wasn't afraid. Out of the corner of my eye I saw some guys approaching to help, but Billy was too quick. The back of my head hit the side of the truck so fast that I barely had time to register the sharp pain before everything went black.

Chapter Five

Frankie

Why the ever-living fuck Megan had gone to the lake was beyond me. All she had to do was lie low for two more days and she would be on her way to a new life. But no, she'd practically thrown a going away party for herself. And it had ended with a fucking bang — her head against metal.

And hiding in the trees had left me as helpless as the unconscious Megan on the ground. Maybe she'd changed her mind. Maybe all the reservations of hotels and rental cars I'd spent my day doing had been for nothing. Maybe she had a death wish.

"You fucking knocked her out!" One of the men from the group came over and knelt in front of Megan. He tapped her cheek.

"What can I say? I don't know my own strength." Billy laughed. "Come on, Meg. Wakey."

Fucking asshole. The knife they'd used to clean the fish glimmered out of the corner of my eye. I could fillet that motherfucker and toss him in the water. Then the fish could eat him, the miserable prick.

A couple more guys came over and swore at Billy, who yelled back and pushed one of them before he fell on the ground.

The first man propped Megan up as she regained consciousness and winced when she touched her head. He asked her something and she nodded slowly.

"Get up, Megan. Stop making a big deal out of a little bump." Billy perched his hands on his hips.

Megan stared at the ground as another girl raced to her side. The group grew and shouted insults at Billy, who taunted them in return. Something told me it wasn't the first time he'd reminded them that he was the law. What were they going to do?

The guy next to Megan stood up. "Get the fuck out of here. Jesus, Johnston."

A third man approached Billy with his hands in surrender and they had a quiet conversation. Whatever he was saying, it was cooling Billy off, and it ended with his arm around Billy and them heading toward another truck.

Megan was helped to her feet, and I slipped back into the woods then broke out in a sprint to the other side of the lake where I'd parked. I raced to the school in Megan's neighborhood where I parked my car then snuck through backyards to her apartment. A light was on, and I peeked in through the window to make sure she was alone. I called her phone and she answered with a groggy, "Hello?"

"It's me. I'm outside. Let me in."

I walked to her front door and slipped in. She closed and locked it behind me. Megan's face was streaked with tears and her hair was a rat's nest.

"Let me see." I motioned for her to step forward.

"It's–"

I dropped my chin before she could go on. *Is she really going to pretend like it's nothing?*

With her eyes on the ground, she walked over to me and turned around in the tiny living room of her apartment. Her thick, dark hair hid the damage, but when I ran my fingers over the bump, it was impressive. I crossed the room into the little kitchen and thankfully found a bag of frozen peas in the freezer. The only furniture was a small, tattered loveseat and I pointed her to it. "Go... Lie down on your side."

She shot me a curious glance but did what I'd said. I followed her over and placed the peas on the bump. Her knees were bent to accommodate for the small space, and she asked, "How did you know?"

I sat on the floor next to her and draped my arms over my knees. "Don't take this the wrong way, but I followed you. Why didn't you just stay home?"

She turned her head and held the bag of peas in place with her hand. "I was trying to be as normal as I could. I didn't want him to suspect anything."

"So Sunday is still on?"

Her eyes widened, like a deer in headlights. "Do you not want to help me anymore because I messed up?"

I offered a tight smile. "Nothing has changed for me. Where are your painkillers? You must have a massive headache coming on."

"You don't need to do that. I'll go in a sec."

I stood. "Nah. Besides, it makes me feel like I'm useful." Not like standing in the trees and watching a woman be brutalized and not being able to do anything about it. I went to the bathroom and found two pills then filled a glass of water from the tap in the kitchen.

"Thanks," she said once she'd swallowed the medicine. "You don't have to stay. I'll be fine."

"Megan, you have a concussion. Someone has to wake you up every two hours — unless you want me to drive you to the hospital, which I would be more than happy to do."

"You know that's not going to happen. Too many questions, too many bills." There was a little waver in her voice. The exhaustion was probably kicking in, and she needed sleep.

"Do you feel like you can walk to the bedroom, or do you want me to carry you?"

She giggled. It was completely out of place and utterly adorable, then she stopped abruptly. "Oh. You're serious. No. I'll be fine."

After a long exhale, Megan swung her feet around and pushed into the couch as she stood, but she wobbled, and I caught her. For a long moment, she searched my eyes for something. If it was goodness she was looking for, she wouldn't find much. *Maybe someday.*

"Come on. Let me carry you. It's the least I can do." I didn't wait for her answer, and she hopped into my arms. Megan laid her messy head on my shoulder, and I liked it. I had never held a woman like that before, and there was a strength and intimacy to it that was instantly intoxicating. I carried her the length of the short hallway. Her bedroom wasn't much — a queen-sized bed with a yellow spread occupied most of the space and on the opposite wall there was a white closet with accordion doors — but it was clean.

As I moved around the bed, her eyes closed, and I was pretty sure she sniffed my neck. Yeah, she was entering the groggy faze. I laid her down and she hummed into her pillow.

"You smell yummy."

Yep. Loopy status confirmed.

"Do I?" I raised my eyebrows and smiled, then covered her with the yellow spread from the opposite side.

She smacked her mouth a few times. "Like a man. Like a *real* man."

"Well, I am a real man, so that probably explains it." I sat on the floor and zipped my hoodie.

She tapped my head a few times. "Your hair is soft. Why is your hair so soft?"

"You need to sleep, Megan. We can talk about my hair in the morning."

"Okay." She sounded a little drunk, but I knew it was just the swelling in her brain.

I set my alarm to vibrate at four a.m. and quietly made my way back to the couch. I turned off the light and tried like hell to find a position on the tiny sofa that was comfortable. No matter how I contorted my body, it was awkward. I tried the floor, and it was worse.

On a scale of 'wrong to pretty fucking wrong', I rated the idea of sleeping next to her. It wasn't like I would make a move. Besides, she was out cold, so she would never know. I tip-toed back to the bedroom and took off my shoes. As carefully as I could, and with my eyes on Megan's back the entire time, I crawled into the bed. When I was as close to the edge as I could get, I closed my eyes.

Billy slamming her head against the truck replayed over and over—and each time I was reminded that I'd let it happen. I had done nothing to protect the delicate woman to my right. I was a coward. I was stupid to not have a gun. My father's voice rang through my head. *"When you get the shot, you take the shot. Any hesitation and the window closes."* Billy's window was closed. *Fucking shame.* But there could be another chance if... If what? I came back and killed him? Killing out of passion was a big no-no for my father. It meant we were emotionally attached. I'd never *wanted* to murder the victims. I'd wanted the big paycheck that came when the deed was done. So, what made Billy so fucking special?

My alarm vibrated before I'd fallen asleep. I rolled out of bed and turned on a bedside lamp. In the orange glow, Megan rested peacefully. Her pouty lips were closed and made a sort of puffy heart shape. I wondered what it might be like to feel those lips on mine. I bet she was soft and gentle—all the things I didn't know how to be.

I knelt next to the bed and shook Megan's shoulder. "Hey. Can you open your eyes? I want to make sure your pupils aren't dilated."

They fluttered open and Megan immediately cringed. Yeah, waking up with a head wound was hellish.

"Head throbbing?"

She gave a quick nod that looked equally painful. I stood and got a couple of more pills from the bathroom, refilled the water glass and was back by her side in two minutes. She'd sat up and was checking the swelling of the back of her head.

I laid the pills on the table next to the glass. "I should probably sneak out before sunrise. Why don't you lie low all day and I'll see you tomorrow at the church."

Megan took the pills then glanced away before turning back to me with a crinkled brow. "Did I tell you that you smelled nice?" She hid behind her hands then peeked out.

I tried to hide my grin. "You did, like 'a real man who has soft hair'."

"I'm not going to lie. I'm pretty mortified. I'm sorry if that made you uncomfortable."

I laughed. "That was by and large the best part of my day."

"I'm such an idiot."

"First, don't say that about yourself. And second, I'm well aware that was the concussion talking." I lifted her eyelids, and everything seemed normal. "Call me if you have any nausea. The best thing for you is rest, so stay put. Tomorrow this nightmare ends. Okay?" I took a final look at her, satisfied she'd make it through the day. Maybe it had been a mild punishment compared to the ones I imagined before it. She seemed to be handling it pretty well.

By the time I got back to my motel, the sun was rising, and with the time difference, I knew Leo would be awake and working out. I popped him on speaker and threw the phone on the bed then started to get undressed.

"Morning, Suzy Sunshine." The small pant in his voice made it clear he was on the treadmill. I was jealous. I missed our morning routines.

Might as well call a spade a spade. "Well, for a man who prides himself on security, I am a total fucking failure."

"Self-deprecation before breakfast? I need to hear this."

I rubbed my eyes. "Her fucking hick of an ex smashed her into his truck last night."

"Oh, fuck. Is she okay?" Leo kept up his short breaths. He wouldn't have stopped running for news like that. It wasn't in our blood.

"She has a concussion. I had the shot, just no firearm. Have you ever wanted to filet a human?"

"Dad is rolling over in his shallow grave, wherever the fuck that is. But you know you did the right thing, as hard as it was. There are countless reasons, big brother."

In my boxers, I lay on the hard bed. Jesus, I missed my thread counts and down pillows, and I didn't care if it made me a snob. Comfort mattered. I let out a puff of an exhale and said, "Yeah. I know. But can you just list some so I can feel better about this? I watched it happen, Leo, and I did fucking *nothing*."

"Wait a second." He chuckled. "Did you just talk about your *feelings*?"

Fucking wise-ass. "I swear, I'm going to hit you so hard when I see you again. But you know how that shit eats at me. I just stood there in the fucking trees. I let her get thrown into a wall of fucking steel." A small whine crept into my voice, and I hated it. It showed weakness, it left me exposed. I froze.

My dad had been more than just a little abusive to my mother. He'd controlled her life from A to Z. She was terrified of him and incapable of stopping what he was doing to Leo and me. I liked to think that one day she'd left, but I feared that he'd actually killed her and buried her body with all the others he'd stacked up. I had been just a little boy, but that helplessness each time my father's temper flared was one of the few things Leo and I didn't have in common. He had been too young to ever really witness the extent of the abuse. So seeing it happen to Megan, with her hair as pitch black as my mother's, had taken me places I tried like hell not to go to.

Leo's breath had calmed, so he must have stopped running. Apparently me sharing my emotions was worthy of his full attention. "Sounds like she needs to get the hell out of there."

"We leave tomorrow morning. I'm going to drive south for a bit then head to Chicago, where I change cars." Thinking about the logistics of the plan relieved a bit of my guilt for not killing that worthless piece of shit Billy Johnston.

Leo sighed. "Listen. I know it sucks, but you did the right thing. It was an impossible situation, but if you would have stepped in, she wouldn't be leaving tomorrow. You know that."

I grumbled. I did know that, but it didn't mean I liked it. "I could kill him today."

"Yeah, probably. But you had the bright idea to try to become an upstanding citizen or some bullshit like that. So, in my book, it's your own fault you couldn't take out that fucker."

That was typical baby brother bullshit. Pin it back on me. "I am so going to kick your ass next week."

"Nah, old man. I'm quick like lightening. I had Myers on his ass in less than thirty seconds yesterday. Was a pity you missed out. It would have cheered you up."

I smiled a little at the thought but went back to reminding my brother just what I was doing for him. "You know, I was just supposed to come here for one damn day, check her out and go back to my life. This has turned into a clusterfuck and dumpster fire rolled into one. When did I get into the business of saving damsels in distress? You owe me big time."

He laughed. "We both know you're doing this for Fi and your newfound love of trying to be a hero. This has exactly zero to do with me."

Chapter Six

Megan

Orange and blue peeked through the white stratus clouds. I drove down the two-lane highway, passing pretty farms and tall golden corn fields. Would I miss the rural beauty of where I'd grown up? Probably. The chances of me ever stepping foot back into the life I was leaving behind would need to be none.

The car radio boasted of a hot summer day, and I turned it off when a classic rock song came on. It was hard to believe that I was going to actually leave, and that, God willing, I would never see Billy again. But it was also with a heavy heart. My community had helped me more than I could ever repay. Was it fair to abandon them?

Ever since I'd decided to leave, a guilty ache had been constant in my gut. And as many times as I told myself saying goodbye was the only route to survival, and as many times as Father Peter had assured me it didn't make me a bad person, the dull pain of cutting all ties remained.

As I turned into the parking lot of my church, my hands slipped off the steering wheel. My palms were clammy, and I had half expected to see Billy's truck waiting for me. It seemed impossible that I could disappear without a fight, especially after that was how Ruby had done it—whisked away by strangers.

I let out a stuttered breath then climbed out of the car. My bag, filled with only a few essentials, was lighter than it should have been. But when I'd taken a look around my apartment that morning, I hadn't wanted to remind myself of the lonely, depressed shape my life had taken. So I had my toilet bag, an oversized T-shirt and three changes of clothes. *Pretty damn depressing.* Frankie had said we could buy some things on the way to New York and my pride didn't want to accept it, but my brain convinced me it was the only way. I needed a handout and help, plain and simple.

And I had the phone—the one line of communication I had with Ruby. I thought back to the day before she'd left. She'd been wearing the yellow dress with the blood stain she didn't think I knew about. The only way I'd gotten her to agree to leave was if we could keep in touch, so I'd bought two pre-paid phones that we'd promised only to use for each other. It was the only thing that kept us sane.

The clean air of the country had yet to turn humid, and I filled my lungs, hoping the molecules also contained some courage. The familiar congregation staggered their way into the church, but I was unable to make out any individual faces. There must have been some remnants of the concussion, because my head spun and I felt dizzy. I knew I was deceiving Frankie a little bit. He didn't know about Ruby and probably imagined that Billy was my ex. And while he could probably keep a secret—he didn't seem like a blabbermouth—I'd decided that the best way to deal with Ruby was to pretend to the outside world like she'd never existed. It kept my story straight.

I said, "Morning," over and over to people I was sure I knew but couldn't recognize or place their names, then sidestepped to Father Peter's office. I slipped in and used the door to hold myself straight.

Finally, I was able to focus.

Frankie and Father Peter leaned over the desk and they both looked up when the door clicked shut. Frankie raked his dark eyes over me before he turned back to the priest. In his khaki pants and tight navy polo, I bet he thought he was some kind of casual. The scent of his cologne lingered in the air, and it warmed me like a bath of sunlight. I hadn't been wrong when I'd bumbled through my head injury that he was all man. *Holy everything…* Testosterone seeped out of each pore of his lovely, tanned skin. His beard was perfectly trimmed close to his face. And, yep, his hair was styled but there wasn't an ounce of product visible.

"Morning!" Father Peter said with a polite nod, startling me out of my dreamboat stare.

"You ready?" Frankie asked in a deep tone.

I was so tired of being helpless, so exhausted of my nerves on constant look-out and so very much over being hunted like a sitting duck. "Yeah. Yeah, I am."

"I worked it out with the priest that we can leave from his garage. Come through this door when you're done with your goodbyes." Frankie crossed the threshold to the private residence, and I stood, alone, trying to fight off the heart palpitations.

Father Peter walked over and placed his hands on my shoulders. "I'm going to miss you. It's not everyone who confesses to planning a murder. You've been keeping me on my toes." He winked.

The bells rang overhead, signaling the start of Mass and my time to go. I held Father Peter's gentle gaze one last time. "Thank you for stepping in when you did. You've saved Ruby's life and mine..." A memory of me sobbing in the confessional flashed in my mind and tears puddled in my eyes.

"Just doing my job. Be well, Megan. Make the most of your new life."

We hugged, and I hoped he knew that he'd done a lot more than just his job. I took a big breath and walked out of his office.

I didn't look back. I couldn't. My heart was already breaking. I wiped away the tears that had fallen and spotted Frankie on Father Peter's couch. He hopped up and said, "Showtime."

I followed him to the built-in double garage and over to a silver sedan parked next to Father Peter's Subaru.

"Get in the back and lie on the floor. There's a light blanket. Hopefully you can take it off when we get to the interstate."

It hadn't occurred to me until that moment how genuinely equipped Frankie was for the job. I did as he said, and once I was covered, the garage door clanked open and he cranked the engine. We backed out and he stopped, opened the window, then closed it again.

"What's happening?" Stopping couldn't be good. I'd broken out into a sweat, and the pebbles on my forehead were clinging to the blanket.

"Just tossing the garage door command into the grass. The priest will get it as soon as Mass is over. Stay down for a bit and relax. The streets are empty."

Sunday morning in small-town USA had indeed been the best time to sneak out. Everyone I knew was either in church or in bed.

But as we drove on, the desire to know where we were, which route he was taking was making me even hotter. I uncovered my face, but from my position, I could only see the roof of the car and the top of the window. Each second passed like a painful hour, and I started counting in my head.

"You okay?"

No. I'm definitely not okay. I was seesawing between the adrenaline that I was finally leaving and a heavy fear in my chest that we would be caught. And I couldn't move. But instead of being honest, I said a weak, "Uh-huh."

Frankie reached back and tapped my thigh twice. "You're gonna be okay. We're only going to Chicago today. Five hours...and there shouldn't be much traffic."

I had no idea how much time had passed when he said, "We're on the interstate. You can move to the backseat if you want. But just to be sure, stay down and don't look out of the window."

Around lunchtime, we crossed the state border, but we didn't stop to eat, which was fine by me. I wasn't hungry. The new state brought a small relief but an overwhelming sense of loneliness. Frankie hadn't said three words since he'd given my little taps of encouragement. But how would someone even begin small talk with the girl they were saving?

I bunched up the blanket and used it as a pillow. The only thing interesting in the car was the driver, so I studied his muscular arms and profile. He had a strong jaw, which he worked back and forth like he was trying to solve a complicated math problem. He was a level of handsome and sophisticated that I had no idea how to compute. Then it hit me... *I have a tiny crush on him.*

Heat spread over my neck, and I was glad he wasn't looking at me because I was sure I was blushing. We drove for three more hours until Frankie pulled into a parking lot of a massive hotel. He killed the engine and swiveled around.

"Coast is clear. I'll go get the room and bring you the key. Then I'm going to drop the car at the airport and take the shuttle back."

I sat upright and nodded.

"Are you okay? Do you need anything?"

Such simple questions, and yet, I had no idea how to reply. I stared into his eyes. Maybe the answers were in those deep, dark pools.

Frankie unbuckled his seat belt and twisted farther in the seat. "You may be in a little bit of shock. That, with the head injury, is a lot to process. I'll be as quick as I can. You can veg out on bad TV while you wait."

He reached for the handle and it struck me that we'd never talked about money. Everything had happened so fast, and it didn't occur to me to offer.

"Umm... I'll pay you back everything once I start working for Fiona. I'm so sorry... I didn't think about..." I was so stupid...and presumptuous.

"I'll work it out with my brother," he said with a wry grin. *What does that mean?* He exited the car and I sat back, still not fully believing that I was out of Iowa. Fifteen minutes later, Frankie handed me a key card and said, "Eight-thirteen. Feel free to order room service if you're hungry."

I stared at the card. Opening the car door seemed impossible. It couldn't have been safe to be so exposed. "By now he knows I'm gone. He would have driven by my place after church then gone looking for me."

"There are hundreds of business travelers staying at this hotel. Not one of them knows you or Billy. Other than the fact that you're pretty, they won't give you a second look. I know you're nervous, but you're safe. I'll be back as soon as I can."

I chewed my lip. "What if—?"

Frankie shook his head. "Don't do that. Don't play that game."

"Okay. Bad TV and a diet soda." I gathered my bag and shoved the blanket in. It offered an odd sense of security. I opened the door and climbed out of the car.

The warm afternoon air was stifling and the engines from a jet roared overhead, causing me to duck. I walked one shaky step after the other toward the entrance of the hotel and gave a fleeting glance over my shoulder to Frankie. He smiled before starting the car and backing out of the parking spot. My heartbeat thundered in my ears, and I broke out in a cold sweat. Inside the hotel, the air conditioning was jolting, and I shivered. After a quick scan, I found the elevator bay then stared at my battered sandals all the way until I was in front of it. Someone had already pressed the call button and the doors to my left rattled open after a ding.

"What floor?" an older man in tan pants and a white golf shirt asked.

"Eight, please." I held my bag tight to my side with one hand and gripped the keycard with the other.

The man got off before me, and I let out a long breath when I was alone. The room was in the middle of the floor, and when the green light signaling the door was unlocked flashed, a small sense of relief washed over me. The hotel room was spacious but nothing special. Two double beds were neatly made with crisp, white sheets and a crimson bedspread. I dropped my bag on the one closest to the window and opened the drapes. A plane took off in the distance and I had to admit the sight of it was exhilarating. I turned a club chair to the window, propped up my feet and watched the air traffic.

All those people were coming from all over the world or leaving on a vacation to somewhere exotic. The possibilities were endless. Would that be true for me, too? I was more in a state of limbo, and at least for the following days I would be. Then I could help Fiona with her new family, and maybe glance at her hottie brother-in-law at family gatherings from time to time. Eventually my old life could be a distant memory, almost like a bad dream — or so I hoped.

No, I wouldn't play the game of 'what if'. I would try to be optimistic. I would be grateful. I would be different. Maybe I would even find it in me to be bold one day. *Bold, that's a goal.*

The click of the door startled me, but Frankie's smile put me at ease.

He tilted his head to the side. "You look better." His bag was flung over his shoulder, and he carried it with two fingers. He dropped it on the bed closest to the door then walked over to the small fridge that was against the wall.

I stretched and said, "I was just thinking about how maybe I can get lost in this world. Also, you have no idea how much your time means to me. I'll never be able to repay you for getting me out of there."

"Drink?"

"Just a water. Thanks."

He grabbed a clear bottle then opened himself a beer before sitting in the other chair and turning it to the window. "To your new life. *Saluti*." He tipped the bottle to me then drank. "And it would have been really hard for me to leave you in that situation. So, thanks for trusting me. Besides, if I went back to New York without you, my sister-in-law would have never forgiven me. And since family is the most important thing in my life, I couldn't have let that happen." He gazed out of the window and a huge plane took off in front of us.

"Well, whatever your motivation, I am very thankful. And I think I'm hungry. Could we order some food?"

Thirty minutes later, I had a burger and fries in front of me, and Frankie picked his way through what he said was overly cooked salmon and a sad excuse for vegetables. After we'd eaten, we set the empty plates out in the hallway and I found an action movie on TV.

Frankie sat on his bed texting, shoes off and ankles crossed. His attention was on his phone, and I wondered if he had a wife or girlfriend. He must have sensed me studying him. He glanced to me then over to the movie. A disgusted frown spread across his face.

"What?" I muted the movie.

"Nothing. Never mind. Just keep watching." He shook his head and mumbled something about letting fiction be fiction.

"Tell me. You've sparked my curiosity. Humor me. Please." Maybe it was pushy to insist, but he'd had some kind of visceral reaction, and I was curious. Also, I was a little bored. The movie was pretty stupid, and it wasn't like we'd had much of a conversation.

Frankie tossed his phone to the side. "Have you ever been hit in the nose?"

"Unfortunately, yes." I'd gotten pegged with a stray volleyball in gym class when I was fourteen. I could still feel the sting.

"First of all, I'm sorry that happened to you. But you know how much that hurts, right? That idiot in the movie just got hit not once but *twice,* and he's still standing. Not possible. Even the best fighters I know would be on the ground after the first blow." He *tsk*ed then stood and walked over to the TV screen. "And fists? Really? What is this, a boxing match from the 1920s?"

The annoyance in his voice was pretty damn cute. That, and the complaining about his meal, made me realize that he had a genuine cranky side. To be fair, he could have been a miserable prick, and I still would have liked him. He was helping me, and anything that might have prevented him from being attractive was wiped out.

I turned on the light between the beds. "How would you have done it?"

He looked at me like I'd asked the most obvious question in the world. "With the heel of my palm. Wide stance, wrist back, fingers separated. Slam up." He demonstrated his technique then shrugged. "Or you could go from the side. That works too."

I stood and walked over to him. "Wide stance, wrist flexed, separated fingers. Slam up." I tried to do exactly what he said, but he frowned.

Frankie moved behind me and kicked my legs together. A lustful shiver ran through my spine and an embarrassing, little giggle bubbled out of me. It hadn't been the first, and it was mortifying.

"Too wide." He held my forearm and jabbed it higher than I had. "The nose is like a triangle. Hit the base."

I immediately missed the physical contact as he stepped away and propped his hands on his hips. "Try again."

In my head, I repeated his directions and was determined to impress him. I inhaled and, on a sharp exhale, I thrust my hand into what I imagined to be Billy's smug face.

"Better."

I tried again then paused. "How do you practice this? It's not like people want their noses broken."

"Yeah. It's more of an on-the-job training one." Frankie let out a small laugh. "I'm gonna shower." He hiked a thumb over his shoulder to the bathroom, grabbed some clothes and bundled them around his toilet bag before going in and shutting the door.

What the heck kind of job lets you punch people in the face?

Chapter Seven

Frankie

Around two a.m. the shuffling of Megan's feet woke me. A blade of a streetlight cut through the drapes and highlighted her silhouette as she walked at the foot of our beds. Her legs were bare, and she wore a long, white T-shirt. It was one of the few items she'd brought. I wondered if it had any sentimental value. It couldn't have been easy to leave everything behind. Turning my back on Chezzie or Leo would never happen, no matter what. Until Fiona and Violet had come along, they were all I'd had. That was part of the reason I'd kept tabs on Leo when he'd gone to Covington Heights, that shithole of a neighborhood.

Megan padded off to the bathroom and I flipped sides, giving a small punch to the unacceptably lumpy pillow. The toilet flushed, the tap ran and I barely caught the flash of the light before she opened the door.

She walked into the small alley between our beds, crawled in next to me and let out a small sigh.

My muscles tensed. Jesus, I hoped she didn't think she owed me some kind of physical favor for what I was doing. *Fuck.* I raced through our interactions. Had I hinted that she needed to repay me in any way? *Fuck. Fuck. Fuck.* I should have gotten her a separate hotel room. Leave it to the evil inside me to find a way to worm its way out. She'd been living a life without choices, and I'd failed to give her any. *What an asshole.*

Plus, I'd barely even spoken to her on the road. Where was my sympathy? My compassion? Had she taken my silence as anger or annoyance? *Yep, total prick.*

Megan mumbled something and pulled on the covers, which exposed my right foot to the cool air in our room. I lay perfectly still. If I went to the other bed, would she be insulted? I sure as shit wasn't going to fucking spoon her or cuddle. Did I even know how to do those things?

Maybe it was just a simple mistake, like she was sleep walking or something. Maybe she was disoriented. And maybe, just fucking maybe, there was a part of me that liked her there…closer.

Shit.

What was that small ping of honesty?

No, it couldn't be. It was probably just my instincts of wanting to protect her, me paying an old debt to a society that I'd stolen too much from, me accepting my new role as security instead of assassin. Yeah, that was it. It certainly wasn't that I was secretly lonely and longed for a quiet moment of intimacy — totally me just doing my job. The closer she was, the safer. That was all.

Her breathing slowed and I carefully turned to face her. In slumber, she was a beautiful stranger. With her eyes closed, there was no past, and the future was a mystery. I hoped she was peaceful. Her chest rose and fell, hypnotizing me with its cadence. She really was lovely. Anyone who would want to lay a hand on her and taint her natural perfection was a cruel idiot.

My hand reached out to touch her before I could stop it. I stroked her cheek—so soft, so lovely. How many times had it received a brutal and undeserved smack?

She opened her eyes slowly, offered me a small, simple smile that pierced my heart before her lids closed again like they were too heavy. I withdrew my hand and searched her face for more information. What was she telling me? Was she even fully awake? She didn't reach out or speak, so I rolled to my back and stared above me while my mind raced. Sleep only came after I resolved not to read anything into the actions by either of us. We were in an unbelievable circumstance, and there was no precedent to judge our behavior.

I didn't want to bother with the morning traffic, so instead of racing out of Chicago, I let Megan sleep in— she was still very much in my bed—and I took the opportunity to use the gym in the hotel. While I ran on the treadmill, I vowed to be softer, kinder. Hell, maybe I would make Chezzie proud and not be my normal stubborn prick of a self.

When I got back to the room, Megan's hair was wet and she wore a pretty romper made for the brutal heat of a Midwestern summer. I'd left her a note stating my breakfast order and whereabouts, and from the platter on the table by the window, she'd read it.

"Sleep okay?" *Is it wrong that I wanted her to say 'the best night's ever'?*

"Not bad." Her little shrug gave nothing away. "Your granola and yogurt are over there. They didn't have espresso, so I just ordered black coffee. Sorry. How far are we driving today?"

I frowned. Black watery coffee wasn't my idea of the proper way to start the day, then I remembered I was a snob and maybe not everyone on the planet considered the lack of espresso a reason to put on a bitch face.

"Pittsburgh. Should be about seven hours." I grabbed my bag and headed to the bathroom where there was still fog on the mirrors from Megan's shower. My mind started to wander... Her naked there moments earlier... *Great.* I'd turned into a creep. I slapped my face a few times. *Leave the poor girl alone, Frankie.* The last thing she needed was me entertaining how damn alluring she looked in her outfit.

I showered quickly, willing myself to think about scratchy sheets and ugly carpet—anything but the woman on the other side of the bathroom door who would smile at me with her eyes in a way I'd never experienced before.

Normally the women I dated were attracted to my money—and I'd hoped my body and looks. I'd picked them for their status, long hair and plastic bodies in designer dresses. A woman like Megan would have normally been so far off my radar that I could have ridden an elevator fifty flights alone with her and still not have thought twice about her.

But there she was, making me fucking caress her cheek in the middle of the fucking night. It was innocent enough but a loss of self-control that I'd never experienced before.

I was dried off and dressed in record time. I checked traffic while I ate my granola and hoped that there might be an espresso at the airport when I fetched the new rental.

"Thanks for ordering breakfast." I rose from the small table by the window and threaded my arms through my jacket. "I'll get the car and come back for you. You need anything?"

She quickly shook her head 'no'. Was that fear in her eyes? What was I missing? Megan glanced away and the tension in her posture gave me the distinct impression that she was uncomfortable with me. When she sat on the bed and turned her back to me, I was sure.

Had I been rude? Cruel, maybe? I had a tendency to be a bit chilly in my delivery sometimes — or so Chezzie liked to tell me. Whatever I'd done, I would probably never guess, but I'd triggered something and I didn't want her to question her safety — not just because of the way it would make me feel, but for her. The poor woman had been through a lot. The bump on her head alone was traumatic. I wondered how long Billy had been stalking and abusing her.

I walked over and stood in front of her then lifted her chin so she had to meet my gaze. In a soft voice I said, "I'm not him. I don't know what you think you've done wrong, but I can assure you I'm not harboring any kind of resentment or hiding any anger."

She stared at me with wide, green eyes before looking away. She opened her mouth then closed it again before taking a breath and saying, "It's stupid. I'm sorry."

I tugged at my pants and squatted in front of her. "I'd like to know, if you don't mind. I don't want to repeat the same mistake."

"You're going to think this is so dumb. It *is* so dumb." Megan brought her hands to her face and hid behind them before rubbing her temples.

I waited. It was important to clear the air. We were going to spend seven hours in the same car together. Awkward silence for that long would get old quick. Also, the idea that I was a safe person to talk to appealed to me.

Megan groaned then said, "I can't believe I'm going to say this out loud." She let out a huff. "The coffee. You didn't drink the coffee. I messed up your order."

Whoa. What? Handle with care, Ricci.

I nodded. "I'm a bona fide coffee snob. Actually, I'm a general snob. My apologies. But I'm not mad that you didn't find me an espresso. Don't worry about that."

A small smile came back to her face and the fear disappeared from her eyes. "It's just you're doing all this for me, and I can't repay you. I bring nothing to the table. I guess I thought the feeling of helplessness would go away…"

"It will take time, but you have your whole future ahead of you."

"Thanks to you."

"No. You're the one who reached out to Fiona. You set the wheels of fate in motion. It just so happened you found an employer who would never leave you in a situation like you were in. Hell, she would have flown out here and gotten you herself and given birth on the side of the road to make sure you were safe."

Megan smiled and a warmth filled my chest. "She sounds pretty awesome…Fiona."

"She is." I stood up. "You gonna be okay?"

"I'm gonna try."

I winked at her. *Holy shit, I winked at her.* That had to have been wildly inappropriate. But it deepened her smile, so maybe she liked it. *Wait. Do I want her to like it?* I swallowed over a lump that had formed in my throat. I needed air. Something was happening to me. I was being…nice.

I hitched a thumb over my shoulder. "I'm going to get the car. Shouldn't take more than an hour."

On my way to the shuttle, I sent a text to Leo, telling him my plan to switch cars again in Pittsburgh and that we would see him the following evening when I dropped Megan off.

At the airport, there had been a bunch of flights canceled, and the line at the rental company was longer than it should have been. I was annoyed, but to my surprise, I was upgraded to an SUV that needed to get back to the East Coast. It was way more automobile than the two of us needed, but it beat the shit out of the four-door I'd dropped off the day before.

I was back at the hotel mid-morning and Megan flipped off the television when I entered the room. "Ready?"

"So ready." She hopped up and swung her bag over her shoulder.

I handed her the key fob. "It's the black SUV in the fifteen-minute spot out front. I'll check out and see you there."

She nodded. "Can I ride in the front now?"

"I don't see why not." I grabbed my bag and checked the bathroom for anything I was forgetting. "Take the stairs, though. I'll go down in the elevator."

I checked out under my fake name and met Megan at the SUV where she was sitting in the passenger seat. Her hair had a natural wave to it, and she looked more relaxed than earlier. Maybe she was eager to get going. I took off my jacket and placed it in the backseat then climbed in.

"Frankie?" Her voice was soft, and I liked how she said my name.

I started the engine and backed out then glanced at her when I shifted into drive. "Yeah?"

"I just want to say that I really, truly appreciate this. I'm sure you have a million other things you'd rather be doing. And…"

To get to the interstate, I needed to turn left at a busy intersection, and she waited until I was headed in the right direction until she spoke again.

"I'm sorry I climbed into your bed. And full disclosure, I did it on purpose. I was sure it was all a dream, and being close to you was the only way I could convince myself it was real. But if it made you uncomfortable, my apologies for not asking first."

It was sweet of her to confess, but it was a mild blow to the ego. "And here I thought it was my soft hair and cologne that brought you there. Damn it."

Megan flushed red. I'd embarrassed her. *Fucking self-confidence.*

"Sorry." I flipped the blinker and merged onto the on-ramp. "My poor attempt at humor. Truth be told, I did the same thing Friday night. I couldn't get comfortable on your couch or floor, so I slept next to you for a couple of hours. Hope that wasn't too audacious. But I'd say we're even."

"I knew you were there." There was a quiet confession in her words, but I had no idea what it meant. She pressed her head into her window and stared out.

I let the silence fall between us, and after being on the interstate for about thirty minutes I said, "I don't want you to think you owe me anything...like, physically. I have my reasons for doing this, and that's good enough for me."

She turned to me and tucked a strand of her long, dark hair behind her ear. There was a scar on her index finger just below the nail. It was small but it was there. "I appreciate you saying that. For the record, I didn't think you were that kind of man."

"What kind of man do you think I am?" My curiosity was piqued. I'd never asked a stranger what they thought of me before. In honesty, I'd never given a shit. Yet, somehow, her opinion mattered.

"One who loves his family." She wasn't as wrong as I'd thought she'd be.

Chapter Eight

Megan

The meaning of the strong, silent type was coming into full focus. Frankie didn't say much. Small talk didn't seem to be his thing, but I didn't mind. Besides, what was I going to contribute to a conversation? Almost everything I'd left behind I was trying to forget. But it had been close to an hour without either of us speaking, and words were itching to leave my mouth and make it to his ear. Questions, actually. I wanted to know more about him, but I just had no idea how to ask.

"Hey," he said, and it practically startled me. "Do you mind if we eat out? I know this Thai place that makes crazy noodles, and now that I've started thinking about them, I'm full-on craving them."

"That sounds nice. Thanks." I didn't know what Thai food was like. I'd had stir-fry Chinese at the mall and liked it. Maybe it was similar.

"If you don't want to risk being seen, they do take-out." Frankie steered the car into the right lane for the downtown Pittsburgh exit. He'd driven two miles under the speed limit the entire day, and I appreciated his caution. Also, I was telling myself a beautiful lie that he was in no hurry to be rid of me on his sister-in-law's doorstep.

The night before, when he'd touched my face, I thought I was going to melt or that maybe I'd gone to heaven. It was the single most gentle gesture I'd ever received. I'd probably cherish it for the rest of my life. He would never know how much his simple acts of kindness were easing the jarring transition in my life.

Without a doubt, Billy had probably torn through my apartment then harassed my neighbors, boss and Father Peter. He would have gotten into a fight with someone who would have told him he'd gone too far on Friday night. He would have called my phone a thousand times. The messages would have started angry, then pathetic and back to him screaming threats. He would have found my car and searched it, as well. Maybe his daddy would have spoken to Father Peter, who would have said I'd gone to Mass and mentioned a vacation.

He would have roared out his frustration then cried in pathetic desperation. Billy Johnston was many things and 'predictable' was front and center. It was also why I knew he'd never stop looking for me or Ruby. But in Pittsburgh at a Thai restaurant? I didn't think he had that much imagination.

"I wouldn't mind eating in public. It's not like I'm going to stay inside for the rest of my life." I shrugged and smiled.

Frankie flipped the blinker with his middle finger and looked over his shoulder. "I don't want to force you to do anything you're not ready for."

After hijacking his life to drive me to my new one, I would be damned if I was going to stand in the way of Frankie satisfying his noodle craving.

"I've never had Thai food."

"Oh, Megan." Frankie's voice took on an awe that was completely out of character from everything else he'd shown me. It was pretty darn charming, like a glimpse at the real him.

"Is it spicy?" I crinkled my nose. I didn't normally do well with anything other than bland.

We exited for downtown and came to a stop at a red light. It was rather impressive that he knew where he was going without GPS.

"It's a little spicy." The quick rake of his eyes hinted that his idea of 'a little' might just be more than I could handle. But the hell with it. I was ready to try something new and happy to do it in his company.

Thirty minutes later we were parked in a massive garage along the river and out on a busy street. The cool air from the bank was a welcome change from the car.

"God, it feels good to stretch and walk. This way." Frankie pointed to the left. His comment reminded me that I was the reason he'd been driving all day. And while he'd said that he wasn't resenting me for the position he was in, the twinge of guilt still pestered me.

A quick zing shot through me when he gently pressed his hand into my lower back to guide me. My heart raced and heat flushed over my neck. Thankfully, he was walking next to me instead of looking at me. *Good Lord. Am I so desperate for an act of kindness that just his touch is making me all mushy? Possibly.*

The city buzzed around us. It may have only been a Monday, but there was a pulse in the energy that could not be denied. All kinds of people walked around with their individual purposes. A young mother pushed a stroller and an older gentleman yapped on his phone without a care for how loud he was speaking. A hipster rode his bike by us with his messenger bag in the basket. No one looked at me.

I grinned from ear to ear. I blended in.

"Here." Frankie's eyes had lit up like a Christmas tree, and he held the door open for me. The restaurant was small, just four tables and a counter, and I wondered how on earth Frankie had found this place to begin with.

We sat at the table farthest from the door and Frankie unbuttoned his long sleeves then rolled them up. His watch was all silver with a simple face — elegant and classy.

A waiter came over, offered us menus and we ordered our drinks. I read through the options but had no idea what any of it meant other than I could choose between chicken, shrimp or tofu. I bit my bottom lip, trying to make heads or tails of it.

"Is there, like, just some chicken and rice?"

Frankie plucked the menu out of my hand. "Trust me. You want the noodles. What's your spice level? One, two or three?"

"One?" I cringed a little. Was there a zero spice level?

"Allow me." He stood, went over to the counter and ordered. The waiter handed him our drinks, and as he carried him back to the table, I wondered if I could slip into a parallel universe where I was on a date with a man like Frankie. With his defined cheekbones, he had that kind of perfectly structured face that made him classically handsome. His body was tight, not bulky but muscular. There was also a sophisticated calm about him that comforted me. *Yeah, I'm absolutely crushing on him.* Good thing he'd be rid of me the following day. I just had to get through one more night in the same room…

Frankie sat, his easy smile making me warm and light. He was comfortable, and I wondered if that would also mean open.

Once I'd had a sip of my soda, I asked, "How do you know about this place? Don't you live in New York?"

"I had a job here for about six months. I found this place, and now I go out of my way to eat here whenever I'm nearby."

"What was the job?"

Frankie frowned and rubbed his short beard. "I'd rather not talk about it. I was a different person then."

If anyone could understand, that it was me. As curious as I was, there would probably be a day when I would say the same thing, and I would appreciate someone obeying my verbal stop sign. "I get it."

He nodded then furrowed his forehead. "Do you need anything before we get to New York? I mean, you're giving traveling light an entire new definition. The shops are open until nine…"

The truth was, I didn't have much money to spend on nonessential items. Once I got a paycheck, I would buy some new clothes. But until then, I had my little jumper, eight pairs of underwear, a bra, a pair of shorts and three T-shirts. It wasn't much, in fact it was downright depressing, but it didn't matter.

"I'm good." I shook my head.

The waiter slid two big bowls of steaming noodles in front of us. Vegetables and chicken were mixed in, and the curry seasoning made my mouth water. Frankie hummed a little contented sigh — it was somehow super sexy — then twirled a bite with his fork and spoon, jutted his chin in my direction and said, "If you don't like this, I don't think we can be friends anymore."

I copied his movements while I contemplated his use of the word 'friends'. It didn't sound all bad having Frankie Ricci as my first friend on the flipside. I tried not to slurp as I piled the small mountain of noodles into my mouth.

Whoa! Burning lava assaulted my tongue and inner cheeks. I chewed as fast as I could and broke out into an immediate sweat. Spitting wasn't an option. The damage had been done, and I didn't want to look like a fool in front of my new 'friend'. Tears leaked out of my eyes. *How in the name of all things human can this be the lowest heat level?* Worse, I had to finish it.

"Shit," Frankie said after curiously eying his bowl then mine. "I think that one is mine."

The fire in my mouth spread to my throat as I swallowed the noodles that had surely been made in the deepest level of Satan's hell. I panted, but the cool air somehow made it worse. A swarm of killer wasps had somehow been transformed into what was disguised as food and were officially attacking my insides.

Frankie dashed to the counter while I fanned the flames engulfing my mouth. More tears mixed with sweat streamed down my cheeks and I coughed, only to be reminded of the burning.

Deana Birch

He came back with a glass of milk, which I promptly guzzled, not caring that some of it ran down my chin, neck and chest. Frankie grabbed a napkin and blotted my mess while I looked at him with what must have been bugged-out eyes.

"I'm so sorry. I should have tested it. Shit. Are you okay?"

I slammed the glass on the table and stared at him. Panting, I asked, "How can you eat that? Holy crap."

The milk started soothing the heat, and I took the napkin from Frankie and wiped away the rest of my sweat mixed with tears. I blinked several times as Frankie came into full focus. He very carefully switched our plates and I stared at the noodles, wondering if they were safe.

"I promise they are not spicy—not like this, anyway." He pointed his fork to the dish in front of him.

"How could anything be spicy like that?"

Frankie swirled a bite and, to my utter amazement, ate it. Not even a single drip of perspiration appeared on his forehead, and he continued. Did he not know he was eating satanical demons whose weapons were flame shooters? He chewed, swallowed and grinned.

"You're not human." I pronged a few noodles, rolled them around the fork then brought them to my nose for a sniff. I wasn't convinced, so I poked my tongue out and touched it to the bite. There was a bit of spice, but nothing like the other plate, so against my better judgment, I opened and slid them in.

What had previously been hellacious heat was now an explosion of new flavors that I was unable to identify. Yes, there was a kick to it, but it was delicious.

I grinned from ear to ear once I'd finished the bite and loaded another.

Frankie smiled across from me. "Good, right?"

"Really, really good. But now I'm going to be craving these too. Surely there's similar in New York."

"I keep looking. So far these are the best." He pointed his fork to the bowl. "But let me know if you find a place."

That implied that we would remain in contact—which I guessed was true. He was my new boss's brother, and they must have been somewhat close if he was willing to drive me across country to make Fiona happy.

We continued eating, and even though I was a bit nervous because my crush lingered in the back of my mind, I tried to play it cool and blend into the casual environment.

"So, what does a man like you do for fun?"

Frankie wiped his mouth with a paper napkin from the metal dispenser on our table and tossed it on his empty dish. A twinkle came to his eyes. "What do you mean 'a man like me'?" He crossed his arms and raised his thick eyebrows.

Uhhh… What do I mean? But there was still a small smirk on his face, so he was playing.

I finished the rest of my soda. "You know." I shrugged casually. I barely recognized the flirty tone in my voice. Where had *that* come from? "Sophisticated, serious, mostly silent."

"Do all your adjectives start with the letter S?"

"Just for you." Who was the Megan Walsh in Pittsburgh at the out-of-the-way Thai noddle restaurant? Because the one possessing my body had almost said, "sexy."

Frankie licked his lips then glanced away for a beat. "I haven't had real fun for quite a while, to be honest."

"I know the feeling." I coughed out a stuttered laugh. "The last time I had pure fun was before...." I waved over my shoulder, trying to put the past behind. "Church camping trip. Such an innocent memory. I think we even sang around the fire. Sounds cheesy, probably. Sorry." I shook my head. I was such a simpleton.

"God..." Frankie stretched out his legs and interlaced his fingers behind his head. "I haven't been camping in ages. Leo and Fiona used to go before she got pregnant. Then that overprotective bastard was afraid she'd fall on a rock."

"Sounds sweet."

"It's kinda sickening. But it makes for good material to tease him about."

"You're close." I dared the assumption. Behind the insults, there was an obvious bond between the brothers.

Frankie deliberated the observation. "There's nothing I wouldn't do for him."

"Thus me."

"Thus you." The way he said it was not annoyed. It was both matter-of-fact and accepting. "Shall we check into the hotel so I can drop off the rental?"

"Frankie?" I dared touch his hand. He clocked the movement but didn't object. "Even though you may be doing it for him, it still means the world to me. I'll never be able to repay you—and I know this sounds trite since I have literally nothing—but if I can ever do anything for you, I'd be happy to."

He narrowed his eyes and offered a tight smile, which brought out the wrinkles around his dark eyes. "I appreciate the offer. Come on."

Chapter Nine

Frankie

I rode the shuttle the short distance from the terminal to the hotel. I hoped my plan of switching cars and dropping them off at airports would work and that I was making Megan hard to locate. A guy like Billy wouldn't be deterred. Abusers had a tendency to think that the person they were abusing was somehow their property. So while Megan would be safe for a while, she would probably spend the rest of her life looking over her shoulder.

More than once during those long stretches of interstate, I'd considered traveling back to Iowa and putting a bullet between his eyes then throwing him in one of the small lakes. But it would be linked to Megan, and besides, I didn't do that anymore.

It was hard to imagine how such a bright young woman had fallen victim to a loser like Billy. I was happy she was getting a chance to start over.

The bus stopped under the awning of the hotel. I stepped off and walked over to the side then took out my phone.

"You're on speaker," Leo said after it had rung twice.

"How is she?" Fiona's voice carried concern. It was a good question. On the outside Megan seemed to be keeping her shit together with ease. But it must be gut-wrenching to leave an entire life behind in such a rush.

"You can ask her tomorrow night. I'll drop the rental in Newark, take the train into the city, grab my Porsche and be at your place for dinner."

The fumes from the planes made the humid air thicker. It would be nice to get to Leo's place and smell the salt water from the ocean. He'd been smart to move out of the city.

"Does she need anything?" Fiona asked.

"She's been traveling pretty light. She hardly has any clothes, but she's refused my offers to get some. I think she's proud and maybe a little stubborn."

Leo laughed. "What's that like?"

I would have bet my Porsche that his snarky comment got him smacked.

Fiona said, "Let me know when you get to the city so I can start dinner."

"You're cooking?" *Shit*. I shouldn't have said that so quickly and with the squeak in my throat.

"Yes. Is that a problem?" Fiona slowed her words. It was a trap.

I needed to tread lightly. While I was grateful for a dinner invitation, Fiona and the kitchen were, well…not compatible. "Let me know if I can bring anything."

"Nice save." Leo had taken me off speaker. "How you holding up? Long drives not in your baby and small talk... I imagine you must be cranky. Poor Megan."

"I don't mind her." *At all, really.*

"Huh. Not what I asked, but interesting." The amusement in Leo's voice rubbed me the wrong way. I would never take advantage of a woman in Megan's situation.

"Fuck off. What's happening with our client?"

Leo sighed. "He banged his manager's wife Saturday after the art opening in the bathroom at the after-party. Jackson said it didn't seem like the first time."

Our client, a former tennis champion, was a sex addict who only got off on other people's women. He'd hired our firm after a husband had come at him with a golf club, and Jackson, Leo and I had taken turns babysitting him for the last couple of months. Andy Cobbler had been a referral from a former client, and if he hadn't been paying us a ridiculous amount of money, we would have given him the boot after the first week. I wasn't looking forward to following him around to his photo shoots and TV appearances. The week away had been a welcome break.

"You're gonna take over, right? Jackson needs a night off and Fi is going to seriously pop any minute."

I rolled my neck. The streetlights kicked on and created a warm glow around the hotel. It would be my last night of freedom for a while. "Yeah. Email me any changes to the schedule. I'll see you tomorrow."

An older couple passed by laughing and holding hands. Happily-ever-after was a destiny I would never meet. I was pretty sure my darkened soul would never find someone who could accept all the shit I'd done, the lives I'd taken for money.

I followed them into the lobby and rode up the elevator. For someone who had done nothing but sit all day, I was tired. The little light flashed green after I touched the lock with the keycard, and I decided to knock with the door just ajar.

"It's me."

There was no answer and my hair stood at attention on the base of my neck. I took a cautious step in. The light between the beds was on and our bags were where we'd laid them after we'd checked in. I reached to the back of my waistband for a gun I wouldn't find then closed the door quietly. I'd told Megan not to go out, and I didn't think she would have. I sidestepped to the bathroom where the door was closed.

Before I could knock, it swung open and Megan screamed. Steam flowed out around her and her dark hair dripped down her chest where she held a towel that barely covered the important parts.

"Oh my Lord, you scared the crap out of me." She fanned her face. "I wasn't expecting you back so soon."

After my greedy eyes had taken her all in, I regained a little bit of composure, spun around and stared at the ground. *Why is all hotel carpet atrocious?*

"I'm so sorry. I knocked and you didn't answer. I went on high alert…"

"It's fine. I'll just get my bag and change." She dripped across the room, her little legs shiny from the moisture, and I just may have caught a glimpse of the top of her thighs, which may have also turned into me ogling the shape of her ass and the light color of her skin. I quickly diverted my gaze when she turned around, and I stepped to the side so she could go back to the privacy of the bathroom.

She'd been in the bathroom. What a fucking idiot I was. I shook my head and went over to my bag. Just one more night of hotel room hard pillows and I would be back in the luxury of my Egyptian cotton and down comforter. I toed off my shoes and untucked my shirt.

The bathroom door opened as I undid the last button and Megan passed by in the long T-shirt she wore for pajamas. *Pity... A woman as lovely as her deserves silk on her skin when she sleeps.* It only seemed fair that she could get a glimpse of my skin—surely that was the reason I was undressing in front of her—so I slipped out of the shirt and tossed it on the bed.

"Damn." Megan's hand flew up and covered her mouth. Her eyes widened. Behind her fingers she said, "I said that out loud. Crap." She moved to the bed designated for her and sat down on her hands. "Sorry. I don't mean to stare at you"—she blinked several times—"but I can't seem to stop. Do you have *any* body fat? Frankie, have you seen your body? You're completely ripped. I'm sorry. I know it's rude, but I seriously can't look away."

Okay, so I'm flattered. I took a lot of pride in my body, and I was mildly vain. "Seven percent." I reached for my belt but thought better than to drop my pants in front of her. "I have seven percent body fat."

"That is a miscalculation." She'd dropped her jaw, and I kinda wished she'd been drooling. It was a nice stroke to my ego, and I didn't care how superficial it was. It had been a while since a woman outside my family had complimented me.

"It's for work." Not totally false. I grabbed my shaving kit and headed into the bathroom.

As I brushed my teeth, I wondered if now that she'd seen me bare-chested if I needed to sleep in a T-shirt like I'd done the previous night. My arrogance decided against it, and I exited the bathroom in just boxers then slid quickly into my bed.

"Goodnight. Will you hit the light?" I asked.

Megan chewed her thumbnail and studied me.

"What?"

"It's just..." She closed her eyes for a long beat before opening and giving them a big roll. "It's just that I know I'm going to crawl into your bed in the middle of the night. I can't help it, and I've convinced myself you don't mind."

I didn't. "So you're wondering...why not just start here?"

"Uh-huh."

I sat up. "I want to be clear that you don't owe me anything. You don't need to repay me somehow." *Like with sex.* Sex I'd been sure thirty minutes prior was something I would never do. But after seeing her in the towel and getting a compliment, there was an entirely different part of my brain, or maybe body, taking over my reasoning.

"I'm not trying to do that. Honest. I sleep better knowing you're close. I feel safe." She shook her head. "I know that's pathetic, and it sounds contrived, but it's true. Being near you is calming."

What was I going to say? No? *Ha.* She was inflating my ego at every turn, and it was about ready to pop.

"You can sleep next to me."

She smiled then turned out the light. I wiggled down and stayed on my back. I wasn't sure a good night's sleep was in the cards for me. Her signals were confusing my morals. I closed my eyes. Maybe the right thing to do was somewhere inside my brain.

Megan crawled into the bed and shifted the pillow diagonally so that she was facing me. "Frankie?" she whispered.

"Megan?" I was glad for the dark. I was pretty sure I was losing the battle at fighting my smile.

"I just wanted to thank you for scorching the inside of my mouth."

That was a pretty fucking adorable way to refer to the noodles. I had no idea if she was teasing or just being funny, but I liked it.

"Anytime." Okay, we were officially flirting—or I was at least. There was way too much charm in my tone. And if I was flirting, I was doomed. Also, we were both practically naked. *Jesus Christ, I'm a terrible person.* She was vulnerable and scared. She was also beautiful and right next to me. My pulse kicked up a notch, which was odd, as I was normally cool as a cucumber, even if I was nervous.

"What happens if he finds me?"

"He won't." I regretted the shift to somber, but the logical, well-behaved side of me was relieved when it came.

"Okay."

"You need to talk about anything else? Probably best to get it out now before the only people you're talking to is a six-year-old and your employers." Against my better judgment, I rolled to the side and faced her.

The streetlights were bright and there was a glow that highlighted her silhouette, like a halo around an angel. It was soft and overpowering at the same time.

"I hope you know how beautiful you are. I hope that asshole didn't strip away every last ounce of your confidence."

She stared at me for a long time then said, "I want you to kiss me."

Not as much as I wanted to do it, of that I was sure. "I'm not going to do that."

She frowned, and it was gorgeous. "That only makes me want it more."

"This is a no-win situation, Megan."

"Or a win-win."

I grinned. She had a point. But as jaded as my conscience was, I knew kissing her was way, way in the 'very fucking wrong' category.

She needed to stop looking at me like a sweet angel, so soft and so fucking innocent. It was killing me.

"Megan." I fluttered my eyes shut. Her pretty face asking to be kissed was more powerful than she could imagine. Because, truth be told, I'd wanted to kiss her the second I saw her. "It's a bad idea."

"No. You don't believe that. It's a good idea but bad timing."

"Fuck." I rolled back and stared at the ceiling. She was drawing me in.

"What if I kissed you? Surely, you wouldn't be cold enough to reject me." Her blend of innocence and mischief was killing me.

"Does the dark always make you this bold?"

"Do you not want to?"

I groaned. What was she? Some kind of Supreme Court kissing lawyer? Her arguments were pulling at my heart strings, toying with my ego and sure as shit arousing my dormant libido.

And way, way, way fucking worse, she was moving on top of me. Straddling me! Leo was seriously going to try to kick my ass if he found out I was in bed with his nanny — not to mention what Fiona would do to me.

"Megan…" I warned.

"Frankie." The tips of her hair tickled my chest as she leaned over and whispered in my ear. "One little innocent goodnight kiss. Then I promise I'll go back to my side and keep my hands to myself."

I whimpered…fucking *whimpered* right there below her. Never had a woman turned me to jelly before. Never had I lost control like I was pretty sure I was about to do and never, fucking ever, was I more sure that I wanted to kiss a woman and absolutely should not do it.

"You smell so good." Her hot breath on my throat and the realization that she was grinding against my crotch with only underwear between us was the needle that punctured the balloon of my common sense.

Megan dragged her cheek against my beard and stopped when we were nose to nose. *Jesus with a jackhammer, we're going to do it.* She brushed her lips against mine softly and I was all in. I would let her kiss me until she didn't want to anymore.

She pecked once then glanced up, with a naughty grin.

Shit.

I threaded my hand below the T-shirt and found silky skin. It was wrong and I was being a very, very bad getaway man, but I didn't see many other ways for the moment to play out.

A short hover proceeded a soft kiss and a long drag of her bottom lip on mine. Jesus, she was sweet. I craved more, probably would have killed for it. Again she teased me with her lips, barely kissing and taking her damn time doing so.

My head spun and I loved it. I ran my free hand up the back of her leg and couldn't help but take a long squeeze of her ass. She moaned into my mouth, and when she leaned down to my ear again, I was sure she was going to convince me to take it further.

"Goodnight." Ever so gently, she climbed off me and lay on her side facing the opposite way.

I licked my lips and swallowed, wanting to keep the small taste I'd had of her with me forever. It wasn't clear if I should regret my actions or rejoice in them. What I did know was that I was officially under her spell.

Chapter Ten

Megan

The rural farms along the interstate reminded me of the Midwest. But my brain buzzed that I was East Coast bound. I didn't even bother fighting the grin. My life was changing and so was I. I'd made a commitment to myself to be bolder and well, the kiss the night before? Yeah. Proof positive. I would have never done that a month prior. But there was also a security I had with Frankie that made room for me to do something so forward.

The white sleeves of Frankie's dress shirt were rolled up halfway on his forearms, showing his dark hair and silver wristwatch. It was a funny thing to find that part of his body attractive, but it was just as tight as the rest of him. Him grabbing my butt during the quiet embrace had confirmed our chemistry was mutual, and I thought I was ready to properly flirt. I just couldn't remember how to do it.

"I need a coffee. Do you mind if I pull off at the next rest stop?" Frankie glanced over at me. It was kinda sweet that he'd asked. It wasn't like I had a choice.

Maybe he hadn't slept as well as I had. "I can drive if you want."

He shook his head. "I have the rental in a fake name. No point putting you on the map if something were to happen."

I narrowed my eyes. There was more to his answer. "Do you think I'm a bad driver because my car was a piece of crap?"

"No. I think we're four hours away from you being at my brother's house and officially starting your new life. I don't want to risk anyone knowing where you are when we've gotten this far already." His tone was firm. Being protected was like a fuzzy blanket I never knew I needed. I wrapped my arms around each other. Was this foreign warmth me starting to actually feel safe?

"So, we drop this off in Newark and take public transportation to the city?" There was a childish excitement I had about taking the subway. How amazing that New York had so many people living without cars, and they got around just fine. I longed to be like that. It rang of freedom.

"Yep." Frankie flicked the blinker and looked over his shoulder. "We can pick up my car downtown then drive out to Long Island."

Hundreds of images flooded my mind. Bustling streets, cat-calling construction workers, yellow taxis — I craved it all.

Frankie took the offramp and pulled into a gas station. "You need anything?"

I shook my head and he got out of the car and headed inside. Four hours, he'd said. As far as we'd come, I was only a matter of minutes away from my new life. My heart raced. I was really doing it.

In the bottom of my bag, I found my pre-paid phone and sent Ruby a text telling her I was almost free like her. I shoved the phone back under my clothes before I could read her reply, and the opening of the driver's door startled me back to the present.

"You okay?" He sipped his coffee and shuddered. It obviously didn't meet his standards. Frankie looked at me with his deep, dark eyes and instead of brushing off what I was feeling, I decided to share.

"Never better."

He turned to me, with a bent knee in my direction. "It's really brave to leave your life. Because, Megan, where you were headed... Statistics are not on your side there."

Oh, I knew the statistics. I'd battered my sister with them for six months before she'd agreed to leave. And I probably could have taken that moment to be honest with Frankie but that would have required me telling him about Ruby, and she no longer existed. That was how I was keeping her safe.

Frankie pivoted forward and cranked the engine. We stayed quiet until the sign welcoming us to the garden state passed by. I was officially on the East Coast. It didn't seem real.

My new life was starting, and it occurred to me that I didn't know much about it. "So...any tips about my employers?"

"Off the record?" Frankie slowed the car and we edged into a line to pay a toll.

"Absolutely."

"Well, to start, they're disgusting."

They're what?

He continued with a frown, "They are ridiculously in love—like saccharine levels. I leave their house thinking I've just eaten an entire candy store. And speaking of eating, Fiona is not to be trusted in the kitchen. Violet cooks better than she does. We've banned her from ever trying meatloaf again."

I laughed. "You can't be serious."

"To be fair, she has impossible standards to live up to. My Aunt Chezzie owns her own restaurant and could make a tire taste good."

There was a pinch in my chest. I wasn't exactly a top chef. Cuisine hadn't been on my list of self-improvements.

"Do you cook?" I asked.

"I can, but I don't."

"Why not?"

He closed one eye and raised the opposite eyebrow. "Cooking for one is a little depressing." Frankie rolled down his window, exchanged a few pleasantries with the woman working the toll booth then, once we were good, gassed the car to the on-ramp.

"I totally see you as one of those guys who cooks for his dates and knows things about wine." *Then gets them into bed with a bat of his eye.*

Frankie chuckled. "Well, you are wrong about that, Miss Megan. My dates usually end very badly—more than once at an empty table in a crowded restaurant."

Not possible. "I don't believe you."

"Oh, I've had some epic fails. The last three women I took to dinner, I did background checks on them and knew too much. My aunt also accuses me of being emotionally unavailable, whatever that means."

"I'm pretty sure I'm going to be emotionally unavailable for decades," I quipped. "What were your deal breakers in the background check? Asking for a friend."

He glanced over before letting out a little huff. "Massive credit card debt and showed up in designer shoes. I couldn't stop thinking about how she couldn't really afford them and wondering if she was a gold digger."

"Okay..." I had my own debt to deal with, but at least I wasn't compounding it with clothes I didn't need.

"Another one checked out okay but just wouldn't stop asking about how I grew up."

Noted. It wasn't the first time he'd mentioned not wanting to talk about his past, which only made the urge to scratch the itch more, but I got it. I wouldn't want to talk about mine on a first date either.

"The last one I went on had a huge social media presence and wanted to snap a pic. Not my thing."

Not mine either. The last thing I would do would be create a profile somewhere. It would be an open invitation for Billy to come stab me in my sleep. *No thanks.*

"So yeah. That little goodnight kiss you laid on me last night was the first one in a while."

Oppressive heat flushed my chest and neck. "Oh, we're talking about that?" My voice cracked.

Frankie shot me a cheeky grin. "Don't get me wrong. I liked it. But we can't do that again. You know that, right?"

No. I didn't know that. "Yeah. Duh. I mean, sorry I put you in that position." I shrugged and stared out of the window. Hopefully I hadn't sounded as disappointed as I was feeling. Before I could stop them the words flew out of my mouth. "*Why* can't we do that again, exactly?"

"Megan..."

"Frankie."

He rolled his eyes. "Because you work for my brother, and you've just uprooted your entire life. You need to focus on you, not a middle-aged lonely man with a charred soul."

Whoa. I would have never guessed Frankie thought that about himself. He was so calm, so well put together.

"Your soul can't be that dark. You basically rescued me from hell."

"A demon knows the way in and out. Don't make me out to be a hero. You will be thoroughly disappointed."

"Well, the good news is that I get to decide how I see you, not you. So thank you very much for your input, but I'll be making my own assessments of character."

Frankie flicked his eyes in my direction. I bet he thought it held some kind of warning. But the way I saw it, whatever it was in his past he thought was so bad couldn't change the fact that the behavior he'd had since I met him showed me someone very different. So, he could have his secrets. Lord knew I had mine.

We got to Newark in the early afternoon, and I waited by the bus while Frankie dropped off the rental car. The sun was bright, and the density of people was like nothing I'd ever experienced. Once on the bus, I glanced around and marveled at the diversity. Each person had their story to tell — or hide, just like me.

At the airport we exited, bought two tickets for the train and were in Penn Station in less than thirty minutes. If I'd thought there were crowds in Newark,

I'd been crazy. People walked past so fast that I was sure were meant for some kind of race. The train station smelled like pollution and urine, but I didn't care. I loved it. Once above the tracks, I spun in a slow circle, taking it all in.

Frankie leaned down and tilted his head. "Like you thought it would be?"

"It's amazing. You can literally feel the buzz of energy."

He smiled and swung his bag over his shoulder. "We'll take a cab to my place."

We exited the station and were hit with a wall of noise. It was just like the movies. The acceleration of a bus, the honks from cars and a swarm of voices. I followed Frankie to the street where he lifted an arm and hailed a cab. Like magic, one pulled over and we got in.

A purple tree hung from the rear-view mirror and a layer of plexiglass separated us from the older driver. I glued my forehead to the window and gawked at all the buildings and pedestrians. New York City was the perfect place to get lost. The scale of everything was astonishing, and I may have been in a state of shock.

Too soon, the driver stopped at a curb and Frankie paid with his credit card. I exited and scanned a building that never seemed to stop growing.

"This will only take a minute."

A doorman nodded to us and opened the glass door. A massive lobby lay spread out with dark leather couches and gleaming marble floors. Not only did I feel underdressed, I was sure I was completely out of place. I swallowed past a lump in my throat and followed Frankie over to the elevator bay where he nodded to a stranger, and I cracked an unsure smile.

We rode up twenty-seven flights. *Twenty-seven.* The ride, the luxury, the shock — it was all making me dizzy. The lights in the hallway buzzed in harmony with the ringing in my ears.

But it wasn't until Frankie unlocked his door at the end of the hall that I truly understood how out of my league I actually was. His apartment had floor-to-ceiling windows and was basking in the afternoon sunlight. He had two massive white sectionals that faced each other and a state-of-the-art open kitchen. Every appliance shined, the stone countertop glimmered and I had no idea what the painting was on the wall but it was surely worth more than I'd earned in my entire life.

"I'll just be a sec." Frankie's tone was entirely too normal. Did he realize where he lived? He disappeared down a hall and I walked over to the windows. A dark river ran into the ocean and if I was right, I was looking at Brooklyn with its own waterfront and bridges. I reached to touch the glass then thought better of it.

Frankie must have been embarrassed for me in my crappy little apartment.

"Ready?"

I jumped. "Your place is stunning."

Frankie grimaced. "It's cold, impersonal and modern — just like me."

Another warning was wrapped up in his tone. He really didn't want me to like him. Too bad…that ship had sailed. And I wasn't sure he was any of those things. His value in family alone negated all three.

"Come on." Frankie held the door open for me and I followed him down the hall. We rode the elevator to the basement, and it opened to a massive garage with luxury cars. One SUV after another lined the lot, but it was the lights of a small, light-blue Porsche that flicked on and off.

That's his car? I would have never guessed.

And boy, oh boy, could he drive that baby. In and out of traffic we zoomed, and my heart pounded. I held onto the roof to keep myself from flying into his lap. After three days of cautious speed on the interstates, Frankie was taking the term 'expressway' to new levels.

It wasn't until he exited into a small town that he was forced to slow his speed and abide by traffic lights.

Cold Spring Harbor, also known as my new home, was nothing like I'd expected. Huge trees lined the rural streets, and old Victorian homes peeked out between their branches. It was somehow both quaint and luxurious.

Frankie turned down a long path, and a beautiful red-brick home came into view. It was the biggest house I'd ever seen, and the grounds and exterior were immaculately groomed. Okay, so these Ricci brothers had *serious* money — all in the name of private security? They must have been the best in their field.

To say I was overwhelmed was putting it mildly. My new home was a mansion.

We came to a stop, and Frankie killed the engine. "You ready? Because chaos awaits."

There was just one thing I needed to do before I walked into my new life. I placed my hand over his on the gear shift. "Thank you. From the bottom of my heart, I will be forever grateful for the last three days. You saved me."

Frankie stared at my hand for a beat. "You saved yourself. I just drove the getaway car."

A dog barked then ran toward the car.

"Ah. Rusty. Worst-trained beast in the history of domestic animals. At least he's housebroken. Keep your shoes off the floor. He likes the smell of feet."

A massively pregnant Fiona stood in the threshold, waving eagerly with one hand and holding the other with a little girl that had to be Violet. Overwhelming emotion caught in my throat but calm triumphed.

I smiled first to her then the girl before getting out of the car. All my problems needed to be behind me. This family had done enough for me. It was time to repay their kindness by being the best nanny I could be.

Shaking off my nerves, I hitched my bag over my shoulder and walked down the stone path to the front door. Fiona took me in for a tight hug then held me at arm's length.

Her eyes softened and in a quiet voice she asked, "You okay?"

For the first time in ages, I was. I really was. "Yeah. Yeah, I am."

She smiled and her whole face lit up. "Good. 'Cuz my water broke literally five minutes ago. Leo's just grabbing my bag." To Frankie, who was standing behind me, she said, "You'll stay and show her the ropes, right?"

The younger version of Frankie—it could only have been Leo—jogged down the large wooden staircase holding a suitcase and with sunglasses in his dark hair.

"You made it. Great." He grinned at his brother then nodded to me. "Hi. Welcome. Sorry to throw you into the fire like this."

Frankie kissed Fiona on the cheek then scooped up Violet and whispered something in her ear. *Holy hotness.* My ovaries needed a fan.

I rubbed my neck then focused back to Leo. "It's fine. It's my job, right?"

Leo tightened his gaze, maybe analyzing the level of confidence in my voice, then turned to his brother. "I know you're probably dying to get back to your lonely life and ironed sheets, but..." He weighed his head back and forth.

Frankie blinked once, their silent conversation agreed upon.

"Holy fucking shit!" Fiona grabbed her stomach and bent forward. She waved Leo over and squeezed his forearm.

"Contraction?" Leo asked.

"You're a fucking genius." Fiona rolled her eyes and huffed through several breaths.

But instead of being insulted, Leo grinned from ear to ear. "My boys have power."

"That's my uterus. It's—" Fiona calmed her breath, and after about a minute, the contraction had passed.

Frankie cleared his throat. "Okay. Why don't you two go ahead to the hospital before Megan decides she can't work for crazy people. Text us with the news."

But I would have never done that. In fact, I was crushing on the lot of them. I stepped deeper into the entry way and Leo passed by.

"Good luck!" I waved.

"I'll need it with this one by my side." Fiona glared at Leo, but there was a sparkle in her eyes that didn't match her tone. Frankie was right. They were so obviously in love, but it wasn't sickening. It was inspiring.

Fiona crossed over to Frankie and Violet. "Hey." She tapped Violet's little button nose. "I don't need to tell you to be good, because you are the best little girl on the planet."

Violet beamed. "When can I see them?"

"I told you, bug." Leo went over and kissed her cheek. "You're third in line to hold them. Me, Fi, then you. I'll call you first." He winked at her then took Fiona's hand. "Come on, beautiful."

And in a whoosh they were out of the door and into white Range Rover. The three of us waved until we couldn't see the car anymore, and Frankie, still holding Violet, closed the door.

"Right. So, what was Fiona planning for dinner?" Frankie asked Violet.

She frowned. "You don't wanna know."

"You still have that patch of basil?"

"Chezzie taught me the secret. It's growing." Violet shot me a side-eye. It was too soon to qualify for Ricci secrets.

"Pesto it is." He turned to me. "Your room is this way. You can get settled, and Squirt and I will make you the best pasta of your life. Right?"

"Yep." Violet wiggled down. "I can give you a tour if you want."

I knelt and offered my hand. "Hi, I'm Megan. It's nice to meet you."

We shook and she said, "I know that. I'm Violet, I'm six and my Uncle Frankie drove halfway across the country just so you could help us. You must be really good at your job."

Let's hope so.

"I hear you're a pretty awesome cook. That's what your uncle said, anyway. I can't wait to taste." I stood then followed Frankie and Violet down the hall. On the left was a huge study with bay windows followed by a half bath. In the back of the house was a stylish, open farm kitchen, a dining room and a sunken living room with a sectional and big screen. The entire house was spotless.

Off the living room was the guestroom assigned to me. On top of a queen-sized bed was a light yellow comforter and several lavender throw pillows. There was no way Fiona could have known that yellow was my favorite color, but the coincidence warmed my heart. The wardrobe would be more than ample for my clothes, and to the side was a full bath, also with yellow towels. Overall, it was a sunny and welcoming room. I plopped down on the bed and my bag fell off my shoulder.

My new life had officially begun.

Chapter Eleven

Frankie

The third glass of wine came too easy. Megan had stopped at one with dinner — very sensible, considering she was literally on the clock — but the Amarone was open, and I wasn't driving anywhere, so I figured 'what the hell?' I topped myself off then sat back in my chair. I couldn't shake the feeling that I was playing house and, worse, that I liked it.

That little glimmer of hope that a life so normal and content would be in my future was a bitch. Experience had proven that women wanted to know about the past before they would commit to a future. And my past? Not pretty. Also, blurting out the murders of more than two dozen humans would not just lose me a girlfriend, it would also likely lead me to prison. I hadn't sacrificed my soul to end up behind bars.

"Do you need help getting ready for bed?" Megan asked Violet as she cleared the dishes.

My phone vibrated on the table and Violet looked over with big eyes. I swiped to accept the camera and positioned the phone against the wine bottle. Leo's face appeared and I waved over Violet.

"Hey, bug."

"Are the babies here?" Violet tapped her cheeks in excitement. Her little white dress was still clean after the pesto, a feat I wasn't sure all six-year-olds could accomplish.

"Not yet. But hopefully soon. I just wanted to say goodnight and I'll see you in the morning. You okay?"

"Yep. Frankie and I made pesto. Megan said it was the best ever."

"Nice." Leo looked at me and jutted his chin.

"Say goodnight to Leo, Violet. I'll be up in a little bit."

"Night! Though I don't know how I'll sleep. I'm excited for those babies!" Violet waved to the phone and Leo blew her a kiss back. The clanking from the dishes in the kitchen meant Megan was still in earshot, and I didn't know what Leo was going to say, so I grabbed the phone and walked out to the back patio, taking Rusty with me for his last sniff of the bushes for the night.

"How's it really going?" I walked down to where the light stones met the green grass. Rusty rolled in the middle of the yard, trying to cover the scent of whatever animal had been there.

"Fucking slow. That's how it's going. She's barely dilated and has threatened to never let me touch her again if this is how it ends up. And she's refusing all drugs, which I respect the hell out of, but it's not easy to watch her suffer. Her insults are pretty amusing, though. How are Megan and Violet getting along?"

"Well." I glanced over to the kitchen windows. Megan was hand-washing the big pot we'd used for the pasta with a contented grin on her face. She'd tied her hair up and it somehow accentuated her cheekbones.

"So, I didn't want to say this in front of everybody and embarrass Violet, but she's been having trouble falling asleep. Tonight will be worse because we're not there. You're going to have to read her like six books and lie next to her until she's out. She won't be comfortable enough with Megan."

"When did this start? She's always been great about bedtime. Is she nervous about the twins?" Whenever I'd stayed later on Sundays, after dinner she'd gone right up to bed without a problem. In general, Violet was a perfect child as far as anyone with the name Ricci was concerned. Fiona and Leo had done a stellar job with her.

"There's a fucking bully at school. Fucking first grade, Frankie."

"What? Why would anyone pick on Violet? And where does this kid fucking live?" It was rare for me to get angry, but messing with my family, with my niece, I had a finger to shake in the face of some parent, and I didn't give a shit if it made me look like an asshole.

"Trust me. I've thought the same thing. But now you have to do everything with a moderator or mediator or some shit. Apparently, Violet let it slip that we weren't her real parents, and the girl now throws it in her face. It's bullshit—but it's also true, so it's not like she's spreading rumors. Anyway, take care of my little girl for me."

"Yeah. No problem. Also, I drank your most expensive Amarone." Despite the information about Violet, I grinned.

"I figured as much. Also, Frankie? Don't bang my nanny."

What the fuck?

"She's, like, half my age." I couldn't tell if I was insulted that he thought I would do that or encouraged that he thought I could. But him telling me not to do it? Forbidden fruit was always the sweetest.

"I need to go back. But I'm serious… I saw the way she looked at you. And you haven't gotten laid since I flunked out of high school. So, you know, keep it in your pants."

"I just drove her halfway across the country and stayed in the same hotel room for three nights. I think I can manage my self-control for one more while my niece is asleep in the same house. Jesus, Leo, a little credit here."

"To be continued. I'll see you in the morning. Lisa said she'd come out and help Megan get acquainted with everything, so it's just a matter of dropping Violet at school."

Oh, I was definitely going to drop my sweet little niece at school. Then I was going to figure out who the bully was and…do nothing.

I frowned. "Keep me posted."

We ended the call, and I rubbed my beard. What had he meant the way Megan looked at me? Had we really been that obvious? I shook my head and decided to worry about that later. I had a six-year-old princess to tuck in.

Back in the house, Megan was drying her wineglass in the kitchen with a black and white striped towel. She'd been barefoot since she'd found her room and the lack of polish on her toes made me appreciate the simplicity of her. She barely wore makeup, had no jewelry and none of her clothes were designer—and yet, she was beautiful. Maybe I'd been dating the wrong kind of woman and had just never realized it.

She smiled as I entered the kitchen. "I can go read to her, or do you think it's too soon to be in her bedroom."

"I'll go. It's been a big day with a lot of changes. No offense to you, but she probably needs someone familiar." I set my phone on the counter.

Megan nodded and replaced the wineglass in the cupboard. She had to stand on her tiptoes, and the action lifted up her shirt and gave me a glance of her stomach. A stomach that had been on mine the night before. Along with an ass—that I'd thoroughly grabbed and enjoyed—that had been grinding my crotch.

"What time do you think she needs to get up for school?"

I blinked hard. *Shit.* Fucking Leo putting ideas into my head. But her lips had been so perfectly soft…

"Frankie?"

"Uh, yeah. She gets up at seven." I knew that because Leo got up and ran on his treadmill every morning. If we were on a call, he always hung up before seven to shower and wake up Violet. "I'm going to stay with her until she's asleep. You don't need to wait up for me."

Violet came out of the bathroom as Rusty and I hit the top step. She smiled and I could tell she was relieved it was me and not Megan.

I tucked my thumb into my palm. "Four books. That's my limit."

"You're supposed to start with your low number, silly. Then I can feel like I won."

"Silly?" I faked insult and followed her into her room. "I am *not* silly. And *I* win, because I get to read to you."

She hopped into her bed and snuggled under the colorful duvet. Rusty curled into a ball on the rug at the end of the bed.

"I want the same four from last night. They're on the table."

I flicked on the lamp next to her bed then turned off the main light. The first book was about a dinosaur with indigestion. There was some kind of underlying vegetarian activism, but the illustrations of the massive beast trying to hold in his gas were hilarious. And I had to admit, Violet's giggle was one of the best sounds on the planet and wonderfully contagious.

The other three weren't as funny, but it didn't matter. Violet rubbed her eyes then turned toward me. She whispered, "Leo told you to stay, right?"

"No place I'd rather be." I offered up my hand to hold and she interlaced her little fingers into mine.

"Do you think those babies are going to like me?" Her blinks were getting slower.

I kissed her warm forehead. "They're going to love you as much as we all do."

Violet closed her eyes and let out a small puff of air from her mouth. I hated the thought of her unhappy and hoped that I was comforting her in some way. The lazy rise and fall of her chest hypnotized me and made my own eyelids heavy…

A gentle nudge on my shoulder woke me up. Megan knelt next to the bed with a sweet smile. She whispered, "Hey, your phone's been vibrating for about ten minutes. Thought you might want to know."

I nodded and looked over at Violet, who was sound asleep. Slowly, I withdrew my hand from hers and followed Megan out of the room and downstairs. Was it wrong for me to be checking out her ass in her cut-off shorts? Probably. But I'd squeezed it and my hand had detected the perfect amount of meat and muscle. Some men liked legs, and others would lose their minds for a nice set of tits. Me? All ass.

Megan's was that perfect upside-down heart. It had fit in my palm like it was meant to be. In fact, my hand was begging for another grip. *Shit.* Both hands were forming hungry claws and I was biting my bottom lip. I'd completely lost control of my body parts. At the bottom of the stairs, I adjusted my junk and focused my gaze upward.

But that plan didn't work either. The nape of her neck—with its dark little hairs that had escaped her ponytail—screamed at me to pepper soft, teasing kisses all over it until she giggled and shuddered. I licked my lips. She'd tasted too sweet.

Enough. She'd just come out of a horrible relationship. I was Satan in a suit. She was starting anew. I was an older, jaded, cranky murderer. *Well, former murderer.* I scrubbed my beard, three full days with a woman had made me horny—reminded me of how soft they could be. No, that wasn't fair to Megan. There was something special about her that appealed to me. I'd liked saving her. It had made me feel like a nice person for a change. She'd brought out some good in me.

Megan went into the living room and curled up with a fuzzy throw blanket. My phone was exactly where I'd left it. I'd bet she hadn't even flipped it to see who called.

There were seven missed calls from Leo and a trail of texts that finished with, *You better not be fucking my nanny.*

I swiped to return the call and downed the remaining wine in my glass.

"Finally," Leo answered. The pissy voice was equal parts annoying and satisfying.

"Sorry. I fell asleep next to Violet. How's it going there?"

"Bad. Very fucking bad." Leo let out a long exhale.

I started to pace around the island in the kitchen. "What does that mean, exactly? Do you want me to come?"

"No. I want you there. Twin A — that's what the doctor calls him — is fine, head down. But B — also the genius name by the doctor — is breech. They say that it shouldn't be a problem. They've seen it before, but they want Fi to have an epidural just in case they have to do a Cesarean. So considering that she doesn't want to take any drugs fucking ever, you can just imagine how that's going over."

"Fuck. I'm sorry. I wish I could do something." I stopped pacing and leaned against the counter.

"You and me both. I'd completely forgotten what it felt like to be scared. And this must also be the feeling of helplessness, something we were taught was impossible."

"There's always a solution." My father's Brooklyn accent rang in my ears. He'd fucked us up on every level, but he'd also engraved survival into our skulls.

I quieted my voice. I didn't want Megan to hear my big brother pep talk. "You're not helpless. You go back in and show that woman why she loves you. You are strength. You are calm and steady. You are her rock. Got it?"

"This conversation never happened."

"Understood."

I hung up and found a seltzer in the fridge then joined Megan in the living room on the opposite end of

111

the sectional. I kicked off my shoes and untucked my shirt.

"The second baby is breech. They say it should be fine, but it's not ideal."

Megan crossed herself. It was the first time I'd seen it done where I thought it actually meant something. We stayed silent for a long time, and I kept stealing glances of her out of the corner of my eye. There was an ease to her energy, some unspoken understanding that we didn't have to say anything. Yet, at the same time, I wanted to know what she was thinking, how she was coping with being thrown into her new life. It also occurred to me that it might be the last time I would be alone with her.

Sure, I would see her again, but it would be surrounded by the chaos of my brother's home. A little smile quirked on her face.

I had to know. "What?"

Megan turned to me and propped her elbow on the edge of the sofa then pressed her head into her fist. "I'm just wondering how a cold, impersonal and modern man makes a delicious dinner and falls asleep holding a little girl's hand."

"You trying to ruin my reputation?"

She stood and the blanket fell back on the couch. We locked eyes as she walked toward me. My heart pumped hard in my chest. *Holy shit, it's going to take every bit of self-control I have not to bang my brother's nanny.* If she straddled me like she'd done the night before, I was done. My hands had already proven they had a mind of their own. My baby brother was having the most stressful moment only miles away and I was actively wondering if he had any condoms in the house and where they might be.

But instead of realizing my desires, Megan bent down next to me and whispered in my ear. "I think you're ruining your own reputation—and it's pretty damn sexy." Her warm breath was followed by a kiss so gentle on my neck that I wasn't even sure it had happened or if I'd imagined it out of desperation. "Night." She stood and walked out. I stared, gawked and eye-stalked her fine, fine ass the entire time.

Chapter Twelve

Megan

The dog barked and barreled down the stairs, waking me from a wonderfully naughty dream about Frankie's beard brushing against my stomach. But why the dog was barking sent a rush of fear up my spine. I threw back the covers and grabbed my shorts from the floor where I'd left them the night before. I hadn't expected Frankie to wander into my room, but I had kinda hoped he would.

I threaded on my bra under the baggie T-shirt and headed down the hall. Leo stood in the doorway scratching Rusty's ears and Violet appeared at the top of the stairs while Frankie emerged from the back living room. We waited with bated breath.

"Dante and Marco Ricci were born at 3:37 and 4:02 a.m. They're both around five and a half pounds and healthy. Their mother is the strongest woman I know and is finally sleeping."

Violet ran down the stairs and threw her arms around Leo who picked her up and kissed her cheek. "Do you have pictures?"

"And videos."

"Congratulations." Frankie walked up to Leo and patted him on the back then slapped his cheek a few times. "I'll make coffee."

I wasn't really sure where I fit into their moment. I didn't want to overstep or force my way but proving myself useful was important.

Leo spun around and I nearly walked into him. "Oh, Megan, you can go back to bed. I'm going to spend some time with my girl, have a shower and a nap then take her to the hospital to meet the boys. Our friend Lisa is going to swing by around ten and walk you through our routine."

"Are you sure? I can make breakfast or walk the dog or…"

"I got this." There was a little edge in his tone, and I wondered if my help was not welcome. Fiona had said I was going to help more with the babies than with Violet.

I nodded and pointed my thumb over my shoulder. "I'll be in my room if you need anything." Looking at Frankie would have revealed my anxiety, so I focused on the floor and went back to my room, which had somehow transformed into a sunny prison. I showered and washed my dirty clothes in the sink then hung them on the towel racks.

At seven-thirty there was a light wrap on my door. Maybe Leo had fallen asleep, and Violet needed something. I plastered a smile on my face and opened with enthusiasm.

Frankie fiddled with his watch then held my gaze with a smile that reminded me of the dream I'd had about him. I let out a stuttered breath and resisted the need to fan myself.

"Three things. One, Leo is extremely possessive and protective of Violet. Don't take that personally. It's their thing, and it will never change. Two" — he pulled out a phone and charger from his back pocket — "this is yours. It has a lot of names and numbers in it that you don't know yet, but eventually will. Also, and we do this to everyone, it has a tracker, so if it's on you, we know where you are."

The phone was brand new and a model I'd never been able to afford. I hoped I wouldn't get addicted to all the stupid games it offered.

"Three, goodbye. I'm going back to my regular life and work. It was nice getting to know you, and I'm glad you got yourself out of that situation."

Goodbye? As in *forever*? I searched his face for more information but came up blank. No, I would see him again. He was committed to his family. He handed me the phone and charger.

"Thank you seems a bit weak for all that you've done for me. Maybe I could buy you dinner once I start making some money."

"Megan—"

"Frankie." I lifted my eyebrows, daring him to reject me.

He shook his head and turned to walk away. "I'll see you around."

That was it? *Ouch.*

As he went down the hall, I thought about how one person could change an entire life. He didn't have to do any of the things he'd done to help me. He could have handed me a bus ticket and wished me luck. He could have even taken one look at my situation and told his brother to run in the opposite direction.

I closed my door and sat on the bed with my new phone. In the browser application, I searched the local library then routed it on the map. It would only take me twenty minutes to walk there. Perfect. Then I routed the train station. It was a little farther away, but still walkable when I would get a day off.

With endless information at my fingertips, my curiosity scratched like an angry cat. I typed in the address of my former county's sheriff's website and my heart leapt into my throat when my high school head shot came up on the screen with the word, 'missing' in all capitals underneath.

I quit out of the browser and tossed the phone on the bed like a hot potato. No good would come from me stalking my former self. I needed to get out of my room and go discover my new surroundings.

In the kitchen, Leo rubbed the back of his head and yawned. Violet and Rusty were in the backyard and she threw a ball. The dog chased it then ran to the opposite side of the grass.

"So no school for her, right?" I tucked my hands into my back pockets and rocked on my heels.

"Nah. I don't have the heart to make her wait until three p.m. to meet the boys."

"Congratulations, by the way. I love the names."

"Thanks." He yawned again.

"You know, I'm here to help, and you're sorta paying me to help. So, I can totally cover this for an hour while you grab some shut-eye."

Leo shifted his gaze to the backyard then to me.

I tried again. "You're just going to be upstairs. We won't leave the property."

A light grumble bubbled out of his throat. "Can I be honest with you?"

Had he been lying about something?

"Please." I swallowed my fear of being fired before ever really doing any work.

He looked down and away. "I didn't want to hire you—not because of what you left. By the way, you're pretty fucking safe here. I have cameras everywhere and my—" He shook his head quickly before continuing, "I didn't want to hire you because I didn't want to admit we needed help. But we do. And I really, really need to sleep. So yes, thank you." Leo grabbed a bottle of water from the fridge and trudged up the stairs.

Violet had succeeded at getting the ball back from Rusty, but when she threw it again, he played his game of cat and mouse at the opposite end of the yard. But I had an idea. My mom had grown up on a farm and used to say, *"A block of cheese can turn the dumbest dog into Einstein."*

I found some cheddar in the fridge and cut it into tiny pieces then tossed them into a plastic bag. I joined Violet and Rusty in the backyard.

"Here." I handed her the bag. "Show me what he can do."

Violet twisted her face and pondered the cheese. "He can't do anything. Leo and Fiona never had dogs before. We love him, but Fi says he's dumber than a box of rocks."

My work was cut out for me then. "They tend to follow the food. Makes sense, right? Gimme a piece."

Violet opened the bag, and I took a few squares of the cheese. Rusty ran up to us with the ball in his slobbery mouth and wagged his tail.

"Sit." At the same time that I said the word, I lifted my hand so his gaze followed the treat and he sat back on his hind legs.

"Whoa." Violet's eyes widened.

I showed Rusty the cheese and said, "Drop it," then brought my hand close to his nose. He promptly let go of the ball and I fed him the cheese while he stood back up on all fours.

"Do it again!"

I had to go back and finish off the block of cheddar, but within an hour, Violet and I had the dog sitting and lying down. He was really crappy at staying, but there had definitely been progress made. In the end, Rusty found a stick in the backyard and wandered off to chew on it, signaling that he was done.

Violet and I washed our hands in the kitchen sink and she went up to get dressed while I cleaned up the breakfast dishes and the cutting board from the cheese.

Leo came into the bright kitchen freshly showered in shorts and a buttoned-up dress shirt. He offered a little nod that I guessed was a bit of a thank you, but I was only doing my job.

Just as I was drying my hands, the doorbell rang, sending Rusty into a barking tizzy, proving I still had a long way to go with him. Leo trotted down the hallway and hooked a finger in Rusty's collar, holding him back while he opened the door.

A pretty blonde held a bouquet of white flowers, and she walked past Leo with a casual, "Hey. Congrats on your healthy babies. But we both know you only planted the seed. It's your wife who did everything else."

"No argument there." Leo closed the door and freed the dog, who sniffed the woman's legs before licking one quickly. Leo shooed him away and they walked down the hall to the kitchen.

"Hi." She tucked the flowers under her arm and stretched out a hand. "I'm Fiona's friend, Lisa. Welcome."

"Nice to meet you."

Violet came down the stairs in jean shorts and white T-shirt that read, 'our kid'. She had brushed her hair and had her little Converse tied. Impressive. At the shoe store it was odd to find kids who could tie their own shoes. I didn't know when people had stopped teaching their kids such a simple task, but Velcro-closure sneakers sold way more than traditional ones with laces.

"Hey, sweetheart. J.J. says the best thing about twins is that you each get to hold one. It's not like with Rusty when you had to take turns." Lisa turned to me. "J.J. is my son and her bestie. My husband, Jackson, works for Frankie. It's all very incestual, but we're not weird. I promise."

I didn't mind that they were friends and co-workers. If anything, it proved that Frankie ran a good company. "Can I take those and put them in water?"

"No." She shooed me away. "I'll do it. You two off?"

Leo walked toward me with a key and a small sheet of paper. "House key and security code, please memorize it. You okay to fend for yourself today? We'll have lunch and dinner with Fiona and the boys..."

"Absolutely." I beamed. "I've already located the public library and am looking forward to checking out the town."

Leo narrowed his eyes then scrunched his face. "Violet, go hop in the car. I'll just be a minute."

She waved goodbye without a second thought while the silent tension crept between the adults. What had I said that was wrong?

"Megan. How you gonna check out a book?"

I shrugged. "I'll get a library card."

"Mm-hmm." Leo looped a finger in the air. "Take that one step further."

"Oh." *Right. Duh.* Showing my driver's license from Iowa. The place I'd just run from.

Leo dug into his front pocket and pulled out an impressive wad of cash. He peeled off three bills and handed them to me. "Buy the books. Much safer."

I didn't want to take the money. "This is an advance, right?"

"Totally." Leo offered a quick, tight smile and was out of the door.

Lisa rolled her eyes and scoffed. "Those Ricci brothers can be cranky-ass bitches. You have to learn to look past it. Come on. I know where Fi keeps the expensive tea, and 'spill the tea' we shall."

Apparently, Lisa knew where everything was in the house because I barely had time to sit at the breakfast nook before she had the flowers in a beautiful purple vase and the kettle on for tea. It was the end of summer and a bit hot for tea, but I didn't mention it. If the woman wanted to sip hot liquid and fill me in on the group of people I had somehow infiltrated, I was down for it.

"Did you have a tour?"

I shook my head. I hadn't wanted to intrude and ask people to show me their bedrooms.

"Let's do that while the water boils. Follow me."

Did we have the right to do that? "Um…"

"Don't worry. I cleared it with Fi." She waved me on.

Upstairs had five bedrooms. Violet's was the first one on the right and it had a beautiful view of the front yard. Across from her was a massive full bathroom with a sunken tub and beige tile. There were two sinks, and each fluffy white towel was perfectly hung. Two identical rooms followed on the right, one set up for the babies and the other with two twin beds. At the end of the hall was a simple double, done in more masculine dark blues and greens. The star of the house was the master bedroom, with windows that overlooked the entire back yard a huge bed, walk-in closets and all done in gray and white. It somehow managed to be modern yet warm.

We walked back down the stairs and Lisa showed me the laundry room, pantry and entrance to the garage, where there was a sleek black Audi and massive black SUV with tinted windows.

When we finally were back in the little nook, she poured our tea and I had to admit to being both impressed and intimidated. It was almost like being drunk on style and luxury.

"Everything is so clean."

Lisa laughed. "That will change with the boys. But yeah, Fiona and I are neat freaks. It's because we came from nothing. We both grew up in the same projects, so now the nice things we have? We take care of them. What made you come here?"

I swirled my finger around the rim of the mug. "Ready for a life change."

"I hear that. When Frankie and Leo offered Jackson a job, we never looked back." Lisa held her cup in front of her face and was lost in a memory.

"Where do you live now?"

"In Queens. Jackson lost his dad a few years back, and we decided we wanted to be closer to his sister. We don't have this kind of money, but we do all right. Jackson is putting his sister's kids through college."

"All from a security company?"

"They're not just any security company. They are the most elite. They guard diplomats and rock stars. Right now, Jackson is Andy Cobbler's bodyguard. Apparently he's a nightmare, but they don't say why. I just know Frankie's taking over this afternoon and Jackson couldn't be happier."

I briefly wondered why an ex-tennis star would need a bodyguard, but at one point I may have heard he was the highest paid athlete in the world. He probably had gold watches that needed their own protection. The world of the rich and famous was beyond me.

"Anyway. I wanted to ask you if you needed anything. I heard you only brought one bag."

"Do you guys tell each other everything?" I sipped my tea. It was sweet and light with a hint of rose. *Delicious.*

"Everything and nothing, I'm afraid."

That sounded oddly comforting. "I'm good. I'm going to walk into town, not use my ID and grab a couple of things.

Rusty barked at a bird through the glass door. The sound made me jolt and hot tea ran down my wrist. I wiped it up with the little napkin she'd set out.

"Best form of security." Lisa thumbed to the dog over her shoulder. I wasn't so sure. Frankie had put me more at ease than Rusty. Twice already that dog had made me jump out of my skin. And he was pretty dang harmless, unless being dopey qualified as protection.

"Thanks for taking the time to come out here and show me around."

"It was the perfect excuse to see the babies at the same time. I'm headed to the hospital now." She stood up and started to clear.

"I'll do that. It will give me something to do." I smiled. Lisa was friendly and helpful, I definitely wanted to be on her good side.

We walked down the hall to the front door, and she turned to me. "My number is in that phone you got. Call me if you need anything." She rubbed my upper arm. "I really mean that."

I had the feeling she did.

Chapter Thirteen

Frankie

It gave me a disgusting amount of pleasure to look into the baby blues of Anton Myers Friday morning for my workout. I hadn't hit anyone in far too long, and he was the perfect punching bag.

He snarled. "Don't look at me like that. You're not a tiger, and I ain't raw meat."

"Oh yes you are." I turned off the treadmill, happy that I hadn't wasted energy lifting.

"You're practically drooling. At least let me warm up. Jesus." Anton dropped his bag on the bench of our private gym and tugged off his hoodie. It was early, the sun was barely out, and I had some rage to work through.

I taped up my knuckles and wrists with care as Anton jumped rope. I had to hand it to him. He'd checked his massive ego just enough to stop being so unbearably annoying and had taken our advice to lose his bulk. What he lacked in skill, he made up for in anger. After all the years of trying to live normal lives and integrate into society, none of us had managed to shake the effects of our dark pasts.

But we were safe about it. We kicked our own asses on a regular basis, and it had served as a healthy outlet. Face-free Fight Club, Jackson had called it. Otherwise, one wrong look at someone we cared about would end badly. We were all addicted to violence and consumed just enough to get our fixes. And mother of all things, I needed a fix.

Anton tossed the rope back into its box where we kept our props and grabbed the tape. "What are you so pissed off about, anyway? Didn't you just road trip the babysitter across the country? Let me guess, hard pillows and thin towels?"

"And the ugliest carpet you've ever seen. But no. You ever wanna kill someone so bad that you dream about it and wake up grinning?" Because Billy Johnston had been playing on loop in my brain. I could still go back and make it look like an accident. No one would ever fucking know.

"All the fucking time. Do I get to know who's living rent-free in that gray-ass head of yours?" Anton reached for the boxing gloves we sometimes used when we were feeling nice.

"No gloves." I pulled off my T-shirt and popped in my mouth guard.

"Fuck. All right. Let's get this over with. Don't think it's going to be easy." After a quick wipe of his nose, he jogged backward and put his hands in defense position in front of his face. He and my brother were always so concerned about looking pretty.

But I didn't want to get it over with. I wanted to savor the punishment. The liquid hate running through my veins pumped through my heart and up to my brain where it transformed Anton into Billy. The more time I'd spent with Megan, the more I hated what he'd done to her.

I started with a swift kick to the kidneys and Anton blocked my jab to his chin. He landed a light blow to my ribs, but it was like being swatted at by a kitten. I knocked his right arm to the side with my elbow and delivered a combo to his gut. He was solid. Leo and I used to tease him about his footwork being shit, but those lead feet were good for his defense.

New tactic. I spun around and waited for the fraction of the second when he attacked — making him open — and whipped my foot into his head. He didn't fall, but he stepped back and blinked several times.

The one thing I really liked about Anton was that he never quit. Sometimes I wondered if we liked getting hit as much as we liked delivering blows. We exchanged punches for another fifteen minutes. That fucker kept trying to hit me in the head, and I kept blocking and getting him in the ribs. I could have kept going, wanted to keep going, but I also needed to get to work. I narrowed my eyes, calculating my final blow. We weren't allowed to intentionally knock each other out — a bullshit rule I'd let Leo put in place after I'd gotten the best of Jackson one day — so I would need to back off a little bit of my power.

Getting Anton on the ground was never easy, but if I hit him just right on the head, in the same spot that had gotten him dizzy at the beginning, he would stumble again.

He came at me, and I smacked him perfectly then went for the swipe of his legs. He landed on his ass. Victory was mine. I reached down and yanked him back up to standing.

"Thanks for that. You go out and meet my nephews yet?"

"Yeah. Sammie and I went out last night. They already have the devil in their eyes. That poor woman has no idea what she's in for." Anton unwrapped his hands and tossed the tape in the trash.

Over the years and on my path of somewhat normal, I'd often wondered about our DNA and if it was just in us to be angry killers. Or how much of our father's abuse — what he'd referred to as 'training' — had turned us so dark.

I showered and said goodbye to Anton, who stayed and lifted weights, then drove Uptown in one of the company's black SUVs to the hotel where Andy Cobbler had officially taken up residence.

The thing about Andy was that he wasn't really in any kind of danger. Yes, he did stupid and shitty things, but no one was threatening his life. We were glorified arm candy. Having a bodyguard made him look more important than he was. I carried a gun and a knife, but I'd never really needed them.

Initially, I hadn't even wanted to take the job, but Andy had too much money. He could literally burn it and it would never run out. Not only was he the continued face of a luxury watch company, but he was also in countless commercials and his father had been a smart businessman. Andy came from a rich family then had made even more money he didn't need. It was a little sickening. So, as a way to get out of protecting him, I'd tripled our rates as a joke. He hadn't even batted an eye.

So there I was babysitting a self-declared bad boy while he was in the city for a few months. My father would be rolling over in his shallow grave. Then again, he'd always liked easy money.

I knocked on the door of his suite and he answered right away. It wasn't unusual to find him in the middle of an orgy or for him to come to the door naked — he was quite proud of his dick, and we'd all seen it way too much — but he was fully dressed in a track suite and his hair was still wet.

"Okay. Good, you're here." He waved a finger at me then checked the hall.

The second I stepped into the hotel room, an ominous chill ran up my spine. On the couch, smoking a fat cigar, was an overweight man in a suit with two thick bodyguards standing at ease behind them. I recognized him — Fat Freddie the Fish. A former client had put a hit on him, and I'd tailed him for two weeks ten years prior before the job was canceled. He had a diet of steaks and ice cream. I was surprised he hadn't died walking up stairs.

Freddie and his goons wouldn't do anything in the hotel — there were cameras everywhere — but they were doing a bang up job of making my client nervous. In my ear Andy said, "I think I fucked the wrong wife."

"So." The man puffed out some smoke, also not doing any favors to his heart and lungs. "Now that your driver is here, you can go to the bank. We'll wait here, maybe pick out some new watches for my sons."

I crossed my arms as a sign that I wasn't quite ready to head to the bank. I'd left Andy the night before at eleven o'clock. I'd practically tucked him into bed. "When did you meet the girl?"

"Last night at the bar. I went down for a nightcap." More proof that he really didn't need a bodyguard.

"And…where is she now?"

Andy shrugged. *God, he's stupid.* I couldn't believe someone hadn't tried this on him before. "She left after we were…you know, finished."

I scratched my head. A flash of understanding glimmered in Fat Freddie's eyes. *Yeah, I'm onto you.*

Andy stepped closer to me. "It doesn't matter. Let's just go to the bank and be done with this fucker."

"Just a sec." I held up my hand. "Tell me, what does this man's wife look like?"

"Young, skinny, dark brown hair, fake tits—no offense."

I walked over to the window. It was a better angle if I needed to shoot. "And you know *for a fact* that this woman is married to him?"

Andy's face fell. Finally, he was catching on. "No. Actually, I don't."

"Freddie." Me knowing his name caught him off guard. "Your wife is a lovely woman who does not fit that description. You have two sons, neither one of which would have had the balls to walk in here and try this scam. That makes you disappointed in them and sad. These two guys are all muscle, but not the brightest lights on the Christmas tree. And I know you think it's three against two but he's a world-famous athlete and I've beaten better odds with my eyes closed. I suggest you walk out of here before this ends very badly…for you."

Freddie studied me. "You look a lot like someone I used to know." His face fell when the final two dots connected. Leo and I were the spitting image of our father.

"Okay." Frankie stood at a speed I didn't think him capable of. "We're done here, boys." To Andy he said, "Sorry for the...misunderstanding." Then to me, "Can't blame a man for trying, right?" The wingmen were out of the door first. They weren't paid to ask questions, and after Andy shut and locked it, he spun around with huge eyes.

"What the fuck was that?"

"That was me getting a very healthy bonus at the end of the month."

"No shit. But how did you know that about him? Who the fuck was he?" Andy scrubbed his face and swore again.

"I don't kiss and tell." I shot him a tight grin.

"Good policy."

"And I would appreciate if this story doesn't make it to your greatest hits. Discretion is how I just saved you a shit load of money and possibly your life."

Andy frowned. He was a motor mouth who loved to tell impressive stories. I'd heard the same ones several times since we'd started his detail. "Fine."

We spent the rest of the day doing all the normal things that were Andy Cobbler's life. I ate my lunch while he did a photo shoot, and he had lunch with a married woman while I checked the door for paparazzi. We drove the married woman back to the hotel and I sat on the floor outside his suite while he fucked her.

On my phone, I scrolled through the pictures of my new nephews and worried they'd gotten the bad-seed gene that went with our last name. Leo was brave to be a father. Maybe the previous years with Violet had proven that he could do it and not fuck them up. I wasn't sure I had the same kind of confidence about me. The look on Freddie's face when he'd figured out who I was had brought back that high of power I craved and did my best to keep at bay.

A new text from Leo popped up saying Fiona and the boys were home and that Megan was a dog whisperer. Attached was a video of Rusty sitting, lying down and staying while Violet distanced herself then shouted out the command, "Come."

At the very end, Megan came in the shot clapping her hands and walking toward Violet. She wore her signature cut-off shorts and that fine ass wiggled all the way over to give a high-five. *Screw the dog*. I watched the end of that video twenty more times. Leo knew not what he'd done.

Chapter Fourteen

Megan

Fiona had been home for two days and the order and calm of the house pre-twins had vanished. Those two little babies ate, slept, cried and pooped nonstop. I'd been peed on six times, three times each until Lisa came by with a Pee-Pee Teepee. Whoever had thought of that was a genius.

And we all looked like battered warriors. I was pretty sure one of us was supposed to be making dinner, but Leo was asleep on the couch with the babies on his chest. I was folding onesies on the dining room table and Violet was using up her screen time outside with headphones on.

We'd learned 'The Doorbell and Rusty Show' the hard way, so I'd placed a 'please don't ring the bell' sign on the front door. I had no idea what time any of us would eat, but it would be after a twenty-minute power nap, of that I was sure.

I left the laundry basket at the end of the stairs — the energy to climb them yet again was gone — and headed to my room. My phone had started serving as my alarm because it was easier to control the volume. I set the timer for twenty minutes, curled up in my bed and passed right out.

The buzz came way too soon. It had been more of a 'power blink' than nap. But as I took hold of my phone, I realized it wasn't the alarm. It was a call. Just the name 'Frankie' had my silly heart going *pitter patter*. I hadn't thought he would ever call me. In fact, I'd chalked up the chemistry and little kiss from our road trip to me making a total fool out of myself and him too polite to say so.

Even my stupid finger shook as I swiped to answer. "Hi." Damn it. My voice was shaky, too.

"Hey, I'm outside. Can you open for me?"

What?

"Uh, yeah. Just gimme a sec."

I flipped off the covers and jumped out of bed. I ran to the bathroom and loaded my toothbrush then jammed it in my mouth. The person in the mirror made me shudder. She had bags under her eyes, knots in her hair and vomit on her T-shirt. She could have won Best Zombie on Halloween. I scrubbed my teeth, spat out the foam and wiped my mouth with the shirt I was taking off. The only thing I could find clean was a tank top I usually wore underneath other shirts, but it would have to do. A clump of hair fell out when I raked the brush through the rat's nest that had formerly been my ponytail and I managed a new one as I speed-walked to the front door.

Rusty was in the backyard with Violet, so at least the no barking would save waking up the boys. I opened up to Frankie, who held a bottle of wine and a bouquet of flowers. For a fleeting second, I thought they were for me.

I could have sworn his eyes raked over me in a very good way, but it was so quick and I was scattered so I didn't count on it. "I didn't realize you were coming." That was an understatement. If I had known, I would have at the very least showered.

"It's Sunday."

Was that supposed to mean something to me? Either way, I opened the door a little farther.

"I think everyone except Violet is sleeping. She and Rusty are in the back."

"Shit. Bad timing."

Or amazing timing. It allowed me a few moments to bask in his safe energy all by myself. Because, after one look at him, I was energized and warm all over. And I already needed more.

"Hey, you want to take Rusty and Violet for a walk? She's getting pretty impressive at her scooter and I'm training him to be better on the leash."

He pressed his lips together, and he knew exactly what I was doing. But I couldn't help myself. Whether he understood it or not, his draw was like a rip current in the ocean, and the worst thing to do was to fight it.

I didn't give him time to refuse and pointed to the flowers. "I'll just put these in water."

The bouquet was bright yellow and elegant—probably the prettiest arrangement Fiona had received. I found a glass vase and filled it with water. Frankie left the bottle of wine on the kitchen counter and went over to the living room where Leo cracked open an eye. Frankie's emotion filled the space. He walked behind the couch, said something meant only for his brother and tapped him on the cheek. For a long beat, he stared at the babies but instead of happiness, worry crinkled around his eyes. *What is that for?*

Rusty barked from outside and Leo covered the babies' ears. It drew Violet's attention and she waved to Frankie through the window with a big smile. He looped his hand, jacked his thumb over his shoulder then walked two fingers on the opposite palm. Pretty impressive sign language. Violet nodded and put down her tablet and headphones.

With the vase full and in the middle of the counter, I grabbed my little baggie of pre-cut cheese and stuffed it into my pocket. I met everyone at the front door and slipped into my sandals. We left in silence and were headed down the path with Violet at a safe distance, leading the way.

"Heel," I said to Rusty as he tugged to be next to Violet then shoved a piece of cheese in his mouth.

"Good God, he's actually listening to you. I'm impressed," Frankie mused.

"It's the cheese. I'm merely the conduit."

Violet stopped at the end of the street with both feet on either side of her green scooter. She looked both ways then back to us for permission to cross. Frankie scanned the area before giving a thumbs-up and saying, "You have a problem taking compliments."

I sighed. "I'm out of practice at getting them." It probably fed the lie of my being the object of Billy's affection, but...Ruby.

Rusty yanked toward a bird and I snapped the leash back. "Heel." The cheese followed and he whimpered to the bird but stayed next to me.

We walked toward the water, the area becoming more populated. Frankie's eyes never left his niece. "I have an idea."

Please let it be a 'what are you doing on your day off' idea...

"Each time I see you, I will give you an honest compliment and you can just answer with 'thank you'."

"A re-entry compliment program?"

He snickered. "Good title."

"Why?" Was he just trying to be nice or were there underlying motives? Motives I wanted to be there.

Still watching Violet, he said, "You don't realize what you are."

Or maybe I did but he didn't. I let his words hang in the air then continued my gentle tugs on Rusty's leash and his cheese compensation all the way down to the waterfront. Violet showed Frankie how she could swerve on the scooter, and after a half an hour, we were back on the path home. Once again, she was out in front of us. Our alone time was coming to an end too soon, and I wanted to make the most of it.

"So my compliment for the day is about dog training? That's all your giving me?" I elbowed him in the arm, praying he would at least flirt back a little.

"Oh, she's greedy."

"Hungry." Or starving for another taste of him. "Can I ask you something and you'll answer me honestly?"

"Maybe." He gave his head a small tilt.

Fair enough. There were plenty of things I wouldn't answer honestly either.

We were at the end of the driveway, and I bent down and unhooked Rusty's leash. He bolted around the front yard in a victory lap before stopping and smelling a specific spot. Violet scooted in a big circle on the concrete in front of the garage.

I stared at the ground, gathering my courage. When our gazes finally met, a flush of tingling energy raced through my veins.

"Ask." His tone was so soft, so gentle, so unrushed.

I hated being *that* girl—the one who needed reassuring that what was happening was real, but I honestly didn't know and I didn't want to keep batting my eyes at a man who didn't feel the same way or worse, only had pity for me. Bold. That was who I'd decided to be.

A small whimper snuck into my long exhale.

Frankie lifted his eyebrows. "Ask."

"Am I crazy to think you might be attracted to me?" I threw my hands to my face. "I'm sorry. You don't have to answer that. I can't believe I just asked you. Sorry." I shook my head and turned to walk away but he hooked a finger in my belt loop and gentle tugged me toward him.

His eyes glimmered, and with his free hand he twirled a lock of hair that had escaped my ponytail. "Why wouldn't I be attracted to you? You're beautiful and sweet and brave. Somehow you make 'sexy as fuck' look like a second skin. But I'm…"

"Out of my league?" My pulse raced and I thought my knees were actually wobbling. Holy crap, the things a man like Frankie could do to a woman. He was barely touching me, and I was jelly.

Frankie dropped his head back and withdrew his touch. A matter-of-fact grimace replaced the intense and magnetic regard from before. "Complex and darker than you can imagine. And you're my brother's nanny. Plus, you should be focusing on you, not starting a…whatever it would be. So, under different circumstances, yeah."

All his compliments were balled up and thrown in the trash. His rejection flipped an anger switch in me. "So those women you've gone on dates with? It's okay for you to be" — I air-quoted — "complex and dark with them but not me because I work for your brother?" The metal hook of the leash hit my shin as I propped my hands on my hips. A rush of power blanketed me. Man, it felt amazing to be angry without fear of consequences.

Frankie grinned, pissing me off even further. "You're mad at me?"

"Yes. Because I thought you had more balls than to let a job and a past get in the way of something you want."

He grumbled. If the prior few weeks had taught me anything, it was that I couldn't sit back and wait for the train of life to stop for me. I had to run like hell next to it and jump on.

A coldness came to his eyes and practically made me shiver. "You don't know me."

"That's only because you won't let me. And if you think you have some dark crap in the past you don't want to talk about, well let me tell you, *Frankie*, I have a laundry list of things I'm trying to forget. The only thing I'm interested is the future." I spun and marched up the driveway.

When I got inside, I was happy to see that Leo was cooking. I set the table, and when Frankie joined us, I ignored him. Fiona had just fed both babies and Frankie went over to formally meet his nephews in the living room. He effortlessly included Violet into all his conversations, the natural kindness boiling my blood because he had no idea the good everyone else saw in him. All his dark and complex crap was a story he told himself. I was sure of it. He caught me staring, and when I frowned, he cracked an amused smile.

Leo announced that dinner was ready, and as he transferred his stuffed chicken breast to a dark-blue serving platter, Frankie came into the kitchen.

"Who wants wine?" Frankie asked then went over to the cabinet for the glasses. I hadn't put any on the table. I'd never seen Fiona or Leo drink alcohol.

"Present!" Leo raised his hand then smiled to his wife who came in with Violet and the babies.

"I can take them while you guys eat. I thought I was hungry, but it turns out I'm not." I avoided the glance to see if my insult had landed and waved for Fiona to give me Dante.

"Thank you," she said. "I'm starving."

"I can wait, too." Violet kissed Marco's little head. She loved holding the twins. So far, she was proving to be an excellent big sister.

I shook my head. "No. Enjoy your uncle. I'll go rock them."

Violet tucked Marco into my free arm, and I went upstairs to their room to have a proper pout while the Riccis ate their dinner. About fifteen minutes into our rock, Dante's face went red as he pushed out what sounded like an explosive present in his pants. Marco wasn't far behind and soon the familiar popcorn smell of baby poo was coming at me in both directions. I put Marco in his crib and hoped his objecting cries would bring in the reinforcements.

I forgot the Pee-Pee Teepee and Dante squirted down the front of my tank while I lifted his legs at the ankles to get a thorough wipe. Marco's cries intensified, which brought in Dante's. We'd realized quickly that the easiest way to get them to wail was to separate them. But for the diaper change, there was no other way.

Fiona came in and quickly picked up Marco, who settled. She eyed the changing table and said, "Well, that onesie is for the burn barrel. Oh God, he peed on you, too. I'm so sorry. I'll do this little rascal."

"All in a day's work." I finished changing the baby and made room for Fiona.

She leaned down to kiss Marco, and I sat back in the rocker. "Can I give you a little advice?"

"Next time use the Teepee?"

"Yes. And—" Fiona scrunched up her nose and said something incoherent to her baby boy on the table in front of her. "If you want to wrangle a Ricci, you've got to show them what they're missing and make them mad as hell."

I bit my lip. "That obvious?"

Marco kicked his little feet at Fiona, and she raised an eyebrow. "It's been obvious since Iowa." She shot me a grin.

But I hadn't spoken to her until I'd gotten to New York, so she must have been referring to him. I rocked while she changed Marco then stood when she gestured for me to follow. "Leo should be done eating by now. He can be the baby police."

I tried to hide my smile. "Is it a problem that I work for you?"

"I think we're all adults here, and we can make our own decisions about our lives. Do I think you should take things slow? Yes. Is that any fun? Nope."

Downstairs, I handed Dante to Leo and went to change my shirt. The only thing dry and clean was the huge T-shirt I wore to bed, and it looked more like a dress or tent, so I knotted it in the back, which showed a little bit of my stomach. Putting on a little mascara would have been too obvious, so I just retied my ponytail and wished myself luck.

I slid into my chair and said, "This looks amazing. Thanks for cooking, Leo."

"So, Megan," Fiona said with a curious smile. "Your first day off is tomorrow. You gonna go into the city?"

A most excellent ally, my employer. I could have kissed her. "Yeah. I may just ride the subway and people watch all day."

"Oh, you'll see some interesting ones there, for sure. I used to work at this hotel in Midtown. Sometimes after my shift, I would sit in the bar and order a drink. I was convinced I would meet a rich businessman who would fall in love with me."

"You did not do that." The glare Leo sent Fiona carried anger, jealousy and disbelief. She was provoking him and laying a perfect seed for me at the same time. The woman was a genius. I worshiped the ground she walked on.

"I totally did." She shrugged a shoulder. "I mean, sometimes people thought I was a..." She glanced at Violet. "Still working, if you know what I mean, but mostly I just met super nice guys who I never saw again."

Leo flared his nostrils and blinked several times before turning to Frankie. "Do you see this?" Then to me, "Megan, please don't go to a random hotel and have a drink at the bar tomorrow. I can't believe I even have to say that." He stood up with a twin in each arm. "Frankie, bring the rest of the wine into the mancave. I want to hear that Fat Freddie story."

"Too bad you didn't have a phone to track me with back then. Right, baby?"

We waited until they left then giggled. Violet joined us and said, "They're funny when they're mad."

"Yes, they are, my darling." Fiona tapped Violet's nose. "Yes, they are. Megan, don't be surprised if Frankie just happens to be at the same bar as you are tomorrow."

Chapter Fifteen

Frankie

I was just making sure she was safe, really — for what was bordering on an obsessive number of times that day. *But, Christ.* She was literally a small-town girl in the big city. I'd seen the mental trap Fiona had laid for me. But had it stopped me from walking right into it? Nope. Not for a damn second.

An assistant pulled off Andy's microphone and he got up from the round table of the sports show he'd just done an interview for. I gave a final check that Megan was still at a department store downtown then slid my phone back into the inside pocket of my suit.

Andy shook hands with the host of the show and came over. "Did you even listen to what I was saying?"

"Not my job."

"Well, I'm not paying you to look at your phone all day."

I tucked my chin. "What do you think I do while you bang wives and I sit in the hallway?"

He loosened his tie. "Wished you were me?"

"Not even for a second."

We walked off the set and down the hall to the elevators. So what that she was shopping? Lord knew she needed some new clothes. But what kind of clothes was she buying? She didn't seem like the type to spend out of her price range. Fiona had probably handed her a wad of cash, though. That was something my sister-in-law would have absolutely done — just like lie about drinks with random men in a hotel bar. That was very obviously made up to ruffle Leo's feathers. Back then, she would have never wasted her money on alcohol. I'd heard the stories about her mother and their financial struggles.

And I'd said just as much to my baby brother to calm him down. He'd said she even worked the night shift, so there was no way the bar had even been open. But it was the *thought* of her with another man that made him crazy.

As Andy and I rode to the garage of the massive building, I knew one thing. Ricci men were jealous idiots. I didn't honestly think that Megan would go on a date with a stranger or end up in a hotel room with one. It was the damn idea of it that was driving me crazy. Hell, on the ride home the night before I'd fantasized about walking in on her and shooting some middle-aged rando with his pants around his ankles. What the fuck was wrong with me? We hadn't even gone on a date.

I blamed Fiona. She had mind fucked both Leo and me. *Clever woman.* At least the day was coming to an end and Megan would be Long Island bound sooner than later.

At the car, I opened the back door for Andy, and he climbed in before I hopped into drive.

"Something bothering you? You're crankier than normal." He bent over his phone, texting.

As if I would confide anything to him. He was the farthest thing from a friend I had. Hell, I'd tell Myers my worries before I'd confess to the jackass in the back seat.

"All good."

We drove in silence back to his hotel until we pulled up and he said, "I can take it from here tonight. I have a date, and since you would only be on your phone in the hallway, I don't really see the point. Her husband's away, so she's going to stay the whole night."

I glanced at him in the rear-view. He had a terrible way of getting into trouble when he was on his own.

"Won't leave the room. Scouts' honor. Go deal with whatever it is that's making you a bitch to be around."

I double parked outside the hotel and nodded to the doorman as I escorted my client inside.

"I'm good. We both know you're mostly for show anyway."

I frowned and watched him get on the elevator. The chances of something happening to him were pretty damn slim, and he didn't have a reason to lie to me, but still. He had hired me to protect him.

I pulled out my phone. Megan was on the move, and from the speed of it, she was walking at a lingered pace. Probably taking it all in. Either that or walking hand-in-hand super slow like in the movies. I frowned deeper.

In the car, I propped up my phone on the dashboard so I could glimpse at her location, which had stayed still for more than five minutes. Was she talking to someone? I pressed my foot on the gas.

The icon had moved her into a restaurant. I knew that restaurant, had eaten there several times. It was actually pretty close to my building. She had chosen it on purpose. Maybe she wanted to be found, see if I would be jealous and what I would do.

But unlike Fiona, Megan could buy herself a drink — or find someone who would offer her one. She was gorgeous after all. Damn it, the internal heat from my body had me sweating. I let out a deep groan. There was nothing I could do to keep myself from checking on Megan — the pull was too strong, the curiosity too high and the jealousy beyond absurd and completely out of control.

Once downtown, I decided to park the SUV in my own garage. It would have taken me longer to find a place on the street, and the short walk would allow me to get some kind of plan formulated in my head.

Fuck. I had no plan. I ran my fingers through my hair and picked up my pace, bumping into random pedestrians and not even bothering to excuse myself. It was the after-work financial crowd, so they didn't seem to care. God, she was on a date with a yuppie prick. He'd probably already slipped her some flunitrazepam. She'd be in a cab in five minutes. Good thing I was going to be there in two.

I checked my phone one last time before opening the big glass door to the restaurant. A small wave of relief cooled my skin.

Alone, at the bar, sat Megan — or at least a version of Megan that had somehow amplified her beauty. She wore a dark-red wrap dress, and, with her legs crossed on the stool, she was showing the perfect thigh. Her hair was up, but styled, and after a sip of her white wine, she scrunched up like she was fully enjoying it.

I unbuttoned my jacket and stuck my hands in the pockets of my pants. The light above the bar hit her just right, and I was sure she was shining. She was definitely beaming. I probably should have left, walked out of the door and kept trying to stay away from her. But I was fooling myself to think I had the power to do that.

No, I set my shoulders and managed a swagger that I hadn't seen since my youth. The second I was next to her, she closed her eyes as if thinking of a wish. Her makeup was subtle, but more than usual—light eyeshadow and mascara with a gloss on her lips that had left a pink print on her wine glass.

Megan turned and opened her eyes. "You're early."

"Early?"

"Our reservation isn't for another hour." She wore her confidence beautifully.

"You were that certain I would come?"

The bartender came over, checking to see if she was okay. I glanced over my shoulder at him. Maybe he'd been hoping she'd get stood up.

"I'll have a glass of whatever the lady's having."

"Pinot Grigio," he said and grabbed an open bottle from the bucket at the end of the bar.

I settled in next to her and could barely believe she was the same person who had sold me running shoes earlier in the month. Hell, Billy Johnston might not even recognize her. The wine came and the bartender seemed content that I wasn't some random stranger hitting on the beautiful young woman in front of him.

I lifted my glass and tilted it in her direction. "*Saluti*. To you. The city agrees with you." After a quick sniff of the crisp citron and hint of peach, I took a sip.

"Thank you. And cheers."

We set the glasses back on the bar and as she blinked over to me, a lock of her hair fell and framed her face.

"So you want to tell me why you're here?"

I scoffed. "Because you and my sister-in-law are wicked women who lay traps for lonely men."

"Strike one."

"Oh. We're playing baseball now?"

She looked up at me with those pretty green eyes and I was done for. "That's the problem. I don't really want to *play* anything. I want you to admit the real reason you're here."

"That's all?" When did she get so demanding? Worse, when did I start liking that? But it wasn't as if she were asking me to reveal a part of myself that didn't have anything to do with her. Quite the opposite. She just wanted to know where she really stood. She didn't want to be dicked over. I scratched my beard and took another drink. She deserved a man who would stand up and prove he was worthy of her.

Fine.

"I'm here because all those things I said yesterday are true. You're beautiful and sexy and probably way too good for me. When I'm around you, I feel like there's some good in me and I like it. Happy?"

"Thank you. Now comes the part where we talk about our days or share a funny story. Do you think you're ready for that, Mr. Dark and Stormy?"

I rolled my eyes, although it was a pretty good nickname. But she wasn't going to get off so easy. "Nope. You skipped the part about why *you're* here."

"Right. That part. Fair enough." She twisted her mouth and studied the high ceiling for a couple of seconds. "I'm here because a few weeks ago a stranger walked into my life and offered me the help I desperately needed. Turns out, I kinda like the way I feel safe around him — and he smells fantastic."

"Some say 'like a man'." I winked at her.

"Only the ones in the know." Her soft grin was something I hadn't seen before, an expression that I wanted to believe was only for me. And that 'feeling safe' comment? That ticked all my boxes.

"So, big city girl, tell me about your day." Who knew I could do small talk?

"It included zero baby poo or vomit, so winning. I met your Aunt Chezzie this morning. I think she brought food for a week. Mostly pasta. How do you Riccis stay so fit with all that you eat?"

We work it off. Too much innuendo. "Genetics." That didn't seem right either, but it was better than explaining the regime our father had pounded into us and how neither Leo nor I had been able to shake it.

Megan described her day, and I couldn't help but marvel at her enthusiasm. And why not? The woman had started a brand-new life in a place she'd only dreamed about. I didn't want to jinx it, but the spontaneous date or forced date — I wasn't sure which was more accurate — was turning out to be my most successful one in a long time.

She asked me adorable questions like 'Is coffee from a deli safe?' and her eyes lit up when she explained how easy the subway system was. Her excitement to discover was palpable, and it made me want to take a day off work and show her all my favorite spots —

which, if I thought about it, there was nothing really stopping me from doing.

Megan refused another glass of wine and instead opted for water, and I followed her lead. But for dinner I had to get a glass of red to go with my lamb, and when I asked if she'd join me in sharing a bottle, she refused.

"I'm taking the train back. I don't want to have a buzz."

"I can call you a car. In fact, I'd very much like to call you a car. You at night, those legs, the train. Not sure I can handle it." I gestured to the menu. "Did you decide?"

"What's the lamb like?" She brought her thumb to her mouth and chewed the nail. I'd forgotten how un-food-adventurous she was. It was really just a lack of exposure. I opened back up my menu.

Risotto with truffles, duck with pistachios and lamb with parsley. I flipped to the fish. "How are you with salmon?"

Megan lifted a shoulder, but the nervous look stayed on her face. She turned to the fish section and counted on her fingers. "Okay. Yeah. I'll have that. Thanks. How am I going to be able to try all these things?"

"Why were you counting?" I took her menu and laid it on mine.

"Promise not to judge?"

"Do I have a history of doing that?" I faked my offense.

She squirmed in her chair. "Well…sorta. I mean you said that woman had credit card debt and came in with designer shoes. Oh, the heck with it. I went over budget on my dress, and I may be a little short for dinner. I'm sorry." She hid her face behind her hands then slid them down her cheeks. "I'm so embarrassed."

Dear God. She'd said 'heck'. And bless her adorable heart, she'd actually used it for a curse word. I laughed. I couldn't help it.

Her face fell. "What?"

"*'The heck with it'?* Really?"

"I don't like to swear. I mean, thank goodness I'm not offended when people do, 'cuz I think we've both met your sister-in-law. But me personally? It has just never felt right."

And now I'm going to have to marry this woman.

Wait. What?

Slightly premature, Frankie.

She reached down to take a drink of water and I stopped the movement with my hand then brushed over her knuckles. "I actually like that about you." My voice was a kind of soft that I'd only ever used on...her, actually. "Don't change just because your surroundings did."

She dropped her head back and fanned herself. "I knew it. I knew you had bedroom eyes."

The waitress came over with a smile. "What can I get you two?"

"Lamb for me. Salmon for the lady. Oh, and whatever you do, don't let her pay. Trust me... I'm a bigger tipper."

"You got it. Anything to drink?"

"Just a glass of the assemblage."

"Two, actually." Megan smiled to the waitress, then me. "I mean..." She shrugged a shoulder. "Since you're getting your way with the check, I assume I won't have a choice about the car, either."

I didn't want her to think I was taking her choice out of the picture. "Too controlling?"

She let out a little sigh. "You're pushy. But I can recognize protection from manipulation. Plus, I can't remember the last time I was on a real date. I plan to enjoy it."

Shit. She was right. It had turned into a real date. My brother would want to kick my ass. And if I wanted a second — which I was already sure I did — I would have to let him do it. She was worth it.

"So" — I sipped the water then tucked my chin — "real dates usually end with a kiss…"

"Can't remember," she teased.

That little buzz between my ears wasn't the wine. It was the pleasure of the innocent flirting. Never had a sensation been so foreign and so welcome at the same time. I ignored all the nagging thoughts about playing with fire, about her being frail and rushing into the arms of the first man who wasn't Billy. It had been too long since I'd enjoyed an evening so much, and I was just selfish enough to keep going.

Chapter Sixteen

Megan

Turned out, I did know how to flirt. Either that, or, like everything else with the man paying for my dinner, it had just come naturally. And Fiona's advice — or plan — had worked like sugar and a fruit fly. He'd come running, just as predicted. But that would be the end of it for me. As much as I enjoyed being the new version of me that was bold, I also didn't want to always be the one in charge and making the moves.

But I needed him to show me his desire. It would be just one more way that he would help me get stronger. I wasn't drunk or tipsy, but after a couple of glasses of wine and looking into his eyes for two hours, I was a little lightheaded. The hard part was figuring out how much of it was Frankie. Either way, I could barely contain my grin. Not only had I spent my day in the city shopping, but I'd also had the first real date of my adult life — dinner at a restaurant with an honest man.

"Fifteen minutes for your car." Frankie slid his phone back inside the jacket of his black suit. How the women he'd dated hadn't dug their claws in him and never let go was a true mystery. "Shall we wait outside?"

"Sure." I stood and reached for my shopping bags.

"I'll get those." He bent down and picked them up before I could object. Seriously, how was he single? Tall, dark *and* polite? *Yes, please.*

"Thank you." I was getting good at saying that to him, accepting what he wanted to give. The truth was, I liked being taken care of. He did that thing where he put his hand on my lower back and guided me out. His touch was both thrilling and reassuring. Maybe this was some kind of reverse Stockholm Syndrome, but I didn't care. A man had never looked at me the way he did. I deserved to know what that meant.

Outside, he set my bags on a free bench then interlaced both our hands before bringing them to his chest. "I want you to know that I will never, ever hit you. My dad used to beat my mother, and while I share many traits with that man, abusing women isn't one of them."

I didn't know why he'd chosen to share a bit of his past with me, but the gravity was not lost. "I've never thought you would."

"But you're right. I am pushy. Years of logic transforming into instincts have also made me quite stubborn—not to mention babysitting a former sport's star who spends the day googling himself has me a little cranky. I'm—"

I pressed my finger to his lips. "I'm not perfect, either. I'm emotional and naïve." *And I don't always tell the entire truth.*

This time it was him who pressed my lips, but with his own. They were just as soft as I remembered and had a faint taste of the wine we'd drunk with dinner. He cupped my cheek with one hand, and I laced my arms around his neck. My heart thumped with the extra work it was going through, pumping all the bliss into my bloodstream.

Frankie slowly rubbed his beard on my chin and kissed below my ear and down my neck. A beautiful shiver tickled my spine. He dragged his nose along my jawline to my waiting lips where he brushed his against them.

"I could fucking devour you." There was no threat in his tone. Instead, it was a confession — one that made me whimper. He grumbled and shook his head. "That?" he whispered. "That little thing you do? That alone could feed me for months."

I didn't mean to, but I did it again. I was pretty sure I was melting in a pool of need right there on the street.

Frankie pulled back and placed his hands on my hips. "You should also know that I'm notoriously bad at sharing. You can ask my brother. So, now that this has officially started..." He shook his head in an apology. "I don't do things casually."

As if I would be interested in even looking in another man's direction. Nope, the one in front of me was more than enough. "Is that your way of asking me on a second date?" I softly scratched the hair on the back of his neck.

"I need to talk to my brother. We have our ways of sorting things out."

"Fiona said we were all adults, that we could make our own decisions." I had a hard time thinking Leo would stand in our way, but their relationship was solid, and Frankie wouldn't do anything to jeopardize that. Family was everything to him. I could relate.

"I'll handle it. But I owe him the respect to talk to him first."

A black town car with tinted windows pulled up to the curb and Frankie glanced over. "This is you." He pecked my forehead and broke the embrace.

It seemed unfair that once I'd gotten into his arms, I didn't know when I'd get back into them. He gathered my things then walked over and opened the back door. He said something to the driver while sliding the bags onto the long back seat then stood and held the door between us. "I'll see you soon."

I nodded. 'Soon' was my least favorite word. It was vague and held zero commitment. I placed my hand on top of his, I didn't want to leave. I wanted to find out what his idea of 'devour' was.

"Don't give me those sad eyes." He shook his head in a small scold. "You got your date. You got your kiss. Manhattan mission accomplished, young lady. We both have to work in the morning."

I traced my finger over a small scar on his knuckle then closed my eyes. He was right. I was being greedy. "Thank you for the date. It was perfect."

His slow blink said goodbye, and I got into the car. After he shut the door, he tapped it twice and the driver edged into traffic.

My phone vibrated in my bag, and I fished it out. Frankie's text said *Sweet dreams*, and I was sure I'd have them. The night, the day, the everything couldn't have gone better. He'd even opened up to me about his past—something I'd never expected—and talked about his job—something I thought I'd have to drag out of him to make conversation. It was interesting that he seemed bored with the tennis guy, but I guessed if he was really just sitting around on his phone, it wasn't very exciting work.

Who googles themself, anyway?

I pulled the phone away from my chest and stared at it. A warped curiosity bubbled in the pit of my stomach and rose to the back of my brain. No one was around to judge, and I had a long drive in front of me. What were the chances of there being news about me? I was no one of importance.

A quick click on the browser confirmed my deed and I searched my name plus the word 'missing'. In less than a second, a link to a local news station popped up with a picture of my neighbor Janet. She wore actual clothes, not her housedress, a light-blue shirt and a pink ribbon pinned to her lapel. The banner at the bottom of the video read, "Distraught neighbor claims deputy sheriff is responsible for missing girl."

My heart raced. The frame of Janet holding a tissue to her chubby cheek screamed at my better judgment to hush. I bit my bottom lip and put the volume low. I couldn't even stop my finger from touching the triangle on the screen to play the clip.

"What do you think happened to Megan Walsh?" a voice off the screen asked.

"I think that boy killed her. He drove his car by her apartment every day. I saw him. This whole town knows he used to beat her sister. She disappeared six months ago and now Megan. People might not say it, but they know it's true."

"That's a strong accusation. Do you have proof?"

"No. No, I don't. But this community stood by and did nothing for those sweet girls. They lost their mama when they were still in high school. Now this. It's terrible." Janet wiped a tear. "I didn't help them, and I should have. Maybe at the very least we can bring the Walsh girls some justice."

If she kept accusing Billy of murder, his daddy was going to make her life hell. The sheriff ruled our small town with an iron fist. The Johnston's would get every neighbor to turn on her if they hadn't already. It was small-town social suicide. Plus, she was wrong. Ruby and I were very much alive. They would never find a body or a weapon. She would forever think I was murdered and that she'd let it happen. That was a tremendous amount of guilt based on a lie—not to mention that if the news went viral, Ruby's and my face would be everywhere. That would lead Billy right to us.

The video cut to a female journalist in front of my church. "The official message from Megan Walsh's local church was only, 'We miss her,' and some speculate that the small Catholic community knows more than its saying. But Janet Klemper insists otherwise."

Back inside Janet's apartment with her medication behind her on the table, she said, "I only knew Megan for two months as a neighbor, but that girl was salt of the earth. There's no way she would have left"—she snapped her thick fingers—"just like that. Besides, everything was in her apartment, and they found her car. There is something foul happening here, and that boy is at the root of it."

The reporter appeared in a television studio at a big desk with an older male colleague. "We should note, Bob, that since filming the story, the Johnston family has filed a libel suit against Ms. Klemper and is threatening to press harassment charges."

I dropped my head into the cool leather seat behind me. Didn't she know to stop? Why would she risk so much just to be right? And she would never be right. She was acting on circumstantial evidence that would lead to nowhere. If only Father Peter could have dropped some sort of hint. But he would never risk our safety.

Just one quick phone call, saying I was alive, telling her to let it go… Otherwise, how would she understand? If I was in her place, I would think the same thing. The entire town probably all thought what she was saying was true, especially after the lake. Worse, the Johnston's were vindictive. They would ruin her and anyone who took her side. The bravery she was showing was honorable and touched me, but the consequences would be devastating. Sheriff Johnston could fabricate charges and put that poor woman in jail in the blink of an eye. And the attention? It needed to stop.

I did a quick search for her phone number and clicked on the line to call it.

After two short rings she answered. "This is Janet."

My chest tightened and even though the driver couldn't hear me I whispered. "This is Megan. I'm alive. Drop it, please."

"What?" she barked. "Megan? Oh my Lord, thank you, Jesus. Are you okay? Is he holding you hostage somewhere?"

"No. But please stop talking about me and Ruby. We're safe."

That would have to be enough. I ended the call and stared at the phone before throwing it against my bags with shaking hands.

When I got home, Fiona was coming out of the kitchen with a cup of tea. Her hair was in a messy bun, and she had on pajama pants with a white tank stained with breast milk. "Hey. Wow. You look killer." She smiled wide. "Did our plan work?"

"Like a charm." My voice lacked the enthusiasm to convince her.

She quirked her head. "You okay?"

"I'll be fine. Big day in the city. It was a bit overwhelming." I shrugged. "Do you need anything?"

"Nope. Chezzie is a fairy godmother, some kind of baby whisperer. Must be the Ricci blood. The boys loved her. Besides, it's still your day off. 'Night."

In my room, I wrote and deleted so many texts to Ruby that they all became a blur. Finally, I decided to call. I locked myself in the bathroom out of habit and dialed, but she didn't answer.

In the end I texted.

Need to talk. Call when you can.

Chapter Seventeen

Frankie

Leo tossed his bag onto the wooden bench and hung his suit on a hook above it. "Why'd you reject my nanny? Or did you bang her and your dick is so old it made her as cranky as you?"

I stopped skipping rope, and Jackson muttered something about the insult from the treadmill. He was right. That was damn cold. But I hadn't done either of those things. In fact, it had been four days since I'd seen or heard from Megan. She was showing a respectable amount of restraint. I hadn't even gotten pictures of the twins from her. I'd thought we'd opened the lines of communication, but she must have been waiting for me to talk to Leo—which I was planning on doing on the mat to let him kick my ass a little bit.

He threaded his arms out of his hoodie and bitched, "She's all... *'Yeah, yeah, nothing's wrong.'* In that singsong woman voice when you know something's obviously wrong."

"I know that voice. That's a scary-ass voice." Jackson stopped the treadmill and propped his hands on his hips. "What'd you do?"

"I didn't do anything. We had dinner on Monday. I haven't talked to her since." Why did these two have me on the defensive? I hated being on the defensive — especially when there was no reason for it.

Jackson *tsk*ed. "You didn't call her after two days. Everybody knows you have forty-eight hours to call after your date. You are ice, Ricci. Poor little nanny. Too bad... Lisa said she would be perfect for you." He shook his head all the way to grab his clothes and headed into the changing room. At least Jackson was on tennis star duty, and I wouldn't have to deal with *that* stupidity. Leo and I were on a one-day assignment for a traveling diplomat, and I had been looking forward to spending the day with my little brother.

Leo crossed his arms and raised his eyebrows. He was pretty adorable when he was angry. Plus, I knew he wasn't really pissed. If that had been the case, we'd already be hitting each other.

I whipped the rope overhead and went back to my exercise. "I didn't do anything to make her mad or cranky. I was worried about her first day *alone* in the city and went to check on her. We ended up having dinner. It's not like it was the first time we've shared a meal."

The corner I'd backed myself into would make it difficult to ask his blessing to date her. But what bothered me more was Megan's mood swing. When I'd left her Monday night, she'd practically begged to stay. Was it the forty-eight-hour rule that I was unaware of?

I kept skipping rope and asked, "How long has she been like…whatever it is she's like?"

Leo had moved to the floor and was doing push-ups. He stopped at the top and said, "Fi says she wasn't right when she got home that night. Seriously, what happened? And don't give me that 'we just had dinner' bullshit. She had or has a serious crush on you, and now it's like walking on eggshells in my own home. It's not like I can fire her."

I threw the rope back in its basket and sat on the floor with one leg out. Leo kept moving up and down, I had to hand it to him. His form was perfect.

"I admit that we are attracted to each other."

"Eww. Gross. Stop."

"We've kissed."

Leo looked over his shoulders with flared nostrils. "What part of 'stop' do you think means 'keep going'?"

I rubbed my temples. It was complicated, but if anyone would understand it would be him, and while he may be saying to shut up, he was only pretending. It was a thing we did to somehow prove we were still masculine. Maybe Chezzie was right. Maybe I was emotionally unavailable.

"I like her," I confessed. "She's the first woman in a long time I've actually liked."

He snorted.

Asshole.

"Nothing to do with all those mommy issues you have inside that cold heart of yours?"

"I don't have mommy issues."

A drop of sweat fell from his nose and plopped onto the mat. "You have mommy issues, and I have daddy issues. Sometimes, we both have both. Our parents fucked us up just like Fiona's mom fucked her up. The woman thinks if she has one drink, she'll be a strung-out addict in a week. You saving Megan from that fucker is you living vicariously and thinking you're really saving our mother."

"Paging Dr. Freud... Someone's wearing your nametag." I rolled my eyes. But he was right. I'd even thought the same thing, but that didn't mean he had to wave his therapy ticket stubs in my face.

Leo pressed into a plank and pinned me with his dark gaze. "Here's the question... Do you like *her* or the idea of her? Because leading someone down a path then bailing is kinda fucked up."

I knew that. I just couldn't figure out where I'd gone wrong, especially if her brooding had started when she'd gotten home.

"You want to spar? I'd love to hit you." He fluttered his eyelashes in a 'pretty please' cartoon motion.

"Nah. I'm going to check a few things before we go. Besides, isn't your boyfriend on his way?" I'd read a text earlier on our group chat about Anton being late but wanting to see Leo. *Sickening.*

Leo made a pouty face that didn't suit him. "You are so cute when you're jealous. I'll meet you at the car in an hour."

I flipped him off with a bored expression then showered and put on the black suit that was our uniform. My aviators were in my office, which was next to our gym, and with a bit of time to spare, I cracked open my laptop.

The guy I used to forward mail through on the West Coast had sent me a late-night email with the subject, 'Interesting'. I clicked the long blue link which led me to a story in Megan's hometown newspaper. Her neighbor, Janet, had apparently accused Billy of murder then suddenly retracted all her claims and blamed it on a mix-up in her medication. Down the rabbit hole I went, watching all Janet's previous interviews where she didn't look anything but legitimately upset, and she pointed a very direct finger at the sheriff's son. Why on earth would she have stopped? The Johnstons had threatened many things, but it didn't look like any of them panned out. Even their libel lawsuit had only really been a cease and desist.

But most interesting of all was the mention of a sister. On the road when I'd asked Megan about leaving her family, she'd said that they were all gone. I'd thought she'd meant they were dead. And the neighbor was claiming that Ruby had been abused by Billy Johnston. Did that mean that Megan had not? No. I'd seen him stalk her, seen him throw her against a truck. He must have been beating them both.

But where was the sister?

I checked my watch then closed my laptop. There was no sign of Leo in the hall, but the gym was locked, so I headed down the elevator to the garage. My brother stood with Anton in front of our black work SUV. It was bulletproof and the interior had been sealed in the event of a chemical attack. It might have been just a tad overkill, but so much of security was image.

I gave a two-finger salute as my hello to Anton, who promptly said, "Word on the street is you're a bad kisser."

Had that thick-headed shit not learned that I had a pristine memory and he would pay for that? I let the insult slide for that reason and hopped into the driver's side. Leo and all his *Psychology Today* articles could be on door duty for the diplomat.

On the way to the airport, Leo jabbered on about his boys and Violet—how good she was with them, how amazing our Aunt Chezzie was with the three of them. I didn't mind the hijacking of the conversation and the one-sidedness of it. The monologue gave me time to think, to question. Maybe *I* hadn't done anything to alter Megan's mood.

Did the existence of the sister change how I felt about Megan? It wasn't like I'd asked her and she'd straight-up lied to my face. I'd assumed the worst. Maybe I'd even projected. All I would have to do is ask.

I turned to Leo. "So I'm going to date Megan. There's really nothing you can do about it."

"Whoa. No. No, fucking no." Leo's face was tight in disbelief, just like the time when we were kids and I told him what our father actually did for a living.

I shrugged as we pulled into the airfield.

"You can't just drop a bomb like that two minutes before we get our client. I don't want you making out on my couch with my fucking nanny. Only *I* make out in my house. No. Bad, Francis. I'm calling Chezzie."

At the toll both I showed my credentials that allowed us to take the car to the private sector where we could go from jet to car without having to deal with the public part of the airport. Man, luxury had perks.

Leo continued his rant, "Just because your DNA popped out before mine does not mean that you get to decide everything for this family. No. I say *no.*"

"You sound like a whiney bitch." I smirked. It was probably the wrong road to success, but it was way more fun.

"Now you insult me?"

A sleek jet skidded down the runway in a smooth and impressive landing. The black-and-gold flag of a foreign country came into focus on the side of the plane before it turned its pointy nose in our direction.

I rubbed my lips together then tapped Leo's chest. "Fifty bucks on us finding an escort for this fucker."

"A thousand."

I turned and stared, that little shit was serious. "Deal."

"You're fucked. He's engaged. I read it online last night while I was doing my homework."

Baby brother was losing his edge. Did he really think I didn't know that? I was making the stupid bet to give him something to rub my face in and distract him from me dating his nanny.

Every minute that passed during the day and it was business as usual, Leo gloated. He sported a smug half-smile in and out of the various buildings where our client had a meeting. When we finally dropped the diplomat back at the airport without him having made a mid-day romp with an unknown woman, I paid the thousand and informed him I was driving him all the way back to Long Island.

"Fiona's cooking." Leo's attempt to discourage me was laughable.

"Chezzie gave you enough food for an army on Monday. I doubt it." As I drove us back through the city and to the expressway, Leo thumb punched his phone and ignored me.

If I were truly honest with myself, it hadn't just been me wanting to talk to Leo before officially starting to date Megan. It was also more than me thinking it was terrible timing and she needed to focus on herself. The real root to my four-day silence was that I had serious doubts about my right to be happy.

The 'normal' life I'd been trying to lead for the past several years hadn't proved anything. I still had the memories, still had taken twenty-seven lives. I wasn't sure a life like Leo's would ever be for me.

"Can I ask you something?"

Leo put down his phone. "You ask if you can ask a question but tell me you're dating my live-in nanny? You're so fucked up."

"Fuck off. But this is a serious question. Aren't you concerned about our DNA? You basically just made two more of us. Doesn't that worry you?"

"You really think I'm going to take them camping, give them knives at five then leave in the middle of the night to see if they can find their way back to the car?"

The memory was vivid. It had been the first time Leo had learned how cruel our father really was. He'd cried all the way down the mountain, poor little shit, then been ridiculed by our dad for his tear-stained face. I could still see it. He'd been filthy everywhere but the wet streaks on his cheeks. It was also the moment I'd decided I would never leave my little brother's side.

"No." My answer was quiet, and even if his question was rhetorical, he deserved to know I didn't think he was capable of an action so cruel.

"It's different, Frankie. You know what made me fall in love with Fiona? She always put Violet first. Always. How many times did we feel that? Fucking zero. That's why it's different."

"I'm not sure I want to be a father. I'm terrified of fucking someone up." I tapped the wheel of the car because a confession was rare for me. I didn't like being exposed.

"So now you're getting married and having a family? Should we send you to Turkey for three months to see if it's the real deal, like you did for me?"

I glanced over with a dirty look. "I sent you to Turkey because you did a bad thing, and I was afraid you would go back to that shitty neighborhood and get caught. You needed daylight between you and Anton."

"So thoughtful. Listen… If you think you're going to have some kind of simple relationship, you are mistaken, big brother. You are a complicated human. And just take it one damn day at a time. Why are you in such a rush? Jesus."

He was right, not that I would say it out loud. He was also sparing me the part about being a shitty communicator. I really sucked at talking.

We pulled into his driveway just as the summer sun set in the dark pink-and-orange sky. Leo reached for the handle and stopped. "You know, you *are* capable of love. Look at the way you love this family. In the end, it all means the same thing."

I frowned. "We don't have to hug now, do we?"

"Don't be ridiculous."

Leo punched in the code to his front door, and we were met with Fiona at the end of the stairs.

"Hey, Frankie." Fiona's greeting was quick and a little cooler than usual. "Um, babe? The boys are sleeping in their own room. Violet passed out thirty minutes ago after a seventh book with Megan. I know you had a long day and are probably hungry, but we have a window."

Leo's eyes went wide before he looked at me. "Bye."

They giggled up the stairs like naughty teenagers and I couldn't help but smile. Their bond was stronger than ever. They'd put all the dark shit behind them and flourished in their happiness. *Can I?*

I made my way toward the kitchen and spotted Megan in the living room, flipping through the channels. She paused mid-click when she saw me, and her mouth went agape.

Not exactly the same energy we left off with on Monday night.

Chapter Eighteen

Megan

Someone must have unplugged my heart, because I was pretty sure it had stopped beating. No one had mentioned that Frankie was coming over.

"Hi." He walked into the living room in his black suit and shiny shoes that I knew cost more than my rent had been in Iowa. He had on a black shirt that was opened at the top button and everything about him was fresh, even though it was close to nine p.m.

Me, on the other hand? I was a mess. Fiona had given me a few hand-me-downs and I was rocking black yoga pants covered in Rusty's fur and my oversized T-shirt that I slept in. I'd also taken off my bra, so the girls were hanging free. The empty bag of nacho chips in front of me had been my dinner, and my fingers were stained orange from the fake cheese. So, yeah, not my best look.

I managed out a stuttered, "Hey."

"Mind if I sit?" His quiet tone was serious. *Crap.* My palms got clammy, and I wiped them down my thighs.

Frankie tugged at the top of his pants and sat to my left with his legs wide apart. He propped his elbows on his knees and scrubbed his beard. "I owe you an apology. Apparently, there is some kind of forty-eight-hour rule that I broke by not calling you after the date. I'm sorry. I was waiting to talk to Leo in person, and that only happened today. I wasn't ignoring you."

I chewed my bottom lip.

"This is the part where you say you forgive me — or just say something really."

I shrugged. "I was never mad at you. I just thought you might not want me to force you on a second date."

"No one forces me to do anything."

I believed that.

Frankie sat back in the couch and crossed his foot over his opposite knee. "Is that it? Leo says you've been acting…guarded."

"Nope. All good here." My clipped tone and his quick glance to the empty bag of chips were evidence to the contrary.

"You sure there's not anything you want to tell me?" He was fishing, so he knew something. Maybe he'd put an alert for my name and had seen Janet.

"I had a really nice time on Monday. And it's totally unfair to show up all dapper when I look like a train wreck."

"Huh." He left me sitting there and tinkered around in the kitchen before serving himself the remaining grilled vegetables from the fridge and a chicken cutlet he ate cold. I watched him until it was borderline creepy then padded off to my room to freshen up.

It would have been too obvious to change my clothes, but I did wash my face and add a thin layer of mascara. I wiped off the pants and tried to remove as much Rusty as I could and was relieved that I didn't smell like vomit or body odor.

With the calmest energy I'd had all week — because that was what five minutes with Frankie did to me — I went back to the kitchen where he sat at the island and finished the last bites of his dinner.

I motioned to the plate. "I'll take care of that. So…did you talk to your brother today?"

"All day." Frankie wiped his mouth with a paper pink napkin that Violet had picked out when we'd gone grocery shopping earlier. It had been her impulse item. Mine had been the chips. "Says we can't make out on his couch." He shrugged and tossed the napkin on the dirty plate.

"Sounds reasonable. I mean, I do work here."

"An excellent point." Frankie stood. "Walk me to my car?"

"Sure." I followed him down the hall and left the door ajar so I wouldn't need to punch the code when I went back in. The solar lights glowed around the driveway.

"No Porsche?" I asked, gesturing to the SUV.

"Work-mobile. It's bulletproof, weighs a ton."

I ran my fingers over the back passenger door before turning and leaning against it. There was a tight grin on his face, and it didn't look like there'd be a goodnight kiss.

"So, I'm just going to be honest about this, because if we are starting something, I'm not interested in lies."

Any flirty energy I'd been clinging to drained out of me. "What's that?"

"I saw a news report with your old neighbor — something about you having a sister."

Shit.

He held up a hand. "Now, if anyone gets not wanting to talk about the past, it's me. But if you are manipulating me or using me — or worse — my family, well, that's gonna be a problem."

I swallowed over the massive knot in my throat. If I didn't throw him a bone, I would probably lose any chance of dating him and possibly my job. It would also mean I had to do something I'd sworn I'd never do. I let out a stifled exhale. *Crap.*

"Yes. I have a sister. She's in hiding and I'd really like to leave it at that."

He scratched the back of his neck.

It wasn't enough. "I'm sorry if I didn't correct your assumptions about Billy. It's really Ruby he wants…not me."

"Apology accepted. Besides, you were still in danger. You still needed to leave."

That was it? "Seriously?"

Frankie squinted past me then looked at me with a little confusion. "Listen." He sighed. "It's not every day that I'm attracted to someone like this. I'd really like to explore it."

If there had ever been a big, fat 'but' hanging on the end of a sentence, it was then.

"But I was holding back because I thought you'd been abused. I didn't want to rush you."

I played with a button on his shirt then gazed into his eyes. For the first time there was a softness there. Every fiber in my being wanted him to rush me. I'd put my entire life on hold for two years while I'd worked out a getaway plan for Ruby then me. The lack of attention had pecked away at me. As much as I was willing to sacrifice myself for Ruby, any healthy selfishness had slipped away. And while I'd been working out details for our departure, it wasn't like a boyfriend would have been a good idea. I would have had to break anything off when I left.

But all that was officially behind me. I was out. I was starting fresh, and Frankie deserved to know I wasn't a fragile mess he had to be careful with. I'd thought about all the ways the small deceit would work in my favor but had failed to see how it would stand in my way.

"Billy pushed me a few times. And yes, it was getting worse. What you witnessed was the farthest he'd ever taken it. But I'm strong. He could hold a knife to my throat, and I would never tell him where my sister is."

I hooked a finger around his button and brought my lips to his. "You don't have to worry about me being ready for all those things I know you're dying to do to me."

"Sounds like a challenge."

I linked my arms around his head and hopped into his arms. His beard scratched against my cheek and his citrus cologne smelled better than home. A happy heat pulsed through my veins as he kissed me slowly. The terrible tease only made me hungry for more and I pulled him in tighter. How was he able to show so much restraint?

In my ear he whispered, "You're so fucking beautiful. But I promised my brother not to do shit like this on his property."

I whined and in return he groaned then pulled away. He had self-control in spades. I slid down his body until I was standing.

Frankie stepped back with a little smirk. "What would you say to a date on Monday? I can take the day off and show you some things."

"I would love that."

"Good." He pecked my forehead. "And until then, if you need to talk to me, just call. I understand secrets, but I won't tolerate lies."

I stepped away from the car with my lips pressed together. There was nothing ambiguous about his warning, and in truth, I was glad to have cleared the air. I hugged myself and watched him drive off. Maybe it was finally my turn for a little happiness.

Inside, Leo sat at the island eating pasta directly out of a plastic container. He'd changed out of his suit into baggy gym shorts and a fitted tank top. Once he finished chewing, he nodded in my direction.

I carried Frankie's plate to the dishwasher and slid it in then looked back. "Can I ask you about something?"

Leo scraped out the last bite and loaded it with the remaining sauce. "If it's about my brother then no. Sorry, I don't do that 'what's he really like' thing."

I wouldn't have dreamed of asking Leo about Frankie. We were far from being that familiar. "No." I crossed the room and leaned against the counter. "This is about Violet."

That got his full attention. "Go on."

"Well, she kinda mentioned something to me today, and I was wondering what your take on it was. She said the boys were so lucky to have you as their real daddy."

Leo scratched the back of his neck and swore. "Okay. So you just broke my heart."

"I told her that real dads are the ones who are there for us every day, like you are. But she said that they get

177

to *call* you 'daddy'. So I'm wondering with that bully and with the boys, if she sees herself as on the outside of something, even though she's very much the center of this family. I don't know. I don't want to pry or overstep. I know she's the apple of your eye."

He frowned. "It's tough. She knows Fiona is her sister, so calling her 'mom' would be weird, but yeah. Thanks for letting me know. I'll talk to Fi about it." He took two bottles of water from the fridge and stopped before going upstairs.

"You really want to date my brother?"

Yes, yes, I really did.

I faked a wince. "Sorry?"

Chapter Nineteen

Frankie

Chezzie slid into the car with a cheesecake in her lap. I eyed it and swallowed the drool that had immediately pooled in my cheeks.

"Orange ricotta?" I asked.

"I can't remember." Chezzie tapped her mouth with her index finger. "Do you like this one?" She winked, knowing damn well I loved that cake. It pained me to share it with Leo. But I also knew she only made my favorite things when I was depressed or she wanted something.

I drove out of the city and waited for it.

Once we hit the expressway she broke. "I met someone."

I spun my head in her direction. Her expression was more confident than I would have thought. She wasn't even cringing. I must have been losing my edge. That didn't stop the grumble from bubbling up. My Aunt

Francesca was not only my namesake, but she was the closest thing to a mother Leo and I had ever had. She was a saint, and I dared anyone to tell me anything different. And Leo and I may have been slightly overly protective of her throughout the years. Some might even say possessive.

She lifted her hand in a full-on stop. "Before you go ballistic and overreact, he's Italian, a widower and loves my cooking."

"Everyone loves your cooking. That doesn't make him special. It makes him human." I pressed on the gas and passed a semi at full speed. "How did his wife die?"

"Breast cancer. Fifteen years ago."

"How did you meet him?"

"He was a complimentary, polite and charming customer." It almost sounded as if she'd rehearsed her answers, because they were coming out entirely too matter-of-fact.

"How old is he?"

"Sixty-seven. He just retired. He was an accountant."

I glanced over. He was seventeen years older than Chezzie.

"Don't. Don't say one word. It's not easy finding a man in his fifties who wants to date a woman his own age." She was giving me that Ricci stare-down. We were all capable of the threatening look, but she just happened to be the most effective. I blamed experience.

I looked back at the road. While Chezzie deserved happiness like the rest of us, Leo and I had always been too selfish to let her have it. We'd basically picked up where our father had left off on scaring the shit out of her future boyfriends. Maybe it was time to break that cycle.

But still, she'd made that cake. There had been some bribery needed. "What's the catch?"

"He doesn't live in the city." By that, she also meant he didn't live in the state. Old, Italian and with some money, my bet was on Florida.

"Naples, Florida?" I closed an eye, wondering how close I was.

"Fort Myers. But you are frightening."

"Thank you."

We had another half hour before we got to Leo's for Sunday dinner, which gave me time to think. Who was I to stand in the way of Chezzie's happiness? It wasn't like I'd listened to Leo when he'd asked me to forget about Megan. If there was a spark, why deny it?

Chezzie continued, "It's just that I realized my only chance at happiness is going to be in a relationship. And I don't know if it will work with this man, but I'd like to try. I don't want to be alone and in my kitchen for the rest of my life."

And I didn't want to be alone protecting strangers for the rest of mine. "I get it."

"What?"

I was just as surprised as she was.

"I'm still going to need his full name and date of birth." I frowned, being reasonable sucked.

She grinned from ear to ear. "Will you tell Leo?"

"Can I have the entire cake?"

"Maybe." She lifted a shoulder and grinned.

But there was more. She was entirely too prepared.

"What's your move here? That is, if mister Italian widow accountant checks out," I asked.

Chezzie interlaced her fingers then twiddled her thumbs a little. "I would close the restaurant for a week and go down for a vacation. I'd stay at a hotel, discover the area and get to know him better. Could be that I hate the humidity or the beach and I come back like nothing's happened."

The thing was, if she'd already gotten to the part of the relationship where she was talking to me about it and planning a trip, she'd already made up her mind about this man. It also meant that she would most likely move to Florida to be with him. Chezzie had been my silent rock forever. It was entirely selfish, but I didn't want to lose her. Screw dinner... I was going to dig into that cake while I still had a chance to eat it.

There was plenty of guilt I could have thrown in her direction, but knowing Leo would shovel it at her in loads about Violet and the babies stopped me. So, I kept quiet for the rest of the ride. When we got to Leo's I opened Chezzie's car door for her and motioned for the cheesecake. It was mine.

Violet greeted us at the door and waiting very calmly behind her was Rusty. I kissed my niece's cheek and said, "Impressive," as I gestured to the dog.

Chezzie bent down and chatted to Violet as I made my way to the back of the house in search of a fork. Leo nodded to me from the grill on the back patio and Rusty trotted into the kitchen then through the open door toward Leo. I couldn't blame him. The meat smelled great.

I opened the silverware drawer and banged it shut with my hip. With my feet crossed at the ankles, I dug into the cheesecake and savored it while joggling through the memories of the unlucky men who had tried to date my aunt in the past.

"Hey!" Leo came in and eyed my dessert for dinner. "Don't get your germs all over that. Is that orange ricotta?"

"Mm-hmm."

Leo reached in the drawer for his own fork and dug in. "Why are we eating this?"

I loaded the fork and piled it in. With my mouth full, I said, "Chezzie's got a boyfriend."

"Nah. No, no. Chezzie's not allowed to have boyfriends. She's *our* Chezzie." Leo gave me a perplexed look. We'd almost finished half of the cake. It was too creamy and light to stop.

"He lives in Florida."

Leo shook his head. My calm tone was throwing him off. That, with the cake eating, meant I'd accepted it. He yanked the pan away from me and hoarded it like it was his first meal in weeks.

"How are you okay with this?" he whined.

I waved my hands around in a grand, dramatic gesture. "I'm not okay! I'm eating fucking cheesecake for dinner! But what am I going to do? Tie her to a radiator? She's a grown woman. We've been sucking the life out of her for years."

Fiona rushed into the kitchen. "Why are you two yelling at each other? And Jesus fuck, are you eating our dessert? Is that orange ricotta?" She crossed over to Leo, who took another bite.

"Oh." A pained look appeared on her face and Fiona rubbed Leo's arm. "You found out about Michael. I'm sorry, baby."

"Who the fuck is Michael?" Leo turned to me, his panic rising.

"Chezzie's boyfriend. Gimme a bite of that before it's gone." Fiona reached for his fork, but Leo lifted the dish over his head.

"You knew?" we asked in unison.

"Traitor. No cake for you. Come on, Frankie. I need to flip the meat." Leo snarled at Fiona, and we went outside and sat at the iron picnic table.

I stuck my fork into the cake. I didn't care that I was getting full and a little sick of it. We would finish it on principle alone. We'd lost all other forms of rebellion.

"This is going to be hard on Violet. Chezzie is basically a superstar to her." Leo stood with a sigh then went over and flipped the meat.

"Well, we maybe overreacting just a little. She hasn't moved there yet."

"But we know she's already serious if she's telling us. When was the last time she mentioned anything about dating? Years, that's how long. You think she sits at home and knits when we're not around? She's a Ricci."

The idea of Chezzie dating without our knowledge had occurred to me several times. It had, indeed, been years since we'd scared off the last guy who I was convinced wanted to marry her for the building she owned then bury her in the basement. He'd been a shifty fucker, and Leo had agreed.

But with Leo married and me starting to date his nanny, the hypocrisy would have been through the roof. I took another bite and sent a sour look to the grill. I'd officially ruined my dinner.

"Hey." Megan came out in the jumper she'd brought with her from Iowa. She was carrying the baby who I thought was Dante, and there was gloss on her pretty lips. "Fiona wants to know — and this is her word, not mine — how much longer you two need to sulk. The babies have both eaten and been changed, so it would be a good time to eat." She eyed the nearly empty cheesecake dish. "Did you guys finish that?"

I nodded slowly. "Did you know about Michael?"

She shifted the baby so his stomach was on her forearm and she rocked him back and forth. "Who's Michael?"

"Chezzie's boyfriend in Florida," I said with over-exaggerated disgust.

"Chezzie has a boyfriend? Good for her. Can we eat or what?"

Leo pressed his knuckle into one of the steaks. "Five minutes. Frankie, go open the wine."

Megan flashed me a confused look but took the baby back inside.

"How long do you think we have to run to work off that fucking thing?" He swiveled around and pointed his long tongs to the table.

"How much cake do you think you'll eat the day Violet comes home with a boyfriend?" I stood and tossed my fork into the dish.

"Hey," he scolded, "that's never going to happen. And if it does, I will kindly give the little shit a tour of my knife collection."

We made a proper display of our disapproval during dinner. Leo sent the Ricci eyes to his wife, and I pouted into my plate. Megan stayed mostly silent. Perhaps she understood that it was a family affair. It was only when she brushed against me in the kitchen while we did the dishes that I ditched my spoiled child act.

"You can't really be mad at her for dating someone. She's a grown woman."

I shrugged. "I'm not really mad at her, neither is Leo. We're terrified of losing her."

"Well, tell her that instead of acting like a big fat baby and stuffing your mouth with cake. Although, it was entertaining…and impressive. How did you manage to eat dinner?"

"Iron will." And one painful bite at a time. I was bloated and pretty sure the food was stuck in my esophagus, as there couldn't possibly have been more room in my stomach.

A twinkle appeared in her eyes, and she hooked her finger into my belt loop. She swayed back and forth like a shy schoolgirl. "What should I wear tomorrow? Is it more of a casual thing or should I be a little fancy? I don't want to feel out of place."

I liked that she'd asked. It showed she'd been thinking about it. "Casual is perfect. Do you want me to get you at the station?"

"No. I want to ride the subway. I already know the route." She clapped her hands together quietly. That she got so excited for something so tedious and mundane was both beyond me and endearing. And as much as I wanted to protect her every movement, I couldn't be irrational about it.

"Two o'clock? I have some cake to run off and lunch with a potential client."

"Perfect. And I'm on bath duty with Violet, so I'm going to steal a little kiss and say goodnight." Megan stood on her tiptoes and pecked my lips. She whispered, "I'm really looking forward to tomorrow. No pressure." She kissed me again and was off. The light energy suited her, and I selfishly thought her carefree mood had something to do with me. I just hoped she'd like my plan for the next day.

Chapter Twenty

Megan

I had to admit that the odor of the subway wasn't great. In fact, a unique blend of grease and urine hovered in a way I'd never experienced before. But I didn't really care. People minded their own business and barely paid attention to their fellow passengers. It was blending in at its best.

As the train whooshed down the tunnel, I pinched myself that I was living out a dream. It had taken a good half hour to get to the stop that was closest to Frankie's apartment, but the time had passed in a flash. The melting pot of different cultures gave me a dorky perma-grin that only widened when I thought about my day-date.

I exited the train and trekked in the slow pace up the stairs with the dozens of other people who'd stopped with me. Above ground, a jackhammer rattled in my ears. The summer sun hid behind the clouds, but the humidity of the day hadn't forgotten to be as imposing as a hot, wet rag slapping me in the face. With any luck, it wouldn't flatten out my hair. I'd tried to make a bit of an effort by blowing it out with a round brush to give it some extra volume.

After a quick check of my phone, the path to Frankie's was clear and I headed east toward the river then south two blocks until I was in front of his massive building. The doorman escorted me in then called Frankie to announce my arrival.

"He's on his way down. You can wait over there if you wish." The man pointed to the large couches, and I nodded. When I sat, the cool leather hit my thighs and I worried that my shorts weren't long enough or were too casual or too cheap. My off-the-shoulder peasant top was new. It had been on sale in a shop in town and my small splurge of the week.

I plopped my bag on my lap, only to feel a phone vibrating on my thighs. I dug in, and sure enough, it was Ruby with her horrible timing.

"Hey. It took you a long time to get back to me."

"Sorry. I lost the charger. But I'm dying to see you. Just knowing you're here is killing me."

Even though there was no reason to hide a phone call in public, I lowered my voice and turned my head from the doorman out of habit. "I know. It's totally the same."

"My therapist put you on the visitor's list. You could meet me here next Monday. *Please.*"

The elevator dinged and my heart stopped. I'd let Frankie know about Ruby, but I wasn't ready to tell him she was forty blocks away. "I'll text you." I ended the call and slid the phone down my chest then hid it back in my bag.

I let out a slow exhale from my mouth, gathered myself and stood.

With an easy smile, and in what qualified as casual for Frankie — dark jeans and a basic white shirt with one more button open than usual — he strode over.

I wiped my sweaty palms on my back pockets.

"Hey." His eyes sparkled and he kissed me on the cheek. A warm blanket spread over my skin in the best kind of way.

"What's in there?" I pointed to the dark bag he was carrying.

"You'll see." Frankie reached for my hand and gently tugged me back to the elevator. "We need the car. Our date is in Jersey."

Jersey? I thought he was going to show me some things in the city. But he had some sort of secret plan, which meant he'd thought about our day, which also meant he'd thought about me. That was good enough.

In the elevator, he flashed me a smile and I hoped my hand wasn't giving away my butterflies of giddiness. I needed to pull myself together a little. It shouldn't have been so easy for him. I smiled back as casually as I could. I probably had no game, but at least I could try.

The baby-blue Porsche stuck out like a massive diamond in a coal mine. We walked over and Frankie opened the passenger door for me. I couldn't be sure, but I thought he checked out my legs quickly before winking and closing me in.

He slid the bag behind his seat then climbed in. Once we were out of the garage, he said, "So what did you do this morning?"

"You didn't track me on my phone?" I teased.

"I managed not to. Progress." Frankie merged onto a highway that led us Uptown and maneuvered the car in and out of traffic with speed and ease.

"I slept in, which was not easy, but it was nice, then took the train in. I ate a hot dog from a vendor on the street for lunch and visited the massive cathedral next to the park. I've never seen anything like it in real life. It was stunning."

"You're stunning."

I rolled my eyes. "So why Jersey?"

"Better laws." He checked over his shoulder before switching lanes. "So Miss Small-Town USA, have you ever shot a gun before?"

Come again?

"I..."

"Oh shit." He deflated. "Don't tell me you hate guns. Fuck. I'm sorry. I should have asked. We can—"

"No." I'd actually wanted to learn how to shoot for a while. I just couldn't find anyone in my circle of friends or acquaintances who would be willing to show me. They were all too worried I'd use it on Billy. And it wasn't like I'd had the money for private lessons. "I take it you know what you're doing with one..."

A cheeky grin replaced the small panic. He glanced over and licked his lips. "I have a steady hand."

I giggled. "Oh! He flirts!" I teased while fanning myself. "What's next? A clever joke?"

He kept his little grin for a while then asked, "But really? Have you ever shot a gun?"

"No. But I've wanted to. So, I'm kinda excited."

"I thought it might be something to help you feel safe. Maybe it's stupid."

We crossed the massive bridge leading to the neighboring state and paid the toll to get on the turnpike. A half an hour later, we pulled up to a thick iron gate and Frankie flashed a card to make it open. There was a long path to a lodge, and only a few cars peppered the lot.

"Mondays are slow. Best days to shoot." He grabbed the bag from behind his seat and we walked to the low brick building and entered. Frankie flashed a membership card and signed me in as a guest. There was an American flag draped behind the counter and a thick layer of glass separated us from the clerk. I guessed when surrounded by guns, one could never be too careful.

Frankie led me down a concrete hallway where his keycard clicked open a door. Inside the room were five shooting stations, all empty. It was like a bowling alley for firearms without the orange and yellow plastic chairs. The florescent lights hummed overhead, and my heart thumped. The idea of shooting a gun was both exciting and scary, and yet the calm of Frankie's mood suppressed any real fear.

On the counter behind the last station, Frankie unzipped the bag. He took out a black handgun, and I wondered how many more were in there.

"This is a 380. It's a little lighter than a 9mm and the barrel is longer. Ideal for beginners." Frankie spun the gun around his index finger then offered it to me with lifted eyebrows.

I blinked several times. Me and a gun… It was the self-defense I'd always wanted and finally with someone who would teach me the right way to use it. I exhaled all my nerves. They had no place there. The moment was serious, and it could one day save my life…or Ruby's.

"Take it," Frankie urged. "Just hold it and get used to the weight. The safety's on, so no worries."

I reached my hand forward, palm up, and the weight of the gun surprised me. The cool, dark steel emitted a sense of power I'd never experienced before.

"It's very basic. Pull the trigger and it shoots. The bullets reload automatically. Come on." Frankie walked over to the last booth, and I followed. The cool air of the ventilation system blew behind me and I shivered.

"The first thing is stance. Show me."

"I don't know. I guess…" I mimicked something I recalled from a movie, my arms straight out, my shoulders hiked up and my back arched. Even I knew it was all wrong.

The heat of Frankie's body warmed and relaxed me as he stepped close. He kicked open my legs just a little, repositioned my hips and used his thumb and middle finger to encourage my shoulders down.

"Relax. Equally distribute your body weight." His hand fell to my stomach, and he tilted it upward. "Engage your core. Next, you aim."

A paper target of a body with lines was at the end of the alley. I saw Billy's beady eyes and aimed between them.

Frankie's beard brushed against my cheek, but I refused to let it distract me. I ran through his checklist of my body stance and took a deep breath.

"The head. A girl after my own heart. Okay, ears and eyes then we can start." Frankie handed me a pair of ear cans and tinted glasses. "There's not much kick-back to this gun, but I'll be right behind you. When you're ready, you have eight shots."

He put on his own ear and eye gear then settled behind me, first with his hands on my hips where he gave them a slight tilt. Then he unlocked the safety button.

It was a sin, imagining Billy's head there — taking satisfaction in pretending. It was one that I'd confessed too many times to Father Peter. I was caving into wrath, losing the battle of ignoring my desire for vengeance. But there was another fight in me that I wanted to win — the one where I had control, where I could *do* something. My nose started to burn, and my eyes went blurry.

The only thing I could control was my breath. I slowed the inhale, and a tear ran down my cheek, its release allowing me to focus again. I squeezed the trigger slowly and pleaded with my arms muscles to absorb any impact to come.

Even with the ear covering, the shot rang loud between the concrete walls and steel ceiling. I jerked back a little and bumped into Frankie's chest. *Seven more.* I shook off the nerves, aimed again and shot again.

With each tug of the trigger, a dangerous excitement built — a taste of a forbidden high I'd never known existed. When the gun was empty, Frankie stepped away and dropped his ear cans to around his neck. He pressed a button on the wall and my paper target zoomed toward us like a bag of clothes at the drycleaner.

There were five holes in the paper, meaning I'd totally missed three times and none of them were between the eyes as I'd secretly imagined. Frankie pointed to the closest one.

"You nicked the ear. That would stop 'em." He smiled then studied me, his forehead creasing. "You okay?"

I shrugged and rubbed my arms. "Yeah, just...emotions."

"Too much?"

"No. But I think I'm done for today. You go."

"Nah." He took the gun from me and opened it to check it was empty then walked it back to his bag.

"Oh no. I go then you go. It's only fair." I put my hands on my hips, I wanted to see what he had in him — perverse curiosity at its best.

He shook his head.

"Is it because I'm better than you?" I teased.

"Yes. It's absolutely that." He was a horrible liar.

But after all his confidence and lack of fear, I was dying to know why. I craved the proof that he was some sort of badass.

"Show them what their missing and make them mad as hell," Fiona had said.

"Okay." I took off my safety gear and placed it next to the black bag then fluffed my hair. "I'll go ask the clerk to show me what he's got. I bet he's got a big gun."

Frankie laughed. "Fine. Put those back on." He pointed to the ear cans and glasses then chose a different gun from his bag. It was silver with a brown wood-like handle. He gave me an annoyed glance before walking over to the booth and sending my paper fake man target back all the way to the end of the range. With the handgun pointed straight ahead, he dropped his shoulder a little. I thought he might take a second, but the first shot went off so quickly that it made me jump with surprise. I didn't even think three seconds had passed and he'd stuck the gun in the back of his pants and was pushing on the button to bring back the target.

Frankie motioned with his index finger for me to approach. Eight perfect holes made two eyes, a nose and a mouth in a smiley face. *Holy crap, he's an expert.* Not that I'd ever doubted it.

"Satisfied?" he asked as he walked back to the counter and stored his gun.

"Getting there."

Chapter Twenty-One

Frankie

Megan swung her bare legs on the island in my kitchen. They had a nice glow to them. She'd probably seen more sun since walking Rusty with Violet. Her feet were bare and she'd hopped up onto the counter to watch me cook. I rinsed the fish in the sink while she sipped her wine, then I dried my hands and sharpened my fish knife.

"That's a lot of knives." She shot a glance at the magnetic band in my kitchen before raising her eyebrows for an explanation.

"They all serve a purpose." It was true that they did, some multiple.

She crossed her arms and it plumped up her breasts. I shouldn't have been thinking about her breasts with a knife in my hand. I was going to cut myself.

"Are you one of those guys who throws knives for fun?"

I gave her a curious look, then sliced open the belly of the fish and began gutting it. "It's supposed to be fun? Huh."

"What *do* you do for fun?" She hopped down and circled the island. I stole a small gawk at her round ass. I would have liked to involve that in my fun. Ever since she'd shot the gun, my mind had been in the gutter. I'd been holding back out of respect, but I was secretly dying inside. Any other woman would have been pinned against the wall in that fucking gun range with my hand in those ridiculous shorts that had been taunting me since I'd first met her.

I fake-frowned. "What? You don't think today was fun? *Is* fun?"

"Today? Well, at least the shooting, was...exhilarating. But also...confrontational."

That was interesting. I stuffed the fish with tarragon and lemon then laid it on the baking sheet. "How so?"

She brought her thumb to her lips, stopped herself from biting the nail and shoved her hands in her back pockets. *Lucky hands.*

"I saw him. Billy."

My heart stopped. "When?"

"At the range. Not him, him. The image of him. I wanted to shoot him."

"Well, you nicked his ear." I winked. Lord, my flirting was borderline pathetic.

Megan's smile stopped halfway. "Revenge isn't healthy. I talked about it so many times with Father Peter. But I can't stop the desire to want him to suffer. I'd like to be better than that."

I washed my hands then went over to her and tilted her chin so she looked me in the eyes.

"We all see someone. Don't beat yourself up about it. You had a human reaction. You're the farthest thing from a bad person I've ever met." No need to tell her that my bar was low.

Those big emerald jewels gazed at me with sadness. She was disappointed in herself. Maybe it had been a mistake to take her shooting. I'd thought it would be empowering, but confrontational? Not what I'd been hoping for.

She blinked then stared so deep into my eyes that I swore she touched my soul. "Who do you see?"

Megan had never asked me for anything. The respect she'd shown for my privacy and secrecy was unparalleled. And she'd trusted me enough to come clean about her sister.

I swallowed hard. "My father." It was a whisper, a quiet truth that would never set me free.

She reached up and touched my cheek. "I'm sorry."

It wasn't her fault or Leo's or mine. I wasn't even sure I could continue to blame my father for how he'd raised us. He was an evil man with an ice block instead of a heart. How else would he have done it? There'd even been times I'd been grateful, as sick as that was.

Megan's gaze didn't offer pity. It was under-standing. She knew why she saw Billy and could only assume I saw my father for similar reasons.

The softness of her touch, her gentle soul... I didn't deserve a woman like that. But I wanted her. The depths of my being hungered—starved—for someone to show me that pure act of sweet kindness. She'd answered all that I'd ever wanted, the opposite of who I was.

It was selfish, the way I leaned down to kiss her like she didn't have a choice. Like I didn't know I was moving too fast. And it was lustful how I deepened it, tasting the tart wine on her tongue. Maybe, one day if she found out how charred my soul was, she'd leave—

horrified of who I was. But in that moment, I would risk it.

She did that little whimper thing and sent me over the edge. As she slid her arms around my neck, I kissed on, trying desperately not to be rough, not to show the aggressive side of me, but the ego was out of the bag.

Down her neck I nipped, while I allowed myself to touch the parts of her I'd been so good about avoiding all the other times we'd kissed.

"Don't stop. Please, don't stop," she begged, and it was music to my warped ears.

I glanced at the timer on the oven. I had sixteen minutes to make her come. If I did it right, the buzzer and she would howl at the same moment.

I pulled back and she clocked the mischief on my face. I rubbed my cheek into hers and tugged her earlobe with my lips. "I'm gonna go until you stay stop. Don't let me do anything you don't want."

"That's hard to imagine."

It was difficult to keep myself from spinning her around and yanking down her pants. I was dying to get personally acquainted with her ass, but that would have to wait. Full Frankie could be frightening. Instead, I lifted her up and kissed her lovely mouth over to one of the sectionals, grinding my erection into those fucking shorts the whole way.

I let her down easy and stole a glance. She was a gorgeous sight—on her back, hair spread out wildly and kiss-swollen lips. But it was her hazed-over eyes that killed me, pulled me into her lustful trance and begged me to stay there.

I groped her. Fucking hell, I could no longer help myself. Her breasts were firm and full and the ache I had for her was too far beyond being a gentleman. I ran my hand over her soft stomach and unbuttoned, then unzipped the shorts.

There was no taking my mouth off hers, I needed to feel her every hitch of breath, every moan of pleasure. We kissed deep, and I slipped my fingers into her underwear.

I hoped my deep groan proved how fucking pleased and privileged I knew I was to be touching her like that. I dipped two fingers into her folds, then found her clit and pinched it.

Megan stuttered out a breath and she arched her back. God, she was on the edge, and I'd barely done a thing. That being said, I was fucking hard as a rock. My dick was desperate to return to the friction of before.

"Do you know what I like about you, Megan?" I whispered on her lips before diving in again without giving her a chance to answer.

She was practically shaking. The rise of her orgasm was building.

"You're so fucking soft." I slowed the rub on her clit and expanded my circle to the silky hair around it. "Everything—your skin, your touch, even this." I cupped my hand and dipped my fingers back in then brought them to where she was most sensitive.

"But me, Megan? I'm a hard man. And sometimes I just can't contain that part of myself." I pushed into her clit then let loose at a frenzied pace.

Megan jolted below me as if electrocuted and gasped several times with shallow breaths. I pressed my palm into her clit and slipped my fingers inside, her inner walls flexing through the final moments of her orgasm.

With my head next to hers, I held her through the last wave then a little longer while she caught her breath. Slowly, I pulled my hand out of her pants as her eyes fluttered open.

The timer beeped from the kitchen, and I pecked her on the lips before getting up and walking over. My dick was mad at me. It somehow knew it wasn't getting any more attention. I pressed the button to stop the noise and washed my hands.

Megan lay still on the couch, and I let her have her moment. I removed the fish from the oven and set the pan on the wire hot plate next to the cooktop. The dish steamed and I added the vinegar and oil to the salad I'd prepared beforehand.

It was impossible to tell what was going on in Megan's head. She stayed put while I took everything over to the table.

I walked over to her as she zipped her shorts. "We can eat."

"Yeah. Okay." She shook out her hair and sat up. "Right."

At the table, she eyed me suspiciously. "So…"

I pronged a bite of fish. "Yeah?"

"Um. Can I ask you something?"

"Anything." *Wow.* That was new. My usual answer was 'no'. Or, 'fuck off'.

"Is it always that easy for you?"

"What do you mean?"

She dropped her head back and the thought of my mouth on her sweet neck send a small rush back to my dick. It was still hoping for some action. I shifted in my chair.

"Like…I don't know. That fast."

"Dinner?" I was fucking with her, but I couldn't help it.

Megan blushed a shade of pink that made me smile.

"I think it's fair to say you were rather tightly wound. And I had a timeframe."

She dropped her jaw. "You timed it for dinner?"

I shrugged and took another bite. Then it occurred to me that it might have come off as insensitive. "Was it okay?"

She shot up her eyebrows. "Uh, yeah." Megan brought her hands on the side of her head and made the explosion gesture.

I stifled the grin forming out of pride and changed the subject. "How's the fish?"

"Perfect. Thank you." She smiled over. "Do you really think you're a hard man?"

I laid my silverware to the side of my plate. "I am."

"Not everywhere. Not in your heart."

She couldn't know that, because she'd never fully seen what was inside me. But instead of trying to make her wrong, I did something worse. I gave her hope.

"Maybe."

After dinner, she cleared the table, even though I objected while I called her a car. I escorted her down to the street where she wrapped her arms around me and placed her cheek on my chest.

"I just want to say thank you." I rubbed her back, the intimacy growing addictive each minute.

Megan laughed a little. "I don't know what for. I didn't do anything today."

That was just it. "You don't push. Not only do I appreciate that, but I also need it. So thank you."

She turned toward me, and I could have gotten lost in the caring gaze she sent back forever. In fact, I was almost entirely sure I wanted to.

"I know."

Two simple words that scared the shit out of me.

Chapter Twenty-Two

Megan

"Are you sure you can manage?" Fiona wrung her hands as she stared down at the boys, each in a swing, each sound asleep. Rusty was curled up at their feet, either protecting or thinking they were in his pack. It was hard to know what went on in that dog's brain.

"It's going to be fine. Plus, you look great. You showered, you have on a regular bra, and you deserve to step away. It's like two hours max, right? I promise, they will be alive when you get back." I turned her around with my hands on her shoulders and nudged her to the front door.

She let out a little whimper. It was her first time leaving the twins, and it was by far harder on her than me or them. "I don't want to go but I *so* need to. I haven't seen Kimberly since before the birth. I have a lot of shit to talk about."

No doubt. But I'd never heard that name before. "Who is Kimberly, again?"

"My therapist. I thought I told you that. She's like a mom, sister and best friend with like, zero judgment. I can't explain it. I just know it keeps me sane." She strained to see the boys. "If I kiss them, it will wake them up, won't it?"

"Yes." One whiff of their mother and those boys were in a screaming competition for her undivided attention—an impossible goal. "The sooner you go, the sooner you're back."

She frowned.

"This is why you hired me. Remember?"

After I shut the door with a gentle click, the house had an eerie silence. In fact, it was the quietest it had ever been. I fetched the book I was reading out of my room, a massive historical fiction novel with beautiful writing, and curled up on the couch above the boys. It was hard to imagine that I was getting paid to sit and read. I would have felt a bit guilty if I hadn't gotten up early, already done two loads of laundry and taken Rusty for a long walk.

My thoughts drifted from the book to what Fiona was doing. A woman who, on the surface seemed so collected, saw a therapist. I'd kinda considered Father Pete free advice back in Iowa and had always walked away from our conversations with more hope than I'd gone in with.

But I hadn't really spoken about my feelings to anyone since the move. I'd spent so much time worried about Ruby, being strong for her, that I'd gotten lost. Frankie was helping me put myself first, but I didn't want to dump old emotions onto my fresh start with him.

Dante let out a contented sigh as he swung below. They were beautiful babies. It was hard to know who they resembled more. Both Leo and Fiona had dark hair and strong personalities. They would be raised with wonderful parents...but no grandparents...

Frankie had said he saw his father's face when he shot, so there must have been something pretty dark in his and Leo's past. I wondered if he talked to anyone. Maybe Chezzie? It could have been why those two men were so afraid to lose her.

I closed my book and dug my phone out of my back pocket. There had to be some kind of affordable counseling in the city. Sure enough, one quick search proposed many options, some even offering online. But I liked the idea of going somewhere, a safe place like a confessional, and leaving my words behind.

I chose a middle-aged woman with sympathetic eyes and scheduled an appointment in her Manhattan office for the following Monday morning then put my phone away before I changed my mind. It would be good for me. Even if I didn't tell the woman everything, I would at least be able to let my guard down.

A movement in the backyard caught my eye and my entire body tensed. It wasn't just Fiona's first time going out. It was also my first time being alone at the house. I climbed off the couch and scratched Rusty until he opened his eyes. I whispered a lie about a squirrel, and he popped up and ran to the glass doors that led to the backyard.

Rusty whined and pawed at the glass. His tail wagged as he did his anticipatory dance to chase a small animal to no avail. Maybe it was cruel to get his hopes up, but I wanted to make sure my mind wasn't playing tricks on me. It had to have been a bird or a random leaf. I walked over to where Rusty was now sitting and staring into a very much non-disturbed backyard. I quickly let him out then locked the door behind him.

Around the yard he went, sniffing, rolling and lifting his leg to reclaim the territory. And while he didn't find anything out of the ordinary — or a squirrel, for that matter — I couldn't shake the fear of being alone.

I searched for Frankie's contact info on my phone. I didn't want to bother him while he worked. Leo had said his brother and Jackson were on a one-day assignment then complained that he'd been stuck with the tennis guy.

But selfishly, I wanted to hear his voice. I knew it would calm me and he wouldn't chastise me for being paranoid. I was overreacting — that, or I was just lonely or a crazy loon who imagined boogiemen when there was just wind. Unfortunately, that did nothing for the tension in my shoulders and tight pain in my chest.

I didn't like being needy, but he'd said I could call him to talk. I didn't want to interrupt his day, so I sent a little text instead.

Two minutes later, my phone vibrated, and Frankie's name appeared on the screen. I swiped and whispered, "Hey. Sorry. It's nothing. I didn't mean to bother you."

"It was actually a good time. Our client is…occupied. What happened?"

"Nothing." I glanced to Rusty, who was rubbing his body into the shrub at the end of the yard. "I'm home alone and I got spooked. It's stupid."

"I think it's probably pretty normal to be a little paranoid, considering you had a stalker. You can call me. It's okay. If I can't answer, I'll call you back when I can." His voice had done it. It had given me back the sense that nothing was wrong. I hated that I couldn't get there by myself. How had I managed in Iowa?

Rusty barked and ran along the perimeter of the yard that touched the driveway. As I walked to the front of the house, I said, "I should go. I'm sorry I called you for no reason."

Fiona's SUV came up the drive and I calmed.

"It was nice to hear your voice during the day. You should call me more often." He was just saying that to make me feel better, I was sure. But I knew the truth. I was a pest. "I'll see you Sunday for dinner."

We ended the call and the second Fiona walked in the door, Marco started to cry—which roused Dante, who also wailed.

Two wet stains bled on Fiona's white blouse. *So much for her regular bra.*

I stuck out my bottom lip in sympathy. "I promise, they've slept the entire time. They must have some kind of boob GPS."

"Fucking Riccis." She dropped her head back. "Will you go grab the pillow? I left it on my bed."

I jogged up the stairs, and when I got to the master bedroom, I marveled at how organized and tidy it was. The bed had been made and the towels were folded in the en suite bathroom. When did that woman sleep? I grabbed the large pillow she used when she nursed them both at the same time.

Downstairs, Fiona sat on the couch with her now-ruined shirt tossed to the side. Her pretty lace bra was soaked in milk, and she waved me over with urgency. "It's actually going to be a relief. I'm engorged. I feel like a damn cow."

"You're a superhero." I slid the pillow onto her lap and did my best not to look at her breasts as I passed her Dante then Marco. Their nosy little swallows replaced the crying the second each one latched on. With a head in each hand and their tiny bodies on her forearms making a V around her midriff, she was helpless.

"Can you put on *The Food Channel*?"

I nodded and reached for the remote then flicked on the TV. If I washed out the milk from her clothes right away, it wouldn't stain, so I grabbed them and headed for the laundry room next to the garage. I filled the sink and dropped them in then went back to Fiona.

"What do you want for after?" I asked. The poor woman, she really was a milking machine.

"The hideous nursing bra, the nipple cream and one of Leo's T-shirts. Oh…and a huge glass of water."

It was so odd to go through people's drawers, a total invasion of privacy. But there weren't any juicy details revealed. I did the laundry, so I knew what I would find. I'd seen Fiona wear a black sports T-shirt of Leo's a few times, so I chose that one. The cream was on her bedside table and the bra she referred to as hideous — a plain white cotton one with flaps — was next to all the pretty ones in her dresser.

I laid them all next to her as she stroked each of the boys' heads with her thumbs. The love she had for her little family pulsed between them.

"You're an awesome mom. A total natural." I sat at the opposite end of the couch. Feeding might have been only her job, but burping required assistance, so I would be needed as soon as they'd finished.

"They're gonna have the worst mouths. Dante's first word with probably be 'motherfucker'." Fiona rolled her eyes.

"Nah. Look at Violet. I've never heard her say anything close to that."

"Violet is exceptional. Plus, these are Riccis."

Everyone kept saying that like it was such a bad thing, but the Riccis I'd met were pretty fantastic. "What does that mean, anyway?"

Fiona shook her head. "Not my story to tell."

We sat there in silence as a chef on TV made a triple layer strawberry cake until Dante had fallen asleep and Fiona motioned for me to take him. I swaddled him then tapped him on the back while I walked around the room. Fiona detached Marco and laid him next to her while she turned and rubbed on the cream.

"I'm sorry you have to see my boobs all the time. There's just no other way to feed them both at once. Hey, do you want to order a pizza for lunch?"

Dante let out a small burp and I congratulated him before putting him in his swing. Rusty had been waiting patiently outside, and I went to open for him. He sniffed his hello to Fiona and the boys then went to the kitchen where he lapped up water.

"Pizza sounds really good, actually."

Fiona took out her phone. "I have them on speed dial. What do you like?"

"Pepperoni."

"Same. I'll get two. I'm starving."

I went into the kitchen and wiped the floor where Rusty had left a mess then went back to the laundry room and put Fiona's things in the delicate cycle and hoped the stains had been caught in time. On my way back to the living room, I grabbed a big glass of water for Fiona and started the kettle for some tea. Normally, she drank the water then had a cup of fennel tea.

She'd put Marco and Dante together on a blanket she'd laid on the floor and was taking a picture with her phone. "This one is for Daddy!" She snapped a few pictures then gave me a mischievous smile. "Is it wrong I wish they knew how to give the finger?"

"You like to give him a hard time, huh?"

"It's how we operate. Always have." She shrugged, finished the message on her phone then tossed it on the couch.

I marveled at the sweet scene she was rubbing in her husband's face. "He'd do anything for you guys."

"He's done everything for us, actually." Her slight frown spoke of past secrets and almost a sadness I wouldn't have guessed. Fiona kissed the boys then peered up at me. "Kimberly says I need to ask you how you're doing and give you two days off instead of one."

Then she would be pleased with my appointment. "Actually, I decided to follow your lead. I found a therapist in the city. I'm going on Monday." Plus, I wasn't going to burden my employer with all the things brewing inside me. If she knew everything I had going on, maybe I wouldn't be the best nanny option.

"Good! If the first one doesn't work out, keep trying them. Kimberly is my seventh."

Marco let out some gas and Fiona's eyes widened. "Oh boy."

I didn't want to pry into Fiona's past and whatever it was that kept her going to therapy. "We can work toward two days off. Right now, I'm good with one. Besides, what would I do?"

"Sleep? Shop? Read? Take a shower that lasted the entire day? Endless possibilities." She bent down and kissed both sets of feet. "Do you know what else Kimberly said?"

It was a rhetorical question, so I waited for her to give the boys more kisses before she continued. "She said all those voices in my head that tell me I'm failing, that I'm not good enough, that everything I worked for could disappear in the snap of a finger—they're all bullshit."

Fiona looked up at me and narrowed her eyes. I hoped Kimberly was right.

Chapter Twenty-Three

Frankie

"Can you get me into an underground poker game?" Andy Cobbler sat in the makeup chair backstage at the sports show he was about to guest on. I'd overheard him in the car with his agent, who said the network had offered him a permanent slot. He'd refused, because doing the same thing over and over had stopped when he'd retired from tennis. His new motto was 'Do as much as you shouldn't and as frequently as possible'.

"Nope. Sorry. Don't know any," I lied. Leo and I were trying like hell to leave our criminal pasts behind, which was not so easy when it was our legacy. And walking back into the dark basements and underbelly of the city so our annoying client could throw money at hungry crooks? Not my idea of a Friday night.

"You're full of shit." Andy plucked the two tissues out of his white collar then spun around to the mirror where he smoothed his eyebrows and dusted his fingers over the short hair above his ears. "That fat fucker who tried to bribe me... You knew him, he knew you and he must know someone with a high stakes' table."

"Those fucks are cheats and liars. There's not one game in the city that wouldn't be fixed to take all your money. You have to go to Vegas or Atlantic City and get in on a legal game. Besides, all those bachelorette parties? Bound to be some married women ready to let of some steam." I pushed off the wall I'd been leaning on and tugged at my cuffs to straighten my shirt under the jacket. Why was I talking him into yet another thing I wouldn't want to do?

"I'm not going to Atlantic City. That place is fucking depressing. But Vegas? That sounds perfect." Andy straightened his dark-blue silk tie and grinned.

No. No, it didn't. It was summer. Why the fuck would he want to go to the desert? And why did he constantly find ways to throw his money away? I followed him into the studio where a stagehand motioned for him to open his jacket so he could attach the mic to his tie.

"It's settled. We'll fly out tonight. And you're coming. You're my good luck charm."

I was pretty sure my forced smile came off like the snarl I was trying to hide, especially since Andy laughed before sitting at the desk and offering his analysis of a game he'd never played. I had to hand it to him. He was a fantastic bullshitter. He would probably be excellent at poker. Maybe the spoiled brat would make money instead of losing it for a change.

While Andy blabbered on and the host of the show hung on his every word, I punched text messages into my phone. First to the business group, congratulating Jackson and Leo on having the weekend off while I flew to the dry, hot land of slot machines that never stopped dinging. The last time I'd been to Vegas, I'd seen too many grandpas with their guts hanging out of their massive T-shirts. They overate at disgusting buffets, and it made me swear I'd never to go back. But luxury Vegas would be different. Sadly, I'd have to leave my gun and knife at home, because the high roller rooms had strict security. Leo replied with a crying face emoji but said he would meet me downtown if we needed a ride to the airport.

My second message was to Megan. I didn't know how long I would be gone. It could be twenty-four hours or three days. Either way, I was going to miss Sunday dinner and might have to cancel our date on Monday afternoon. I'd actually planned a proper date, not shooting a gun. According to Leo and Jackson, that had been the worst idea of my life. Museums were closed on Mondays, so I was going to prepare an afternoon picnic in Central Park. *Color me fucking romantic.*

As I was about to hit send, I second-guessed myself. A text was cold and left too much for interpretation. It was the wrong move. I stepped out of the studio and back to the makeup room, which was empty and private.

"Hello?" Her neutral accent was so much prettier than the harsh East Coast one Leo and I had.

I couldn't help but smile. "Hey, you. Is this an okay time?"

"Just a sec."

Static came through the small speaker in my ear as she rustled on the other end. A door closed before she said, "Hi."

"How are you?"

"Twins slept for four straight hours last night. That's a record."

I made a note that she hadn't told me how *she* was but didn't have a ton of time to dive into it. "I have to go away for work. I'll let you know when I get back."

"Oh. So, no Monday?" Her voice cracked, revealing the sliver of disappointment.

"Not sure. Depends on how long I'm gone and how much sleep I get. Trust me. I'd rather be with you. But the guys and I have a deal that all out of town jobs are me. I'm sorry."

"Okay. No worries. Have a safe trip." She was too quick to dismiss it. Did she think I was hiding something?

"Megan."

"Frankie?"

"It's not what you think."

Megan cleared her throat. "I don't think anything. Besides, I have plans on Monday already."

What?

"Is there something else going on here? It sounds like you're mad at me, I'm not following…" I stopped myself from apologizing for something beyond my control, which would have been very much out of character. And what were her other plans?

She let out a dramatic sigh. "There's nothing else. Let me know when you get back."

"Are you sure you're not pissed?"

"Wait! Do you want me to be mad?"

No. Yes. Possibly. I shook my head. I was a hopeless communicator. "Actually, I think I'm pissed about going and am probably taking it out on you. Thanks for understanding. The good news is that now I get to make it up to you."

She laughed. "I gotta run. I hear babies."

We said goodbye and I stuffed my phone back into my coat pocket. No wonder I'd never had a serious relationship. I'd projected my annoyance onto Megan when there was nothing wrong with the way she'd reacted. Jesus, I was a cranky bitch sometimes.

"Hey, man." Andy strode down the hallway. "I'll call my manager in the car. We're going to Vegas, baby!" He wiggled his phone in my direction, and once he'd passed, I gave him the frown I usually only reserved for Anton Myers. Sometimes I wondered if my old job of murdering people hadn't been a better fit for my demeanor.

By the time we got to his hotel, we were on a deadline. We had three hours to get to the airport, packing for both of us included. I dropped Andy off, then went downtown to get my things and meet Leo, who would drive us, then take the company car home.

On the way back Uptown, Leo shot me a look. "You that pissy about going to Vegas?"

"Can you please tell your nanny—?"

He held up his hand. "Nope."

"I called her to tell her that I probably had to cancel Monday. She was totally fine with it. Like she didn't even care—"

"Here we go," Leo said under his breath, and I ignored him.

"As if I *want* to go to Sin City with the world's biggest douchebag. And since when does she have other plans on her day off? What's she doing in a city where she knows no one?"

Leo looked over his shoulder and changed lanes. "You done?"

"No." I thought about it. God, I sounded like a bitch baby. "Yes."

Leo closed one eye and looked over at me. "How do you think Megan is doing, bro? Like *really* doing?"

"How the fuck would I know? You see her every day. You tell me." I crossed my arms. Jesus, I was having a proper fucking tantrum.

"I actually don't see her much but Fi does—and she's a little worried. Thinks we may have forced her into a situation she wasn't really ready for and wonders if it's too much."

I'd thought about the same thing, especially after she'd called me earlier in the week when she'd been freaked out. It was also why I'd tried so hard to pump the brakes on anything between us. But at a certain point, chemistry and attraction couldn't be denied.

"You know," Leo said with a confused look, "you really fucking suck at dating."

We were almost to Andy's hotel when I finally asked, "So what do I do?"

"If you have something to apologize for, do that. Then give it some space. Fiona says maybe we should let her stay at Nana's on the weekends. You cool with that?"

"Yeah. Sure."

"Look… It's normal that she got a little crush on you. You're almost as good looking as me, and you went in there like a hero and pulled that girl out of a dumpster fire. But I think I have to pull a Frankie on you."

That didn't sound very promising.

"You were right to send me to Turkey. Fiona and I needed that time to breathe." He was telling me I was right and wrong at the same time, tricky little shit.

"You know what Fiona told me? That if I would have taken her out of Covington myself that she wouldn't have been able to get to the point where she thought she deserved me. Megan's not going to walk away from you to become her own woman. She's going to cling to you because she's convinced you saved her."

"We both know I'm not a hero. She saved herself." *And her sister.* But I wasn't telling Leo that part. Not unless I had to.

Leo stopped the car in front of Andy's posh hotel. "She doesn't know that yet."

I grabbed the door handled and paused. "You little shit. You put Andy up to this, didn't you?"

Leo shrugged. The bitter taste of my own medicine slid down my throat and turned my stomach. I fucking hated it when my baby brother was right.

Chapter Twenty-Four

Megan

The doctor shook my hand and motioned for me to take a seat in the matching leather chair opposite her. Her office was simple, no family pictures or fancy artwork. The wall opposite me had three framed diplomas with gold seals and illegible signatures. Was that meant to be reassuring?

On the train ride into the city, I'd pondered how much I would tell this stranger. But her kind smile had put me at ease, and after speaking in broad strokes with Fiona, I knew I needed some tools to move on and create a better life. I'd been naïve to think a new location would wipe away the sadness in my soul.

Carla Godfrey folded her hands into her lap below her light cream cardigan and small wrinkles folded on the side of her hazel eyes. "So, Megan, what brings you to see me?"

Spin the wheel of emotions.

My throat tightened, I wasn't quite ready to let out all the feelings and truths I'd been stuffing down for so many years. They wanted out, but my body and mind were clinging to them.

"I guess you could say I'm trying to start my life over, and I'm not really sure I can." I rubbed my palms on my thighs.

"That sounds exciting. What do you think is holding you back?"

"Me. Well, the me I was trying to leave behind." *And looking over my shoulder for a stalker.*

"And why would you want to forget about her?" Carla had those kind of eyes that brought comfort and lacked judgment.

"Because she was boring and didn't put herself first."

"I doubt she was boring. You're a vibrant young woman. But why did she not put herself first?"

I bit my lip and reminded myself that this woman kept secrets for a living. She was just as safe as Father Peter. Besides, I was there, so I might as well make an effort.

"I barely remember my father. He left when I was about five. My mother did her best to raise us, which meant that she worked herself to the bone. She died in a car accident when I was in college and my sister Ruby was in high school. I started working extra jobs and Ruby…? Well, no one was really paying attention to her…until someone did."

The guilt of never being enough for my sister bubbled up as the image of her with a black eye came clear in my memory.

"He was, *is*, the sheriff's son, so untouchable in our small town. I begged Ruby to end it with him so many times, but she just kept going back. The vicious circle of life."

"That must have been horrible to witness. What happened to your sister?"

I stared over her shoulder as the movie played in my head. "I walked in on him choking her, and she was barely conscious. After that, I managed to convince her that if she stayed, her fate was sealed. I told her that he was taking away my most precious connection in the world."

A tear puddled in my eye, but I wiped it away before it could fall. I usually stopped my memory before I opened the door and saw my sister almost dead below Billy Johnston.

"But you're both out." There was more hope in Carla's voice than I allowed myself. The image of Frankie standing with Father Peter behind his desk flashed in my mind. He got me out.

"Yeah, we are. I got a charity to help with Ruby and managed to get out on my own recently."

"But…"

"He's gonna find us."

Carla studied me before saying, "That must be a hard way to walk around, all that fear."

It was unless I was with Frankie. Then I was safe. "Mind if I skip that one?"

"Megan, you have permission to say or not say whatever you want to in here. This time is about you. I ask questions because I wonder if you've ever thought about them, not because I'm looking for an answer."

I nodded. Saying my story out loud made it somehow more concrete, which was terrifying. There had been times when I'd convinced myself it had all been part of my imagination. But if I'd learned anything by trying to erase the memories, it was that I wasn't going to be able to heal until I confronted them.

I looked out of her window, the leaves of a tree blurring into a green mass. "The first time I found out he'd hit her, she begged me not to say anything. He'd been drunk and blamed the whiskey."

Carla nodded.

"Then she started hiding the bruises and cuts from me. I felt her slipping away. My baby sister… I'd have nothing." The tears I'd been holding back for too long puddled in the corner of my eyes and I tried to swallow but couldn't.

"Tell me about where you are now. Are you safe? Do you need help finding a job?"

I appreciated the change of subject and took a long inhale to gather my emotions. Yes. Talking about facts and realities was much easier. "I'm a live-in nanny in Long Island. Newborn twins and a six-year-old. It's a young couple, so the lines of employer and friends are kinda blurry." *To say the least.*

"Right, so that's work." Carla made a gesture with her hand as if putting the subject to the side. "Personal life needs to be something else. Do you have any friends? And I'm not asking because I don't think you're capable of having them. It's coming from a practical point."

"The brother of my boss and I hang out sometimes." *And kiss.* I wasn't going to mention that, because she'd tell me to stop.

"Do you have friends not related to your employer?"

I shook my head.

"So let's work on that. Let's work on getting a support system for Megan that's going to be there even if the job isn't and is also a place where you can complain about work without it getting back to them. It's important to have safe places that don't overlap."

Making friends? As if I had time for that.

Carla recrossed her legs and wiped the wrinkles out of her pants. "What are your interests?"

I shrugged.

"Okay. Well, if you'd like to come back, we can brainstorm and think about building your future—not around your sister or your employers."

That sounded pretty dang wonderful. "I like that idea."

"Thank you for trusting me with your story."

I scheduled an appointment for the Monday two weeks later then walked along the busy streets and to the cathedral I'd visited the week before. I went in and dabbed myself with holy water then genuflected and found a seat in the back. There wasn't much activity, an older woman praying at the lit candles and a few tourists snapping photos. The cool air was a nice relief from the hotter streets and the high ceilings and stained glass a prettier picture.

I thought of all the times I'd cried in the confessional to Father Peter, nothing ever changing, no matter the frequency or intensity of my prayers. The church had offered shelter to me but few solutions.

In the end, the only person who could help me was me. It hadn't been fair for me to look outside of myself. And as good as it felt to be safe in Frankie's arms, it wasn't right to put him in charge of my happiness. I stood and crossed myself. I didn't know if I would get back to church the way I had in Iowa. Time would have to tell. But I wouldn't forget the help it had offered me.

Outside on the busy street, I grabbed a hot dog from a vendor and sat on a bench in the park to eat it then headed to the address that Ruby had sent me. Inside the brick building, the woman at the reception welcomed me and pointed me down the hall to double doors.

The massive room reminded me of my high school gym, but there were picnic tables in the center and a library of books on one wall. I spotted Ruby, who sat facing the entrance. She waved frantically and popped up with a massive grin.

I had to stop myself from running over to her, the tears already flowing in both of our eyes. I hugged her tighter than I ever had. She still smelled like her favorite vanilla body wash, and I was happy to see she'd put on a little weight.

Ruby sniffed and wiped her eyes, taking a streak of mascara with it. I pulled her in for another embrace. "I missed you more than you know."

"Same." She gestured for me to sit opposite her. "You look good. How do you like the city?"

I grinned. "I love it. But I only get to come in on my days off." I reached for her hands and took them in mine. "It's so good to see you. There were days I thought this would never happen."

"Tell me about it. But one day at a time, right? That's what my counselor says. I told her I was ready for a job, but so far it's just here helping out."

I smiled softly at her. "No rush, right?"

She shrugged. "It's just that I'm so bored. I get that I need to put the work in and get stronger, but if I'm not here doing dishes or alphabetizing the books, I'm in my room staring at the walls."

"Well, I'm here now." I sat up a little straighter, as if my presence would somehow make a difference.

"You always dreamed of living in New York. Tell me about your job. What's Long Island like?"

The Riccis' luxury house and perfect life settled in my mind. "It's like everywhere else. The family is young and nice, though."

The program that Father Peter and I had found for Ruby was almost like rehab. It was designed to keep battered women safe, but from the look of the center, I could see that I was living a better life than Ruby. They required one-on-one therapy, group therapy and strict curfews. It was the only way I could have peace of mind without being with her. It had seemed ideal at the time, but I could see how it might come off as a bit of a prison. The good news was that once they thought she was ready for a job, she would start to phase-out all the restrictions. It was all paid for by the church, as long as their rules were followed.

We chatted for another hour, and I promised to come back the following Monday. She was going to ask permission to go off campus and we'd have lunch in a cool restaurant. I hugged her goodbye, equal parts happy to have seen her and nervous that she was miserable.

I walked to Grand Central, taking in the bustling energy of the city. It was true that I'd always dreamed of living in the city, not that I'd ever said so to my friends at home. It was a secret wish I'd only shared with Ruby.

To get home, I'd chosen rush hour by mistake and the crowd on the platform was thick. Men and women in business attire either chatted on their phones or listened to their headphones as the trains whooshed by before ours screeched to a halt. The sharp noises and the variety of people mixed together and sang to my soul. I was living my dream. My dopey smile carried me on-board behind a short man in medical scrubs. We were shoulder to shoulder like sardines, all the way until I turned around as the doors shut. Then, and only then, did I fall into the depths of hell. Two hauntingly familiar blue eyes stared at me from the platform. *Billy*.

The train left the station with a jolt, and I grabbed a pole to steady myself. A tightness in my chest made it impossible to breathe, and I bent over gasping for air.

"Watch it!" a female voice said over my shoulder.

My vision narrowed to the size of a pin and everything went black.

Chapter Twenty-Five

Frankie

The wheels of the plane touched down, and I'd never been happier to be home. Andy had boundless energy. Fucking boundless. And that peppy shit had been good at cards. Lucky he'd gone to Vegas instead of an underground game in the city, because nothing had been rigged against him.

We rolled our bags through the airport and at the VIP pickup, there wasn't just one company car, there were two. Jackson hopped out of the first one, nodded to me then took Andy's bag. I loaded my own suitcase into the back of the SUV with Leo behind the wheel then climbed in.

My brother, in his black work suit with his aviators slipped into the collar of his shirt, pursed his lips and did the little grumble thing we Riccis did when we weren't happy. I waited for his explanation. It would come as sure as the sun would rise.

We stopped in the long line of cars to exit the airport, and he frowned. "Megan fainted on the train. Some med school hero was right next to her and insisted she get checked out. She's at an ER in Queens."

That was bad. That was all *very* bad. It was scary that she'd fainted and worse that she was at a hospital. Police had easy access to those records in missing person cases. "Why would she faint?"

"How the fuck would I know? She told Fiona it was nothing, but whoever the wannabe doctor is got on the phone and said she hit her head, so he was ethically obligated...*blah blah blah*." Leo made a talking gesture with his hand then accelerated forward. "I'll drop you."

What? "I thought I was Megan-banned? What happened to your Turkey revenge plan?"

He pinned me with a scary stare. I knew it too well, because I had exactly the same one. "You wanna go change diapers?"

Did that really require an answer?

"Fi said it had to be you, 'cuz you know her better and are more sympathetic." He said the last word in a baby voice. "Which is hilarious on its face."

I let the small insult slide, mostly because it was true but also because I was exhausted. Babysitting in Vegas for three days straight had me showing my age. I checked my phone as Leo navigated through traffic.

I glanced over to Leo, who was tapping the wheel with his thumb. "Are you sure it should be me that goes?"

"According to my wife and our aunt—yes. But be my guest... Call them and make your case. I could use a good laugh."

It occurred to me that Leo had been a bit bitchy since the boys had been born. Or was it just since Megan had been forced into his life? He flipped off a minivan that swerved into our lane and swore under his breath. *Definitely bitchy.*

"What's eating you?"

He looked over at me for a beat, his dark eyes almost showing some kind of gratitude that I'd asked, then puffed out a breath. "Ever since I met Fiona, I've only wanted to keep her safe. Back in Covington I knew, *knew,* that Mac was up to no good. I failed her then and I've lived every day knowing I could fail her again at any fucking moment. Megan is a security risk. She comes with trunk-loads of baggage. And this little episode is a flashing red light that there's only more drama to come. She's nice and kind and all that shit, but I don't want her in my house. I don't want anyone in my house."

Well, that was a motherfucking predicament if I'd ever heard one.

"Does your wife know how you feel?"

"I'm not fucking stupid, Frankie." He cut me a look that could have been funny if it weren't so serious. And, holy hell, he *was* grumpy. This had obviously been eating at him more than he'd let on.

I scrubbed my face and ended with rubbing my temples. I had the start of a headache pulsing behind my eyes.

Leo continued, and once he'd started unloading, it was plain to see it had been building for a while. "What happens if the fucker finds her and she's alone with Violet or the fucking boys? You think that twisted idiot gives a shit about my family? My instincts are screaming for her to get out of my house. I have to listen to them."

It wasn't wrong, what he was saying. In fact, it had been me who'd said he shouldn't hire her to begin with. *My* instincts didn't like her around my niece and nephews with her potential stalker somewhere out there in the world either. I knew I should have killed him. "So what? You're going to fire her?"

"You know I can't do that."

"You're fucked." There was no pleasure or teasing in my voice. The battle of keeping his wife happy and safe at the same time would be impossible for him to win.

"Unless you convince her to quit." Leo winced. He knew what he was asking. He also knew I would put him first, no matter what. Problem was, I was pretty sure I had that same kind of sense of protection for Megan. Welcome to my own fucking predicament.

"Oh, you're a little fucker." The words were a mix of a whisper and a long sigh. The pressure in my forehead only tightened as we got closer to the hospital where Leo dropped me off with a small, sympathetic smile. Before I went in, I called Chezzie.

"Hey. Did you get her yet?" Just the sound of her voice, even if the concern wasn't for me, helped ease a bit of my tension and fatigue.

"No. I just got here. Can you go outside for a sec?"

"I answered outside. What am I? New?" Her sass made me smile. I thanked every star in the sky for Chezzie. Without her, my days would have been a hell of a lot darker.

"I'm not asking this to be a menacing little prick, but can you postpone your trip to Florida? Leo wants me to get Megan to quit, and it will fly better with Fiona if you're around. I'm sorry, Chezz, but I'm doing all the dirty work here and could use an ally."

Chezzie hummed. "I wondered why he was so testy, but I get it. Her quitting is the only way to get Fiona on board. Upgrade me to first class and a suite and you have a deal."

I didn't even bother with a fight. It was a small price to pay. "Sure."

"And be nice to Michael when you meet him. None of that grumbly Ricci bullshit."

I wondered if she was shaking a finger on the other end of the phone. She liked to do that when making a point. Leo and I had mocked the way she'd done it for years.

"Same goes for Leonardo. Best behavior."

"Yeah, yeah. I'll call you tomorrow." I appreciated that she didn't tell me to be gentle or wish me luck. I tucked the phone into my suit jacket and plastered a smile across my face.

"Hi," I said to the older woman at the information desk. She fluttered her eyes from her computer screen to me and a light pink blushed her cheeks.

"My little sister was brought in from the train. She fainted. Megan Walsh?"

The woman typed on her keyboard, and the tapping of her long nails was some of the quickest I'd ever seen. She reached for the phone next to her then crooked it between her chin and shoulder. The nametag on her chest read, Ophelia White, RN. Odd that she was at reception, but maybe with the late hour, the reception staff had probably all gone home.

"Hi. Megan Walsh's brother is here." Ophelia raised a finger to me as if a reminder to wait. "Oh. Okay. Got it. Thanks."

She hung up the phone and pointed to the seating area behind me. "You can have a seat over there. They'll bring her out."

"Thanks."

A few minutes later, a young man escorted her through the double doors, and a wave of relief in seeing me passed over her face. From the red eyes and blotched skin, she'd been crying, most likely telling her story or part of it to a trusted medical professional. She nodded to the man in scrubs, who patted her on the shoulder then flashed his badge to open the doors before disappearing behind them.

With her head hung low, Megan shuffled over to me, and I stood. "I thought Leo was coming."

"Sorry to disappoint you." I tilted my head to try to meet her eyes. Yeah, she'd definitely been crying—and I had to get her to quit her job. *Fucking great timing, Leo.* "What happened?"

"I just got dizzy with all the people. Silly, really." She was downplaying and possibly lying. But why?

I pulled out my phone and texted for a car. "Ten minutes."

"You didn't drive?" She narrowed her gaze then looked away. *Why is she nervous?*

"Just landed."

"Right." Megan walked out of the hospital to the curb and sat on a bench. The large metal ashtray at the end was overflowing with butts. It always shocked me how many people smoked at hospitals. Then again, if a loved one was having a triple bypass, maybe a cigarette was the only thing to calm some nerves. I would have hit something, but that was me. I'd been raised on violence.

I kept a little distance from Megan and sent texts off that I was going to take her back to my place. If we went to Leo's, she'd go into work mode, and I wasn't sure we'd ever get to the bottom of what actually had happened to her. Plus, Leo didn't want her there.

The town car pulled up and we got in, a cold, awkward silence between us. After five minutes, Megan turned to me. "Aren't we going the wrong way? This is the way back to the city. No?"

"I had a long flight and day. I'll drive you out tomorrow. My place is closer. You can take the guest room if you want some space."

For the rest of the ride, she stared out of the window and we were in front of my building within a half an hour. My stomach growled, and I became painfully aware that I hadn't eaten dinner. With the weekend away, there was nothing in my fridge and I didn't have the patience to cook.

"You hungry?" I asked as we rode up the elevator.

"Nah. My head's still spinning. I don't think I could keep anything down." The version of Megan in front of me was worrisome at best. She'd retreated into a shell, and I wasn't sure why. The spunk she normally had was gone.

In my apartment, I dimmed the lights and the city glimmered below. I tossed my keys into the little bowl where I kept them and plugged in my phone. Riffling through the fridge confirmed my earlier suspicion of zero food, so I ordered take-out from the quickest Chinese in my neighborhood.

Megan took off her sandals then walked over to the couch where she sat and hugged her knees into her chest. I hung my jacket on the back of a barstool before sitting on the coffee table directly in front of her.

"So. No bullshit, no skating around or brushing it off. What the fuck happened?" I didn't like using that tone with her, but she hadn't given me a ton of choice. Plus, I may have been a little salty for a variety of reasons.

She twisted her lips and her nostrils flared. "I think I saw Billy."

Whoa. Okay, that's huge.

"Where?"

"At Grand Central. I had a panic attack and couldn't breathe. I guess I fainted and hit my head in the same spot as last time. I'm sorry. I wasn't thinking straight, and the guy who helped me was super insistent. I know it was stupid going to the hospital." She blinked several times, the tears pooling.

I dropped my head into my hands. At least she knew the hospital had been a mistake. Maybe that was why she was quiet. She was being hard on herself. But how had I become the person that had to clean up all the shit around me? My life had been simple, stark, unattached.

I didn't want to doubt her story, but Grand Central saw millions of people a day, so she could have been mistaken. Then again, Leo's instincts had been poking at him, and I'd never known them to be wrong.

She stared out of the window with a disgusted look on her face. Her anger was refreshing. Playing the victim was an ugly shade of gray. There was more to her story. I was sure of it.

I stood and opened a bottle of wine. I poured her a glass, though I wasn't sure she'd drink it. As the liquid coated my throat, it dulled my nerves at the same time. I walked the two glasses over to the couch and set one in front of her before taking a seat, leaving some room between us.

"Shall we start at the beginning of your day?"

Her reluctance to share reminded me of when we'd first met, when she didn't know me, and I had to admit it stung a little.

Megan turned to me, and her emerald eyes bore into my soul. "Why did you bring me here and not home?"

I didn't know if she thought I had ulterior motives or if she'd deducted there was something more. But I did think she deserved the truth, however deep it might cut. "Leo feels it's safer."

She nodded slowly. "So I'm fired?"

No point in beating around the bush. "He'd like you to quit. Think of it as saving their marriage."

She let out a small sigh and shook her head in disappointment. I wasn't one to apologize for shit that was beyond my control, so we sat in silence as the truth settled between us.

The buzzer from my door startled her, and she put her hand to her chest. "Jesus."

I'd never, ever heard her swear before, and its meaning wasn't lost on me. I stood then answered the door, paying for the take-out then plating it and setting it on the island.

"Come and eat a little something."

Megan joined me but just moved the rice and chicken around on her plate, taking maybe one small bite the entire time. Eventually, she pushed the dish away and it bumped the wine glass, which was still untouched.

"Do you think I could have a bath? Do you even have a tub?"

I did have a tub—a really nice fucking tub, to be honest. And while I was still hoping to get to the bottom of her story, I could sense she needed a break from it all, and a little time for me to think wouldn't be horrible either.

"Come on." I stood from the island and led her to my bedroom. The en suite bathroom was pretty spectacular, if I did say so myself. There was a massive oval sunken tub opposite a walk-in shower and, on the connecting wall, a double sink. The toilet was its own smaller room at the end of the tub. I'd seen a similar design in France when I'd been there on business and couldn't help myself but to recreate it. The lavish design was showy, but I was a fan of the finer things in life.

"This is your bathroom?" Megan rolled her eyes, and it was the first real sight of her in the entire evening. "Makes perfect sense."

I went over to the sunken tub and started the water. "Hot or scalding?"

"Just hot. Thanks."

I pointed out the towels, soaps and left her one of my T-shirts and a pair of boxers before going back to the kitchen and cleaning up. It was a shame to dump her wine down the drain, so I took it to the couch and tried to devise a plan where everybody won, including me.

My clothes stank of the recycled air from the plane, and I needed a shower before slipping into my cool, clean sheets. With Megan in my bathroom, I went to the smaller second one and scrubbed away my day.

We met in the hall, her hair wrapped in a towel and me in a pair of joggers, my chest bare. One of those stupid shuffles of one person going the same way as the other happened and the oddity of having an overnight guest in my home struck me. Leo had slept in the spare bed maybe once or twice, and the room was more for show than necessity. But I was grateful for it, because that would give a sweet little country girl some privacy.

"We'll work things out in the morning." I offered her a warm smile, knowing it was far from enough. We went our separate ways and I turned off all the lights except the small one above the stove, in case she needed something in the middle of the night.

I lay awake, too tired to sleep and my mind spinning. It didn't surprise me when her silhouette appeared in my doorway. Maybe that was what I'd been waiting for.

"Frankie?" she whispered as she fiddled with her fingers. Her hair was out of the towel and she rubbed one foot over the other.

"Come on." I lifted the duvet.

Megan padded over and slipped in next to me. She laid her head on my chest and played with the drawstring of my pants. "Part of me wants to tell you everything, but I'm having a hard time finding the courage. I know I can trust you, but I'm not sure I'm ready."

She wrapped a leg over mine and holy shit, she wasn't wearing underwear or the boxers I'd left her. That, with the gentle tug of my drawstring was enticing a beast that had no business in my bed with her. My dick was already at half-mast when I said, "You can't tease me like that. It's not fair."

But she didn't stop. "This morning I saw a therapist. I was so sure she'd helped me. I talked to her, you know—like more than I've let out in a long time. I thought I'd had a great day and now I have no job, no home…"

I rubbed between her shoulder blades with my thumb then gave a reassuring peck on her head. Her wet hair was cool on my lips.

I hadn't realized that she'd actually untied my joggers until she pressed a long, warm kiss into the center of my chest.

Megan ran her fingers back and forth just under the waist of my pants. "I just want to forget about everything, just for a little bit."

How could I say yes? Worse, how could I say no?

"Megan, you've had an exhausting day. This is not the answer." My words were so see-through it was pathetic.

She gazed up at me, her pretty eyes sad. "Please."

I dropped my head back, arching my spine. That only made my erection more evident and it brushed against her arm. *Shit.* After physical contact, my dick had hope.

"Frankie." She climbed on top of me and hovered over my lips. "This is the only way I can think of feeling better right now. Don't say no." She interlaced our fingers and drew my arms toward her.

"This will complicate everything." Was I even resisting? She guided my hands to her waist then around to her ass. *Lord help me.*

Megan leaned down, her breasts skimming my torso. She brought her mouth so close that when she whispered, her lips brushed against mine. "How could anything possibly be more complicated than it already is?"

Checkmate.

Chapter Twenty-Six

Megan

In one swift and graceful swoop, Frankie flipped me to my back. Even in the darkness of his room, a guilt haunted his eyes.

"I don't know how to be gentle — not with this." His words were more of a warning than apology.

"That's not what I'm asking for." *Not in the least.* I wanted raw, pure emotion. I wanted to feel alive and forget about anything but the moment. Most of all, I wanted him. But he needed a final nudge before letting loose.

"Can we just stop trying to be that better side of ourselves for a night? Let out a little of the darkness?" If he denied me, I would explode or something far worse, I was sure.

He gave a long shake of his head and swore. But his gaze shifted from doubt to confidence in a flash, and the promise of him devouring me became more than real. He didn't wait to kiss me deep—his tender side replaced by a forceful lust and answering my every aching need. I wrapped my legs around him and crossed them at the ankles.

His normally soft beard was rough against my skin and the fire inside him lit my own. We would burn in our desperation together. I'd known exactly what I was doing playing with the drawstring of his pants. I'd planned it out in the tub when I'd decided to stop feeling sorry for myself, stop being the weak victim and go back to bold. When I'd seen him in the hallway with the lights still on, I didn't quite have the courage to act. But once the darkness had seeped into the night, his lure had been too strong. And without light, we were safe to be our true selves.

I dug my fingers into the strong muscles of his back. I needed him closer. He rubbed his erection between my legs then whipped off the T-shirt he'd given me as a nightgown. There I was, fully exposed and never more at ease.

Frankie slid his hand down my chest and circled a nipple with his thumb. He took his time, and I wondered how long he'd been wanting to touch me like that. I arched my back and goosebumps spread over my skin—half from the excitement and the other from the cool air in the room. His little loops were deliberate, pensive, as if he were savoring the moment. He was transfixed with his own actions and not rushing them in the least. Finally, he dipped down and twirled the nipple with his tongue then tugged ever-so-slowly with his teeth. The pleasure mixed with a gentle pain and my want for him grew. While staring deep into my eyes, he copied the tease on the other side. As he spread his palm and guided it from my ribs to my belly to even lower, I ached for him.

He trailed kisses and small nibbles over my torso until his gentle shove opened my legs wider. It was the perfect amount of force — decisive and dominant.

"Jesus Christ, Megan." His hot breath between my legs made me clench with anticipation. When he dipped his tongue into my folds and licked me deep inside, I shuddered, and my breath caught. Up he went, wonderfully slow in the most erotic gesture I'd ever experienced. I propped myself on my elbows and lifted my hips. More. I needed more. I needed deeper, faster, everything.

I closed my eyes and dropped my head back, focusing purely on that man's mouth and the magic it was working.

"Nuh-uh," he said as he trailed his tongue back and forth, his beard scratching my inner thigh. "Watch me."

I did as he said as fire flushed through my body. We were beyond embarrassment, so it must have been fueled by unbridled lust. Frankie knew how to use it all, pressing his chin into my lips, the beard creating a beautiful friction and the patience in his pace winding me up slow and steady.

My bottom lip quivered, and my lack of confidence screamed at me to look away, but I was mesmerized.

Frankie started a gentle sucking of my clit, and I was done. I couldn't help but clamp my eyes shut. It was the only relief to the spinning in my brain. My breath was shallow, just tiny gasps through my mouth that barely reached my lungs. If his hands hadn't been holding me down, I would have sworn I was floating above the bed.

The suction intensified and a wave pulsed at my core, waiting, wanting its release. It only took the penetration of his fingers and their sleepy tease to put me over the edge. I pinched my nipples and bucked against him. My long, primal moan echoed through the room. He gave me a second to recover then blew cool air on my clit, which sent residual shocks all over my body.

For a brief second, I worried we were done. But Frankie pushed my ass so I was lying on my side and replaced his tongue with his fingers. He pressed my knee into my chest and furiously rubbed my clit up and down for him but back and forth for me. I clamped my eyes shut, barely realizing that a second orgasm was threatening to crash through me. My mouth was parched, and I struggled to swallow into my dry throat. I said something nonsensical that even I couldn't translate.

He slowed everything but kept working his fingers. "You good?"

He had to be kidding. I didn't even know what planet I was on.

I managed an "Uh-huh."

The new pace was somehow better and worse than the faster one. I was exactly where I'd wanted to be — lost with the perfect guide — and I allowed myself to drift away on our stormy cloud.

"Do you want more?" His words were a challenge, a dare he couldn't understand how badly I needed to take.

While Frankie may have hinted at a troubled past, the truth had been in front of me all along. Those dark, soulless eyes told his story. A good man would have left me alone. An honest one would have never brought me back to his place. And a saint would have thought having sex with me would be wrong. But Francis Ricci was no saint. He was a sinner.

I looked over my shoulder, I hadn't even realized he'd taken out his erection and was stroking it at the same pace he teased my clit. "I want it all." There was a truth in my words I hadn't quite expected. It whipped in the air and caused us both to pause before Frankie worked his jaw in contemplation, all the while holding my gaze, all the while getting us both off. Finally, he reached over me to the side table and dug out a condom. I liked that he didn't ask me twice, didn't second-guess me.

"I can do that." I flipped my palm and waited.

He quirked a half-smile before handing me the small, square package. With a deceitfully innocent smile, I opened the condom and put on the tip but instead of rolling it down with my fingers, I rose to my knees and placed my mouth around the head of his cock. I glanced up and Frankie's lips were parted just enough to confirm he hadn't been expecting my action. He quickly shut his mouth and narrowed his eyes, their authority back in place.

I squeezed my lips tight around his thick shaft and rolled the condom as far as I could then finished with my hand.

My heart pounded. I'd upped the stakes by showing him a glimpse of my naughty side. The sweet, church-going girl from the Midwest had done a lot more than he probably thought.

I laid back and Frankie moved on top of me. Being under him tingled my every nerve to attention. He trailed his hand up my leg, watching the movement all the way around my breasts until he cupped the back of my neck and drew me in for what I thought was a kiss.

"Just say no or stop." *Instructions or a warning?* I didn't know.

He moved his hand back to my body then stopped at a breast. This time it was a little less gentle. He pinched and I whimpered.

Between my legs, his tip pressed for entry but before he pushed in, he rubbed it hard on my clit, the barrier of the condom a new, cooler sensation. Slow, so torturously slow, he entered—my walls expanding to take him all in. I exhaled through my mouth, creating a small breeze in his dark hair.

Frankie licked and sucked my neck until his mouth was on mine and we were back to kissing as deeply as we'd started. His thrusts were slow and controlled, and with my eyes closed, I was lost again in the physical. I pushed away all the thoughts of this being too soon, wrong, that I was too fragile. I'd wanted him since the moment I'd seen him.

Something inside me needed to prove to him that I could take more, that I was stronger than the woman I'd been when he'd picked me up at the hospital. That woman was no one's choice. I wanted to be a fantasy, an unquenchable thirst that drove him mad.

I pressed my hands into his chest, and he paused.

"Let me flip." I turned under him until I was on all fours and looked over my shoulder. Frankie's hand was already caressing my bare ass and I smiled, remembering he had a little thing for my butt. He seemed to be pondering what he was really going to do with me. My naughty grin gave him the all-clear. This wasn't about my broken parts. It was about honoring what I had left, proving that I was more like him than he'd ever thought.

There was a small grumble to his exhale, as if he were contracting his throat and solidifying an intention. He slipped a hand between my legs and worked my clit with strong pressure in circles before pinching it tight between two fingers, all the while still rubbing my ass with the opposite hand.

A rush of need shot through me, and I almost swore. Frankie pushed in and the energy was instantly different. He dug his fingers into the creases in my hips and rocked me fast and hard. I didn't care that I was practically yelping. I was free, and so was he. He was unrelenting, pounding into me in a furious rhythm.

I fisted his sheets and fought back screams. I told myself five more pumps and I would tell him to stop. I would be raw, and I would regret it. But five came and went and I started to lose count, the need for him to consume my entire body, mind and soul blocking out any pain. I understood that he was working out as many demons as I was, and after all he'd done for me, this was the only thing I could give him back — not out of obligation, but out of unadulterated need and longing.

Frankie's breath became labored, and instead of speeding up, he edged out bit by bit until only the tip touched my lips. It burned, but I was beyond that. With a meticulous control, he pushed back in as if lavishing each inch. He repeated the act a few more times before crying out his release. My body collapsed below his, the sweat of his chest mixing with the beads on my back.

He panted in my ear and moisture finally came back to my mouth, allowing me to speak.

"Don't you dare *ever* say we shouldn't have done that."

He let out a small laugh. "Nah," he said, kissing around my back and still inside me. "I was going to say we should have done it sooner."

Chapter Twenty-Seven

Frankie

It had been ages since I'd slept naked with a woman. I'd forgotten how the smell of sex lingered and enticed for more. Megan's skin was like soft silk on top of me, clinging in the night sweat like a gentle glue.

She snoozed with her head on my chest, faint snores indicating that she was deep asleep. I grinned. So there was a bit of mischief in her. I'd been so blind trying to fight the depths of our attraction that I'd hadn't stopped to realize how perfect our chemistry might be. Her coy little look while putting on the condom had revealed a whole new world of possibilities.

Looking back, it made perfect sense that she wouldn't want a gentle Mr. Nice Guy. And I was a million doomed miles away from that. But beyond the physical, what did *I* want?

The alarm on my phone vibrated. On a normal day I would have been first at the gym. I shimmied out of bed and Megan flipped to the other side and replaced me with a pillow. Her round ass was on full display, and I tried to put it out of my mind while I blasted my skin with cold water in the shower.

I threw on some track pants and went into the kitchen for some coffee—real coffee, none of that capsule crap. It percolated out of the Italian kettle, filling the apartment with the aroma of its dark roast. I poured a cup and went to the leather chair I had by the window and watched the sun rise.

An orange and pink glow covered the sky as I pondered what to do. I couldn't just send Megan on her way. I was too attached and worried for her safety. Leo didn't want her in his house, which was bitchy but understandable. And by Megan quitting, Fiona might suspect Leo was behind it, but she would eventually agree with him. She'd even said her therapist had hinted that Megan needed more time. My little brother understood about picking battles, and his instincts had proven right so many times in the past that Fiona could only concede.

They'd risen from shit and were happy—really, truly in love. It almost made me believe it could happen to me, too. But I was different. I was on or off, hot or cold. I saw what I wanted in life and grabbed it. So it didn't matter if I had a next move or planned shit out and tried to date Megan like a normal person. It would never work. There was only one way.

The sun was fully out and reflecting on the river by the time I heard her shuffling toward me. "Well, that's a dichotomy. You basking in the light." Megan plucked the coffee cup from my hands and set it on the floor then crawled into my lap. She had on an oversized V-neck, and even though it was big on her, it wasn't doing a very good job of covering her bits. "You eat?"

"Not yet. Listen… I'm just going to say this, and you can debate or negotiate or try to change my mind, but you won't. And I know it's fucked up. I know —"

Megan's face fell and her eyes darted back and forth. "You want me to leave?"

"No." The complete and total opposite. I'd sat there for hours thinking about what would make me happy. It all came down to her. "I want you to stay. And I don't want to do all the shit we should be doing. I don't want you to get your own place or just meet on the weekends and go to the fucking movies pretending like last night didn't happen, play along with a made-up timeline before some unknown relationship god has given us the blessing to live together. Get a job, don't get a job, I honestly could care less, but when I walk through my door each night, I want to see you. That's what I want."

A small smile pulled toward her lovely eyes. "It's rushed."

"Yep. Total cart before the horse." I nodded, but I was still sure what I wanted.

She shifted a little in my lap. "People would say I should take this time for myself. Start fresh."

"They will. They're probably right, too." *Definitely right.*

"I have a stalker."

I shrugged. "I can kill a man with my bare hands." That shouldn't have sounded like a brag. It was meant to be a bad thing.

Megan swallowed. Her chest rose and fell slowly, like she was forcing herself to breathe. In a quiet voice she asked, "Do you know that for a fact?"

"Yes." It was all she'd ever get from me. I couldn't risk anything more. But if she was going agree to all that shit I'd laid out, she deserved to know something. She deserved to know what she was getting.

"Okay." Her tone was even. There was no way to read it.

"Okay, what?"

Megan ran her fingers through the short hair around my neck and put her chin on my upper arm. "Okay. Let's do everything wrong. Playing safe only ever made me miserable."

"There's one condition."

She pulled back then shifted so her wrists were on my shoulders, and she straddled my lap, an overall effective negotiating position. "I thought that was too easy."

"You have to let me take care of you. You have to understand that it makes me happy to do it."

She looked away. "I don't want your money."

"I know." And that was exactly why I wanted to spoil her. "But it's not just that I'm talking about. You need to tell me what's going on in here." I tapped her head.

"You sure about that?"

"If you're afraid I'm going to judge you, I encourage you to revisit my track record."

Megan chewed her lip then shook her head. Her dark locks brushed over her shoulders, a stark contrast from the white cotton. She climbed out of my lap and went over to the window. "Are you sure about this? Me?"

I rose and placed a long kiss on her forehead. "I'm sure I don't deserve you."

She wrapped her arms around my torso. I could have dragged her back to bed. Hell, I could have hoisted her over my shoulder and thrown her down on the mattress and had my way with her. But she needed to see that she was more than that to me.

It was a lot to ask. Maybe she needed more than a minute to make a life-changing decision. I shifted my tone. "Let's get dressed and grab some breakfast. I have the day off and I want to spend it with you."

That smile—that shy, sweet smile—was doing things to my heart. Tugging at it, then seeping under my skin and giving me a kind of feels I had not previously thought possible. *What the hell is happening to me?* I'd gone from single to hopeful boyfriend in less than twenty-four hours.

"Come on." I tapped her ass and followed her to by bedroom where I headed to get dressed.

"Do you have a hair dryer?" Megan walked into my closet carrying her white cotton underwear. "I need to dry these."

"Under the sink." I buttoned my baby-blue shirt and scanned my closet. I was a clothes whore. She was re-washing her underwear in my sink and had come to New York with practically nothing. God, I hoped she would let me spoil her.

If I didn't want this relationship to end in a dumpster fire like my previous ones, I would also need to control my need to control. Most of the gifts I'd bought for women over the years had been apologies more than anything else. I'd never been with anyone where I wasn't making up for something I'd done or said. And while I was pretty sure I wanted to buy Megan a closet full of clothes and whatever else she wanted, I didn't want her to think that she wasn't good enough exactly as she was.

We met at the door, and I held it open, an easy smile on both of our faces. We weren't alone in the elevator, and I reached for her hand. It was such a small, simple gesture. And yet it meant more, as if it solidified in public what we'd decided in private.

In the lobby I led Megan over to the front desk where the head doorman was seated as he logged in a package for one of my neighbors. Jimmy nodded a quick hello.

"Hey, Jimmy, this is Megan."

Megan waved and I wondered if she wasn't disappointed that I hadn't given her a label. I wasn't very good with pleasantries. God, I was going to have to get better at a lot of social skills I didn't have.

We walked to a small café and sat at a table outside. My phone vibrated in my pocket and Leo's name flashed on screen.

"I need to take this." I walked toward the curb then winked at Megan. "Hey."

Rusty barked in the background. Leo was probably outside and away from curious ears. My father's voice screamed in my head. *If you have to talk on the telephone, for fuck's sake keep your voice down.* It was just one of those things all Riccis did, ensure privacy. No wonder Leo didn't want a stranger in his house. Fuck, I was about to have one full-time in mine. But was she really a stranger?

"How'd it go? Fiona is insisting on talking to her. Is she going to quit? Chezzie said she's staying for the week."

"Yeah. You're good. I'm gonna keep her with me for a bit. She thinks she saw that prick so…"

"What do you mean, you're gonna keep her with you?" Leo's words carried a rightful accusation. It was my bullshit way of dancing around the truth.

"Tell Fiona that I'll drive Megan out tomorrow to talk and get her things."

Leo laughed. "Francis Angelo Ricci, did you grow a heart? Did you catch some...*feels*?" His sing-songy tone could go fuck itself.

"Can you put Chezzie on? I need to ask her something."

Leo hollered away from the phone and there was a small ruckus on the other end.

"What the fuck is going on, Frankie?" Fiona's voice was unamused, but the lack of anger was encouraging.

"Hey. How are you feeling? How are those boys? How's my niece?"

"Tired, fuckers and amazing, as always. Your turn to answer questions. What happened to Megan?"

I glanced over to her at the table, the easy smile still on her face as she sipped her ice water. She studied the laminated menu, blissfully unaware that I was talking about her behind her back.

I turned back to the street and rubbed my neck. I didn't want to lie to Fiona. The truth would come out sooner or later anyway. But I could bend the details just a little. "She went to a shrink in the morning then thought she saw the stalker dude on the train and had a panic attack. She's going to be fine, but it's probably best if she takes a little time to sort through things. Not sure working with precious lives is the best call right now. I'm going to talk to her today. See where her head's at."

"Fuck."

"What?"

"This is my fault. I told her to go to therapy. I forgot how hard it is in the beginning."

I couldn't even imagine what a therapist would do with someone like me. Thank God my skeletons were buried at the bottom of rivers or fed to Hungarian pigs.

"It's no one's fault, Fiona."

"Still...I feel responsible. I'm the one who insisted she come here. Maybe she could just live in the guestroom for a bit, and I can find someone else to help."

Yeah, sure. Her husband was going to love that idea.

"Fi, you have Violet and the boys to take care of. Plus, my brother can't be easy. Let me handle Megan. I feel just as responsible, since I'm the one who convinced her to leave." That wasn't *exactly* the case, but it would help Fiona to believe that Megan could be somewhere else.

In truth, I admired my sister-in-law. Walking into the Riccis was not an easy task. But she'd fit right in and she was constantly helping people. She didn't make a huge deal out of it, but I'd seen her hand over her doggy bags to more down-and-out people on the street than I'd ever thought of doing. And the way she'd always fought for Violet? She was fierce but compassionate.

"Yeah...but...you *like* her, right? It's not just guilt. 'Cuz if she's fragile and you're...well, you—no offense—but I'd rather she be here."

No offense taken. It was me who had kept Fiona and Leo apart once she was out of Covington. It had also been me who had followed her to make sure she was okay. That part I'd never told her or Leo. Sometimes being the bad guy was so much easier.

Megan was speaking to the waitress and motioned over to me. I nodded to her. She'd been waiting long enough.

"Yeah, I like her. Don't go gossiping to Chez about it like two happy hens."

"He said he likes her," Fiona said off the speaker then to me, "Here's Chezzie."

"Don't," I warned before she could tease me. "Just tell me where I should take her clothes shopping that won't intimidate the shit out of her."

"Lower Fifth is good. Lots of shops and you could walk west to the open market. Oh, I had a text from Sal, my fish guy, and he has some beautiful skate. Should I ask him to put some aside for you?" Her voice was chipper but didn't mask her intentions. She knew I loved skate and she was pushing me to cook for Megan.

"I know what you're doing." I shook my head and walked back to the table.

"And?" From her tone, I could tell she was smiling.

"Text him back."

"You're welcome."

"Mm-hmm." I swiped to end the call then sat opposite Megan. "Sorry about that. What did you decide on?"

As we crept closer to fall, the summer heat was becoming tolerable, and the streets smelled less like sour garbage and urine. In fact, it was a gorgeous day. After breakfast, the first thing on my Megan shopping list was shoes. She loved to walk around the city and her sandals looked like they were at the end of a pilgrimage.

She put up a little fight, but after the slip-on sneakers were on her feet, I couldn't help but notice an added pep in her step. I wondered of all the shoes she'd sold in her old job, how many times she'd wished she could take some home.

Chezzie had been right about the shops. They were middle-of-the-road enough that Megan wasn't intimidated but unique enough that she wouldn't come away with bland items without personality. On the lower level of one there was a small lingerie section, and I found the perfect match to Megan's personality.

The set was a dusted pink lace, classic and sexy without being raunchy. She blushed a little when I showed it to her but swiped it out of my hands to try it on.

"I'll meet you upstairs," I said when she got in line for the dressing rooms.

"You don't want me to show you?"

"Nope." I kissed her cheek. "I want you to choose what you like, and I'll pay for it. Remember that this makes me happy, so no feeling guilty."

"I know. It just doesn't feel right." She frowned.

"Perfect. We're doing everything wrong, remember?"

When she joined at the cashier, I was happy to see that she hadn't been shy. There were four dresses and two more sets of the underwear. After she laid it on the counter, she threaded her arms around my waist for a hug.

"Thank you. I've never been this spoiled. I don't know if I can get used to it." Those stunning eyes beamed at me with honesty and gratitude.

"You're going to have to. It's just the beginning."

The young clerk rang us up, and I paid with my private card. As she was putting everything in the bag, Megan stopped her.

"Um… Your colleague downstairs said I could take the receipt and change into one of these once we'd paid. Is that okay?"

"Yeah, sure."

Megan chose a periwinkle baby doll dress and skipped away. I carried the bag outside where I couldn't help but look around with scrutiny. What if Megan *had* seen Billy? What if he'd located her? He was a police officer, after all. He would have more resources than the average bear. And that was *before* the hospital.

.

Chapter Twenty-Eight

Megan

It wasn't the golden wine in the long-stemmed glass, because I'd only had half a glass. It wasn't the new clothes or the amazing day in the city that I was rapidly falling in love with. It was him. Frankie. He was making me happy.

And happy was something I'd pretty much given up on, like a bad habit at Lent. I'd craved it but found a way to live without it. I'd put Ruby first since our mother had died, and I'd charged down the path of survival without much thought for myself. It wasn't as if I'd had much of a choice.

But being pampered? Although it had been a bit awkward at first, I'd given in, because a man like Frankie—and oh boy, was he all man—deserved a woman with a certain amount of style and sophistication on his arm. Not that I had either, but I was gonna try. I would still need to figure out what to do about money and Ruby, but sitting there listening to Frankie tell a story about a man who had wanted to date Chezzie made me smile. And I thought I deserved a little break from worry, stress and being the big sister, especially after the train wreck of the day before.

We ate at his formal dining table off the kitchen, facing each other, Frankie's ease at all things both impressing and comforting me. He'd made quite the confession that morning, but I didn't want or need to know more. The devil was in the details. I was going to choose to believe that it was in self-defense not cold blood. After all, he was in private security. Maybe he'd been defending a client.

At the end of the meal, I finished my glass and said, "I'm doing the dishes. No way you cook like that and have to clean up."

"I hate doing the dishes, so fine by me. I should probably check in with the boys. You mind?"

I shook my head, smiled and cleared the plates. Frankie's life was pristine, and I didn't want to upset that. I rinsed everything to the point of it already being clean before carefully loading the dishwasher. Then I wiped the counters, cupping my opposite hand to catch any crumbs so they didn't hit the floor.

He was off in a corner of the open space speaking quietly on the phone. Funny, I'd noticed Leo doing the same thing. Eavesdropping wasn't going to happen to the Riccis, that was for sure. It didn't matter though, because I wasn't interested.

I went to the bedroom and walked into the massive closet. Frankie had cleared a spot for me when we'd returned, and I still couldn't quite believe that I had agreed to live with him. The decision went against all norms and logic and yet made perfect sense to my soul.

Previously, I'd been attracted to how safe he made me feel, but adding happiness and sexually free to the list had me convinced. I just didn't want to do anything to mess it up.

The lacy fabric of the new bra and skimpy panties was soft under my fingertips. It wasn't the particular one Frankie had chosen but the style was the same — almost like classic lingerie from the 1920s but with a modern touch. Without much thought, I slipped out of my dress and old, embarrassingly boring white cotton underwear and into the lingerie.

On my way out of the room, I stopped at the bedside table and nabbed a condom, which I stuck down the cup of my bra.

The sun was setting, and a dark orange filled the sky. Frankie took one look at me and said into his phone, "I'll see you in the morning," then ended the call and tossed the device behind him where it landed on a leather chair with a light *thud.*

"You like?"

"That is an understatement. I almost don't want to take it off."

"Let's not then." My playful tone piqued his curiosity, and he tilted his head to the side.

I walked over to him then led him to the sofa. With a quirked smile, I pushed him back and he sat obediently.

Frankie narrowed his eyes with a devilish grin and motioned for me to come over. Him wanting me was a shot of confidence. I couldn't help but think he was building me into a stronger woman. With as much grace as I could managed, I lowered into his lap. His scent sent a ripple of lust through my skin, and I gently kissed from his neck to his ear.

"Thank you for today." I started unbuttoning his shirt then pushed it open, making sure to let my hands run over his muscled stomach. *God bless his ripples.*

"You're welcome."

All the complications fell to the wayside. When we boiled it down, we both knew we were a fit. And in the private walls of his loft, that was all that mattered.

A raw heat pulsed between us, and the air grew thick. I flipped my hair over my shoulder and leaned in to kiss his soft lips while I guided my hand between my legs and over his shaft. He was already hard, which made me smile. I peppered kisses along the groomed line of his beard and moaned into him. It was hard to believe it was all real. Two months prior I barely had hope to walk to my car without being harassed. I wasn't sure how I would end up, but the road to freedom had never been so sensual.

Frankie reached between us and cupped my breasts, his tender touch unexpected but welcomed. Maybe he didn't think he knew how to be gentle, but that was a lie he told himself and I intended to show him how wrong he was.

I abandoned my original plan to tease him long and hard, because the desire to have him inside me was too strong. I fumbled a little with his pants, but as he lifted his hips and pushed them down, his erection sprang free — only the thin layer of my lace between our heated skin.

I reached for the condom and kissed him deeper while I put it on. His quiet moans encouraged me, assured me of how mutual our desire was. Once in place, I stood on my knees. Frankie pulled down the cups of my bra and sucked one nipple while twisting the other. I moved the lace of my panties to one side then lowered onto him.

We locked eyes and I brought one of his hands to my mouth. As I rocked my hips back and forth, I sucked two of his fingers until guiding them down my chest and stomach into my panties where he pinched my clit. I gasped. So maybe he wasn't so gentle after all. Didn't matter... I liked it.

Two fingers replaced the pinch, and my eyes may have rolled back into my head. Frankie whispered little words of encouragement—some dirty, some sweet— and moved both hands to my hips to deepen my grind. So much for me being in charge. I braced myself on his shoulders as a whirl of pleasure circled inside me. His pelvic bone rubbed my clit in the perfect angle and my inner walls clenched and throbbed around him.

My pained whimpers caught in my throat, but Frankie didn't ease the pace. Instead, somehow, we went faster, and a cool bead of sweat dripped down the arch of my spine. My lungs begged for air and my hips ached from their stretched position, yet the pleasure purring inside me would not ask him to stop. I had a certain pride that I could take him and his force. Even more was my need to prove that I not only accepted it, but I was eager for it.

Frankie's exhale matched each thrust forward until he clenched his eyes shut and cried out. He stiffened inside me, and the tiny movement made me scream.

His eyes flew open. "You okay?"

I smiled and ran my fingers through the sweaty hair along his forehead. "Never better." I rested my head on his shoulder while we caught our breath and he made small paths around my back with his fingers.

We sat like that for a while until he finally said, "Let's go. Shower and bed." Frankie tapped my ass twice in a 'giddyap' motion.

"No. I like it here. Not moving."

"If you stay like that, there's gonna be a round two."

Sounded perfectly acceptable to me. I wiggled in deeper.

"Oh. It's like that, huh?" Frankie rocked forward and in one heave, I was over his shoulder, and we were upright. Not only was he strong, but he was incredibly graceful. I couldn't help but giggle. "Round two shower!"

Somehow, the shower had taken hours, and by the time my head hit the pillow, my thoughts were a blur. I still didn't know if I was going to tell Ruby that I was pretty sure Billy had found me. One thing was for sure, I was going to have to cancel our lunch on Monday. If he really was in the city, I wasn't going to lead him right to her. I put aside the worry, assuring myself it would be there in the morning.

I thought I heard an alarm way too early then the warm body in the bed was replaced by cool space. But it wasn't until I smelled coffee and heard the shower that I was fully awake.

A used dress shirt was on the floor in the closet, and I threaded my arms through and shook out my hair. I smiled. This was my new life, and it was better than I could have imagined.

"Morning, gorgeous. That's a beautiful smile to start the day." Frankie's hair was still wet, and his torso glistened from the shower. That was my man? Boyfriend lottery. Wait? Boyfriend? *Yes, Megan. Boyfriend.*

"I'm just taking it all in."

Frankie tossed his towel on the dresser, and for the first time in daylight, I got a good look at his thighs — and they were insane. Instead of the normal one, meaty muscle, it looked like there were three separate ones somehow working together. I had no idea muscles could do that.

He got dressed in casual navy pants and a crisp white shirt. I would need to up all my games, body and wardrobe to start. If he caught me gawking, he didn't act like he noticed or cared. Maybe he was used to it.

"I usually eat eggs and a carb for breakfast. That okay?" Fully dressed, he came over and pecked me on the cheek then opened a thin drawer with several watches and chose one.

"I can make it if you want. I feel like you're doing everything for me. Also, how are you so awake?"

"I'll do it. But yeah, eventually that sounds like something I could get used to. Get dressed, baby cakes. You have a job to quit and today's my last day off for a couple of weeks."

Did he just call me 'baby cakes'?

"Is the old you aware that this version is chipper?"

Frankie walked over, and not only was he in a good mood, there was also a softness to his eyes. "If the version of me since I've met you includes 'chipper', so be it."

In the car on our way to Cold Spring Harbor, I wrestled with my old friend guilt. No matter what I did, it seemed to follow me like a shadow. The only saving grace of quitting my job was that if Billy had truly found me, Fiona's family would not be in danger — something I should have thought about before crashing into their lives.

Rusty greeted us with a wagging tail and one small bark. I made him sit before scratching under his chin.

"God, I don't know how you do that." Fiona held the door at arm's length, a sleeping baby cradled in the other. She looked good. She'd showered and had on fresh clothes, which hadn't always been the case in the mornings.

"Hey, Fi." Frankie kissed her on the cheek. "How you feeling?"

"Better now that I've laid eyes on this one. I was worried." Her tone both hit me hard in the heart and warmed me all over. For whatever reason, Fiona really did care about me. It was a gift I intended to hold precious.

We followed her to the back of the house where Chezzie was on the couch with the other twin in her arms. Frankie sat next to her, and they started a quiet conversation, presumably about the baby.

"Tea?" Fiona asked after she'd put Dante into the swing.

"Yeah. I'll start it."

In the kitchen, I set out the cups and miniature butter cookies that Fiona liked in the breakfast nook while the kettle boiled. She came in quietly and sat at the table. We made a little small talk about Violet and the babies' night, but once the packets of tea were infusing, it was time.

"Are you okay, Megan? Like, really okay?" The concern in her voice only deserved the truth, as complicated as it was.

"Yes and no, if that makes any sense."

She let out a small laugh. "I actually know exactly what you mean."

"I'm so sorry about all the fuss. But it got me thinking... I'm not sure I'm the best person to be caring for newborns."

Fiona studied me and a heat crept up my back. It wasn't that I was lying, just not saying that her husband didn't want me there. I sipped my tea. "I'm sorry. I don't want to leave you hanging, but I'm not as together as I thought I was."

Her eyes narrowed a bit. "I understand. No one ever thinks about post-traumatic stress. I should have known better than to force you into this job. Leo reminded me that I get pretty obsessed when I want something."

So he'd been working her from his side, *smart.*

"Also" — she sighed and shook her head — "I should have warned you about therapy and opening a can of worms. Actually, it's more like one of those fake peanut cans where everything pops out." She spread her fingers wide like an explosion.

"No. It was good. It's just my mind is playing tricks on me..." I sipped my tea. "I am so grateful to you and Leo for getting me out of Iowa. I don't think I could have done it alone. I'm going to find a way to repay you."

Fiona waved a hand. "Nonsense. But I'm curious, why do you think your mind is playing tricks?"

I wanted to lie or brush it aside, but I also thought that if anyone would understand, it would somehow be her. "I thought I saw him, the guy who was stalking me." The image of the platform flashed in my mind, and I shuddered. "Those beady, soulless eyes... I could have sworn it was him. But that would mean he was way smarter than I thought. No one knew I was coming here."

The energy shifted as Fiona stared out of the window to the backyard. "Eyes have a way of marking you, don't they?"

Whatever she was thinking about, it didn't seem far away from my own experience. But I wouldn't pry. Some skeletons deserved to stay in the closet.

"So what now? I can't just throw you into the world without some support." Her smile was back, and she wasn't mad or disappointed. If anything, she understood.

"Well…" I hid behind my hands then opened them in a peek-a-boo. "I'm going to move in with Frankie."

Fiona's jaw dropped. "Oh, this is some good tea. Keep spillin'."

I dropped my head back. "I know it's a terrible idea. It's sudden and stupid—all those things."

Fiona shrugged. "Maybe."

"I just feel so safe with him. Can you imagine going on a date with a guy and explaining, 'Ya, so my sister's ex is probably following us and might pop out behind the next corner and scream in my face. That's cool, right?'"

Fiona tilted her head to the side. "Wait, your sister's ex?"

I froze. I'd gotten so comfortable with Fiona that I'd slipped up. "I…"

She gave her head a tiny tilt. "We were all under the impression that we pulled you out of an abusive relationship…"

Yeah. I'd deceived them. The nervous laugh that bubbled out of me didn't do much to cover my infraction.

I closed my eyes tight. The Riccis had only ever helped me, so they deserved honesty. "I'm really sorry about that. No one ever really asked, and it seemed like my only chance to get out. I never lied per se. Billy was—probably still is—genuinely stalking me. He's desperate to find my sister."

Fiona held the cup next to her lips for a long beat then took a sip. "Well, if anyone can relate to protecting a sister, it's me."

I could tell she was still a bit stung or hurt from the deceit, because her tight smile didn't reach her eyes. I wanted to tell her more and win her back over onto my side, but I just had to hope she would get there in her own time.

One of the babies cried from the other room and Fiona stood then froze when there was silence. She reached for her cup then studied me for a beat. "Word of advice about Ricci men?"

"Sure. Considering you have three of them, you're pretty much an expert."

She smiled but a sadness came into her eyes. "Whatever hell you think you've lived, theirs is worse. You'll never save him, but you can help him stand back up if he falls."

Chapter Twenty-Nine

Frankie

"Harder than you thought?" I glanced over to Megan as we drove back to the city. It hadn't taken long for her to pack at Leo's — all her possessions had fit into two grocery bags. It was downright depressing. Maybe that was why she had the worried frown on her face.

"I told her about Ruby and that I hadn't been totally honest."

"She'll come around. Once Fiona takes someone under her wing, she's loyal for life."

Megan rubbed her arms and shrugged like a cat stretching. "I hope so. I'd like to have her as my friend."

I let the moment hang in the air before asking, "Do you really think you saw him?"

"Yeah. I do. I can feel it."

"I just don't get how he would know you're here. It's New York City."

She stared out of the window. "It was my dream. Ruby probably told him. They might have even laughed about it behind my back. She really thought they were in love. It was almost impossible to get her away from him."

It sounded dumb and cliché in my head, but the words still came out of my mouth. "Well, if he's in the city, I'm not going to let him lay a finger on you."

Megan let out a long breath.

"Or her?"

Another man would have paused with the confession. *Ruby is in the city, too.* But not me. If there was one thing I understood, it was protecting family. "Or her."

As we drove through the dark tunnel into the city, Megan explained how she and Father Peter had gotten her sister into a rescue program sponsored by the church and in total secrecy—that she'd seen her the week before for the first time in six months but feared she'd led Billy right to her.

When we got home, she went to put away her few things and I stared at a contact on my phone as bile bubbled in my belly. I hated calling in a favor—especially to him—but it was the only way to know if Billy was in town or not.

He answered on the first ring.

"Hell has frozen over." Myers laughed on the other end.

"Yeah, and the devil must be handing out lollypops, because I'm about to ask for your help." I couldn't believe my own words.

"Jesus Christ, Ricci. Do you even know how to do that?"

"It's actually from your wife."

"I still want the credit. She's *my* wife."

"Whatever... Listen... I know Leo filled you in on the background from the nanny. There's a chance that the sheriff-slash-stalker might have found her. If he's in the city, he would have tried to make contact with some other cops. That's how they work. Have Samantha poke around, will you?"

"Yeah, sure." He clicked his tongue. "Two things. One, in my experience, our cops won't share any information with an outsider. They know how this city works. And two" — he lowered his voice — "if he is here, can I find him?"

I laughed. I was pretty sure I knew why but asked anyway. "You bored?"

"Fucking stiff. Plus, Leo said the hick likes to hit women. I don't look very kindly on those types."

Megan walked into the kitchen, saw that I was on the phone and motioned if I wanted her to leave. I shook my head. I was almost done.

"Keep me posted — and do whatever you want." I ended the call and walked over to Megan.

"Shall we order in?"

"Sure. Besides, I don't think I can compete with you and Chezzie in the kitchen." She offered a soft smile, and I was reassured that she was feeling better about sharing that her sister was close by.

I ordered sushi and answered a few emails while Megan read on the couch. When the delivery came, we laid it all out on the table. We danced around the elephant in the room, me telling her that I'd leave early in the morning to work out then go directly to work and subtly asking her to stay in. I casually dropped the line that I was going to use some connections to see if I could find out if Billy really was in town.

In bed later, with her head on my chest the way I liked, she whispered, "You're not going to let anything happen to us, are you?"

"No." I circled my thumb on her back. "I'm not."

"I know this sounds insecure, but I need to know. Why me? What do you see in me? I have nothing to offer."

That wasn't true, and I hoped she didn't feel that way. But on paper, she had a point, so it must have been eating at her. I wasn't used to talking about these types of things, but for her, I would try.

"You're sweet and kind and thoughtful in a way that I could never be. I need that goodness. I need that light inside you to pull me out—to make me better. And I like protecting you. I know that sounds weird, but that's a part of it."

She turned to look at me, and even in the dark, her green eyes were stunning. "Where do you think it comes from, your desire to protect? Were you in the military?"

Hardly. But we'd started this being open shit and I had to keep going.

"It comes from Leo. You think you have guilt about your sister? *Pfff...*"

Megan stroked my cheek and asked, "Will you tell me a little?"

"You don't want to hear my shit. Trust me."

"You know mine." She trailed her fingers down my neck and stopped at my heart. "Please. It helps knowing I'm not the only one."

I rolled my shoulders, debating. The memory looped in my mind. I barely registered that I'd started narrating it. "He was only a baby the first time I had to hit him." I cringed. "He was still in fucking diapers, just this dopey little version of me who shared all his toys and let me open his birthday presents. Happiest kid alive. He literally used to lick his damn plate clean. He was the cutest thing I'd ever seen."

I continued, my words haunting me as much as the vision, "I remember it so clearly. *'Either I smack him or you do.'* Pop knew I would do it. He knew I was soft on Leo and my blow would be nowhere near as brutal as his was. So I hit him right in his chubby, adorable cheek. He was shocked, poor little guy, and went running right to our mom. She was still there at that point. Then they fought, Pops beat the shit out of her in front of us and we had dinner. Pasta Fagioli."

The story hung in the air like a storm cloud until she whispered, "You were just a boy."

"Yeah, but I knew better." There were so many other times I'd hit him. Over the years it had been harder and harder with the eventual realization that we were becoming a mighty force. Our drive had always been our mutual hate for our father. The twisted fate of it was that we were becoming exactly what he wanted, despite never wanting to answer to our destiny.

"I'm sorry." Megan's voice pulled me back to the moment.

"Me too."

She kissed my stomach and I let the realization sink in. Chezzie would shit a brick, because I was pretty sure I'd just made my 'emotions available'. Everything about me was different with Megan. It was true what I'd said. She had a softness that somehow comforted me. And if I could keep her and her sister safe, maybe my past didn't matter for my future.

Chapter Thirty

Megan

My new life of leisure didn't suit me at all. As massive as Frankie's apartment was, being confined to its walls when there was so much happening in the world below was maddening.

I'd wiped every counter three times, cleaned out his already-spotless fridge, paced and tried my best to read. All the activities were half trying to keep me occupied, half avoiding the phone call to Ruby that I knew I had to make.

Mid-afternoon I couldn't delay it any longer. I sent her a text asking her to call me back, and an hour later the pre-paid phone rang.

"Hey. How are you?" The frog in my throat wasn't helping me sound confident.

"I'm awesome. Got approved for our lunch! I wish I could speed up time." The hope in Ruby's voice sank my heart.

"Yeah, about that. We need to postpone. I have a conflict."

I hated bursting her bubble, but a few more days of playing it safe while Frankie found out if Billy really was in the city was worth it. Billy might have even been looking into Catholic women's centers already. Maybe he wasn't as stupid as he came off to be. The only thing I didn't understand was how he'd guessed right on New York, if indeed he had.

"No. Meg, I'm dying here. It's like I went through all that crap with Billy and now I'm the one being punished. It's not fair. You're here and free to do whatever you want. I need that lunch. Whatever your conflict is, fix it." The strain in her voice pulled at my heartstrings but we'd come so far, and I trusted Frankie would protect us.

"Just another week. That's all I'm asking."

She scoffed. "Well, lucky for you it's not your permission I need. It's the center's. I'm getting out of this prison. I've done my work. I've done my time. You have no idea what it's like here." The bitchy whine in her voice was forgivable. She was right. I had no idea what it was like to be her.

That didn't stop me from trying again. "One week… It's for your own safety."

"Bull. You've used that excuse time and time again. Billy has no idea where I am. I need to get out. I need to see strangers and people and places. It isn't fair."

My eyes fluttered shut as I walked over to the massive window overlooking the river. It *wasn't* fair. I'd scored a cushy life with a strong man, and in return for being abused, she'd gotten solitude. Maybe I could convince Frankie to come with us. Surely there would be way less of a risk of anything happening.

"Let me see what I can do."

She didn't even say thank you, just a goodbye. Her frustration had only grown since I'd gotten to New York. It probably stemmed from me being able to come and go as I pleased and her having stricter rules — or so she thought.

I registered the rattle of his keys, but it wasn't until the door shut that I turned to face him. Frankie's work suit did nothing to hide the solid body below. All black, fitted and somehow un-wrinkled after a day in it, he looked just as handsome as the moment he'd left me earlier in the day.

He plugged his phone into the charger on the counter and walked over with narrowed eyes. "You don't look very happy to see me."

I offered a small smile and pulled him onto the couch next to me. "I promise it's not that. In fact, hi." I kissed him. "How was your day?"

He pulled me into his lap. "I'm guessing better than yours. Cabin fever?"

"Guilt." I nuzzled into him. The way his beard scratched was the perfect kind of home.

"Explain, please. I don't like seeing you sad."

In his arms, it was so easy to be honest. It was as if he replaced the wall I'd build around myself. I was no longer afraid to speak my truth, tell my story.

"Ruby's going stir-crazy. I'd promised her lunch in a fun restaurant then canceled. She doesn't understand, and I didn't want to tell her that I thought I saw Billy."

"Uh-huh. And?"

I liked that he was really starting to get to know my ways, how he encouraged me to say more but never demanded it.

"I have you. She has nothing."

He tapped my nose, and it may have been the most endearing thing he'd ever done. "She has you. You're far from nothing."

I turned around to face him. "She'll never understand. And I'm already sure she resents me for making her go away. What if…" I shook my head. I was asking too much.

"Say it. What am I here for if not to listen?"

To protect…

"I don't know. What if you went with me to the lunch? I would feel so much safer. Then she gets her way and will maybe be chill for a bit, and I feel a little less guilty for having freedom while she is at the center." I offered up my sweetest eyes, which got him to crack a smile.

"You're going to introduce me to your sister?" The meaning of his words hung in the air between us. Yes, it was me trusting him more than I'd trusted anyone else in ages. I didn't know if we were in love or falling in love, but one thing was clear as far as Francis Ricci was concerned—he would never let anything happen to me. And since I'd let him in fully, that also included anyone dear to me.

I held his gaze and nodded slowly. For all he gave me, it was a small return.

He licked his lips. "All right. But you must be going stir-crazy yourself. Go put on a pretty dress and let's go to dinner."

His little tap on my butt was an encouragement to move, but I stayed put and skimmed his beard with my fingers. "What have I done to deserve you?"

"Ha! I ask myself the same thing every morning when I wake up to your beautiful face. Now go. I can hear your stomach rumbling."

I smirked climbed off him. "That's *your* stomach."

"Huh. You're right. It misses Chezzie." His smile and gaze followed me down the hallway where I threw on a dress and slid into my new one pair of heels. I met him at the door where he took my hand. In the ride down the elevator, I told myself to enjoy the night, to seize the day and to live in the dang moment. My mountain of problems — or Ruby's problems, for that matter — didn't seem to be going away anyway. But with Frankie next to me, the climb was far less strenuous, and I was sure I would get to the other side.

Chapter Thirty-One

Frankie

When I walked into our private gym, I was pleased and surprised to see that the gang was all there. Leo and Anton were at the bench press and Jackson ran on the treadmill. I really should have looked into getting a larger one. His long legs and longer strides barely stayed on the revolving mat. They all nodded a hello, and I dropped my bag on a bench then took off my light jacket and hung it on a hook just above.

Skipping rope was my favorite warm-up. I blamed my childhood appreciation for boxing movies, which had also led to an obsession about boxers. Sometimes Leo and I even spoke in codes. We used great fighters to explain something. If a situation had been a 'Tyson', it meant that it was quick but violent. 'He'd Sugar-Ray'd it' meant someone had danced around the subject and an 'Ali' meant it had been epic.

As I whipped the rope around, I glanced at Anton, wondering if he had any information for me, but I knew the rules. Hell, I'd made the rules. We worked out, we sparred, then we talked business.

That morning it was Jackson versus Myers, and there was no need to guess whose side I was on. I loved the idea that Jackson was no longer an underling and could finally hit his old boss how he'd probably dreamed of doing for years.

As they taped their hands, I huddled next to Jackson. "Remember that he's not as slow as he used to be. But you are strong, and he has to come at you to reach you. When he lunges, anchor your body weight then block and attack."

Jackson winked then chewed his mouth guard in place. On the other side of the mat, Myers cracked his neck and smirked. Yeah, we all liked a good fight.

"Go!" Leo said before sitting on the bench with a wooden stick on his shoulders, his hands draped over the ends.

I took a few steps back toward the door as the two circled in center ring. To my surprise, Jackson attacked. Myers easily blocked the punch, and while it was a miss, we all appreciated the move.

Back and forth they went, each blocking the other before Anton discovered a quickness he'd never had before. Three swift blows to Jackson's chest landed perfectly before Anton was tripped and on his ass from a wide sweep of Jackson's leg. I didn't even understand how the giant had done it. But on your ass meant you lost, and Anton sat on the ground with his knees bent.

He spit out his mouth guard and chuckled. "How the fuck did you do that?"

Jackson grinned and tapped his head. "Been planning that one for three months."

"Let's shower. Jax and I are on early duty with the douche." Leo's comment was by design. It meant that Anton and I had a conversation for our ears only. Not that we couldn't trust my brother and employee — we could and did so with our lives. But information was a need-to-know basis. We all understood and respected that in a world where darkness crept into most of the things we did.

I offered my hand to Myers and pulled him to standing with a tight grasp. He was a lot lighter than he'd been when he'd first started coming to us. Of all the things he was, a hard worker had always been one of his best traits.

As he untied his tape, he offered a tight, disgusted frown. "So I'm pretty sure he's here. Sammie got word that there was some hick poking around HQ, blabbering on about a missing person, even though the Feds don't have it in their system. But Mr. Small Town got nothing. Rumor has it he went to O'Reilly's snooping around and the off-duties just told him to fuck off."

"But he's here."

"Seems so. Listen... I know it's been a while since I've been in that part of the game, but my ma's contacts are endless. I can call Gus, her old number two..."

I tilted my head and raised my eyebrows. "And what? Kill him?"

Anton shrugged.

A chuckle escaped before I could stop it. "Your wife okay with that?"

The light blue in Anton's eyes twinkled just before he narrowed them. "My wife knows exactly who she married."

He jutted his chin in my direction before heading to the showers. I stood in the same spot for a long time. Megan had no idea who I was, had been. Surely if she knew the greatness of my sins, it would be more than she could bear.

"Hey." Leo tapped the doorway, dressed in his work suit and hair totally dry. How long had I been in the gym by myself?

"I hate to gloat." He raised a shoulder in a fake shrug.

"No you don't. But get it over with. You've been saying Jackson was going to surprise us for a while now." I rolled my eyes. Baby brother loved being right.

"Nah. I mean about my instincts. I knew Megan wasn't safe."

"I told you that the first day I saw her." I opened my arms. What? Did he want some kind of medal for stating the obvious?

The smug grin on his face annoyed me and turned my stomach. "And now she lives with you. Good luck with all that." He turned to walk away.

"Leo?"

My little brother turned around and we locked eyes. His were sympathetic, but I was sending an entirely different message—a desperate one. His tone downshifted from his mocking and went serious. "Yes, you *can* kill him. Should you? Probably not. Will you? If you have to. Don't dig deeper. You won't like what you find." He brought a finger to his forehead. "We know this."

After a tight-lipped frown, he left. I showered and dressed in my suit, even though I was office-bound for the day. I answered all my lingering emails, but Leo's warning haunted the back of my mind until lunch when I had to let it out and fully examine it.

We'd been trained to kill by one of the best there'd ever been. But with all our skill, all our technique, one large fear remained — desire. If I *wanted* to kill Billy Johnston, it would cross some kind of blurry line Leo and I had made in the proverbial sand.

The politicians, crime bosses or just random hits I'd carried out over the years were not personal. They had been mere business transactions. But Leo had killed Mac out of desire. We could wrap it up in a protective ribbon and give it back and forth to each other for Christmas until the end of our days, but we both knew the truth. Leo had crossed the line and he had to live with what that meant. The part of our father that we never wanted to see again was very much still in us.

I skipped lunch and went back to the gym, taking my frustrations out on the heavy bag in the corner. I didn't want to be a murderer. My killing days had been put behind me for a reason. But my urges weren't listening to my brain.

I kicked and punched the bag so hard I was sure I was bruising my bones. There was a calming rhythm to my motions, and I worked up an impressive sweat. When the door to the gym opened, it startled me, but not as much as who I saw standing in the threshold with a bag from Stephano's in his hands.

Anton wore a suit that five years prior would have been laughable. But what was more impressive was the lunch. The line to Stephano's was always around the block, and he served so slow that it took ages to get an order filled. Also, the second the old Italian decided he was done, he just closed. It was anyone's guess if they'd get a sandwich. Some days, he didn't even bother. Myers was holding 'food gold'.

I dropped my arms from their fighting stance and caught my breath. "You miss me?"

"Never. But I stood in line for two hours and canceled an appointment for these sandwiches. The least you could do is share them with me."

After my third shower of the day, I met Anton back in my office where he was sipping on a bottle of water. He'd taken off his jacket and rolled up the sleeves of his white button-down. I had to admit that he played the role of respectable citizen pretty well.

I opened the bag and halved the two sandwiches. It didn't matter what they were. They were going to be delicious, and it was tradition to eat half of one and half of the other. The last thing to do was get two of the same, and even Myers seemed to know that.

"So," I said after my first wonderful bite. "Does this mean we're going to be nice to each other? I'm not sure our relationship can handle that."

"Or your ego." His joke made him laugh.

"You're one to talk."

He finished his first half—*how is he already finished?*—and raised his hands in surrender. "Let's not fight. We're on the same side here."

If he'd brought me Stephano's, he deserved my attention. It was an effective yet rarely used Ricci bribe. "I'm listening."

Anton's leg twitched, an unusual tell that made me smile. I loved making him uncomfortable. He rolled his eyes, and I slowed my chewing, thoroughly enjoying all my senses.

He cleared his throat. "It has not escaped me, the debt I owe the Riccis. Your brother basically saved my crew and the way you let me back in when all that shit was happening with Ma. You hated me, and you didn't have to do that."

It was a big confession from a bigger man, not that I would acknowledge it. "I may still hate you a little bit."

"Fair enough."

I reached for the second half, focaccia and Mortadella. My mouth watered. "Your point?"

"Let me help. We both know this bozo's fate. He touches one hair on one head..." Anton's eyes widened as if the rest was so obvious because, yeah, the rest was painfully obvious.

"Don't you have condos to build or some shit? Palms to grease?"

He huffed. I'd apparently reached my limit of insults. "We both know that you don't want to bring Leo into this. And Jackson? He doesn't have our..."

"Darkness?" I offered.

"I was going to say 'past', but that works." He reached for the rest of his sandwich, and it was gone in two bites. His muscles may have shrunk but his appetite hadn't.

I sat back in my chair and studied Anton Myers in a way I never had. I didn't need proof or a confession to know he'd taken lives before. He couldn't have reached where he had in Covington Heights without spilling rival blood. The only question that remained was if he had the same cold soul as I did.

"When you close your eyes at night, do you see them? The faces?"

The slow shake of his head sent a chill up my spine. He was more like me than I'd ever thought.

Chapter Thirty-Two

Megan

"Wait here. No men allowed." I positioned Frankie next to the lamppost outside of Ruby's center. "And look pleasant. No scary face." I wiped my hands down the front of my yellow sundress.

"I don't have a scary face."

That made me laugh and helped my nerves a little. I gave him a quick peck on the lips.

"You're going to be fine. Nothing is going to happen to you or her." His voice was calm and reassuring — as was the gun I'd seen him slip into the back of his pants when he thought I wasn't looking. I knew first-hand what kind of shot Frankie was, and even if Billy had somehow found us and came out guns blazin', he didn't stand a chance against my Frankie. It wasn't the first time I'd been reassured by the thought of Billy dying. I shook the dark thoughts away, gave a fleeting look over my shoulder to Frankie — who had stuck his hands in his pants' pockets — and went inside to fetch Ruby.

She was waiting in the lobby, makeup on and wearing her favorite shirt. I really should have thought about asking Frankie for a little budget to get her some new things. It would cheer her up. Besides, I was in all new, stylish clothes and her quick once over when she saw me was evidence that she'd noticed.

"Thank you so much for agreeing to make this happen," she said after our tight hug. "You have no idea what it means to get out of here."

I hooked my arm into hers and led her to the door. "So, just to be safe, we have an escort."

Ruby stopped and scrunched her face. "Why?"

"Makes me feel better." I nudged her to keep going and she stumbled a little but came along.

Outside, Frankie peered at us from the lamppost, and I let out a long exhale. Everything would be fine. He was there, so it was probably better than the entire police force.

We walked down the steps and I guided her in front of him then released her arm. "Ruby, this is Frank Ricci, our security. Frankie, this is my sister Ruby."

"Nice to meet you, Ruby." Frankie held out his hand and Ruby shook it with narrowed eyes.

She turned to me. "Can I talk to you for a sec?"

"Sure." Dear Lord, the high pitch of my voice was entirely too revealing. I held up a finger for Frankie to wait and was promptly yanked to the side by Ruby.

"Is that your boyfriend? Do you have a boyfriend, and you didn't tell me? And why is he here?"

So many questions to avoid and swat away like pesky flies. "Look…" I took her by her shoulders. "I got a little spooked, that's all." Especially after Frankie had somehow confirmed that Billy was in town and snooping around. But he'd assured me that there were millions of people, and since Billy had seen me on the train, he'd be looking for me there. If I avoided Grand Central, it would be much harder to track me down — and therefore her. I continued with a warm smile. "You've come so far. We're going to keep you safe and give you a great lunch at the same time." I motioned for Frankie to follow us. I'd found an Indian restaurant not far from her center, and Frankie had assured me that there were plenty of not-too-spicy options on the menu.

He trailed behind and I let out a soothing breath. I'd been right. Having him there was putting me at ease — an ease I was discovering only he had control of.

"Oh, I love Indian!" Ruby smiled when I presented her the restaurant.

"Since when have you tried it?" Our small town had diners, tacos and pizza — thus, my entire noodle experience in Pittsburgh.

"We try new styles all the time at the center. It's actually the one thing most of us look forward to. We have some pretty amazing cooks."

The host offered us a place by the window, but I caught the quick shake of Frankie's head and suggested a table in the back instead.

When we were seated with the menus in front of us, Frankie said, "Do you mind if I just do a quick walk around the block? I'll eat whatever you ladies decide."

"Sure." Somehow without him by my side, I was a lot more exposed, but he was right to check the perimeter. I wasn't going to doubt his experience in keeping people safe. It was what he did for a living.

"Meg" — Ruby slapped her menu into the table — "that is your boyfriend. You can't hide it. And, whooey he's like a…a…man." The last word came out as if she were a little disgusted by it. Good to know she had some age-gap limits. I hadn't been so sure.

She snarled her lip and shook her head. "How did you even meet him?"

I let out a breath. "It's complicated. *We're* complicated. But somehow it works. I didn't tell you because it happened, *is* happening, very fast. Don't worry about me. Let's focus on you." I grinned from ear to ear, happy to change the subject and give her the treat she'd been waiting for. "What are you ordering?"

"Everything!" She wiggled her fingers in delight and went down list, explaining the dishes she knew about and excited for the ones she'd never heard of.

"All good." Frankie slid back into his chair while he unbuttoned his jacket. A calm spread over me. I was having lunch with my sister in the city of my dreams with a man who might have also been part of my dreams. No, he was better than anything I could have imagined.

The food was fantastic, and Ruby made sure we understood she thought so too by rolling her eyes back and making satisfied groans every other bite. Frankie paid, because he wouldn't have it any other way, and as we walked back to the center, he gave us the space to have a private conversation.

"I confess," Ruby said with a little sigh, "that I'm horribly jealous." She pinched at my dress. "New clothes, new life, new boyfriend—or should I say *man*-friend? I'm so tired of being at the center. It feels like everything is on hold and I'm waiting for something, but nothing ever happens to change my situation."

I pulled her a little closer and squeezed her arm where I'd hooked mine. "Just a few more weeks. We'll get you an apartment and a job. You're gonna start your new life soon, I promise." I promised? How was I going to manage that?

Ruby frowned, doubting my plan. I couldn't blame her. "The only thing keeping me there is that I have nowhere else to go."

Such a sad truth, but it was for her safety — and that was what mattered.

"Let's make a deal." I tried a cheery tone, hoping she would follow. "Let's talk every night. What's the best time for you?"

"I don't know. Like eight, maybe? Then we're done with dinner and chores. We go to bed at ten."

I'd known her schedule, but it hadn't been until that moment that I'd realized how depressing it was and the toll it was having on her happiness. The entire point of getting her in the program wasn't just to break the bond between her and Billy. It was also to try to build her back up. The second part didn't seem to be working. What if she got out of the center only to latch onto any man for happiness again and he turned out to be the same as Billy — or worse?

"I'll find a way," I promised. "I always do, right?"

We stopped before the steps of the center and I hugged her tight. She was limp in my arms, maybe showing her how well I was doing had backfired into her realizing that, once again, *she* wasn't *me*.

The memory of her screaming those words at me made my mouth go dry. It had been a fight about her leaving Billy and a revelation that me judging her was never going to get her out of the situation she'd found herself in.

I rubbed her shoulders. "Tonight, eight o'clock. Call me, okay?"

She nodded and sent a weak wave to Frankie then went inside without looking back.

Once the door closed, Frankie came over and put his arm around me. "I think that went well."

"I have to get a job."

Frankie fluttered his eyes. "What?"

"I have to get a job," I repeated then started walking to the parking lot where he'd left his car. "I have to get her out of that center. It's crushing her spirit."

"Megan…wait."

I spun around and crossed my arms, daring him to oppose me.

He grinned. "First of all, that pout is sexy, so I'm not sure you're effectively achieving your goal of being stubborn. Second, can this wait until we get a better read on the situation? As in, we find him and convince him to leave?"

I dropped my head and released my arms. "It's one thing for me to accept your charity—"

Frankie raised a hand and cut me off. "That's not what this is, and you know it." He stepped closer and lifted my chin. "Can I please have a week to track him down? Is that too much to ask?"

I stared deep into his eyes, afraid to ask the question but needing to, nonetheless. "Then what?"

Without skipping a beat, he said casually, "Then I convince him to leave."

That would entail violence, but I'd run out of sympathy for Billy Johnston.

"I'm just so ready for this to be all over. I'd like one day to go by that I don't worry about Ruby."

Frankie took my hand and kissed my knuckles as we kept walking. "I know what you mean, but if you're anything like me, it probably won't happen anytime soon. Sorry."

I didn't hate him for being right, but I loved the fact that he understood.

Chapter Thirty-Three

Frankie

From the sound of the eight-o'clock-nightly calls with Megan, Ruby was doing her best to hold on. It was true what Megan had said. Her sister was getting the raw end of a deal to keep her safe. If I wanted Megan happy—which I very much did—I was going to have to find a way to keep her *and* Ruby safe. I might even have to go back to my previous ways.

It wasn't that I wanted or didn't want to kill Billy. I just could. It would be so simple. It was one thing when we were on his territory, but this was a giant metropolis where the missing person's list was a mile long.

But Billy was doing a good job of lying low. I didn't think he was gone, just looking for Megan in the wrong places. She wasn't out on the street or riding the subway to a museum like she would have very much liked. No, she was pacing a hole in my wood floor and going absolutely stir-crazy—and I couldn't blame her.

She'd waited and dreamed about living in the city for years. Having it at her fingertips then being forced to sit on her hands must have been torturous.

That was why I had my gadget guy come up with an extra dose of security for both her and Ruby. Statistics showed that the first thing abductors take from their victims was their phone. If, and it was a pretty big 'if', Billy managed to get a hold of either of the sisters, phone tracking would no longer be reliable to trace them.

"Hey," Megan said with a big smile as I came through the door. She'd taken an interest in cooking and a hint of rosemary and thyme came from the oven.

"Smells good." I shrugged out of my jacket and hung it on a barstool then took the small box out of the inside pocket.

Her green eyes sparkled as she clocked the present. She'd gotten better at accepting gifts, especially after I'd explained that it was part of the way I showed I cared.

"What's that?"

"This is your ticket to freedom." I kissed her on the lips then held the box high above my head. "How bad do you want it?"

She hopped but couldn't reach then tried a new and way more effective approach. Megan slid her hand to my waist and untucked my shirt before hypnotizing me with her sultry gaze.

The need to touch her back was too strong, and I forgot about our little game and lowered my hand to grab her ass. A millisecond before contact, she snagged the little box out of my hand and ran over to the living room. I told myself I'd let her win on purpose, but I wasn't so sure.

"Earrings?" She scrunched her nose with the question.

"Not just any earrings. GPS earrings…connected to my phone. One more layer of security that makes me feel okay about you going out."

A huge grin spread across her face. "Really?"

I nodded. "We can't let him dictate your life anymore. You see him, you call me." The other thing I wasn't mentioning was the conversation I'd had with Myers about drawing Billy out. We weren't having much luck locating him through the usual channels.

And, quite frankly, I'd had enough. Selfishly, I was ready for Megan and me to officially move on. The only way to do that was to solve the Billy Johnston problem for good.

She removed the small gold hoops from her ears and replaced them with the round-jade studs. "Can we get Ruby a pair?"

"Already working on it. You can fetch them in the morning and drop them yourself if you want."

Megan's eyes widened. "That much freedom? Me, on the street alone?"

"Yep."

"Oh my God, I love you!" She immediately clamped her hand over her mouth. "I'm so sorry. You don't have to say it back. It just kinda slipped, well…blurted out." Her chest flushed below her white peasant top and the pink crept into her cheeks.

I walked over slowly and placed her hands behind my neck. "But is it true?"

"Pretty sure. But seriously, no pressure. I don't—"

A kiss was the only way to celebrate being told you were loved by a beautiful woman, so I gave her the most tender one I could. Her lips were just as soft as the first time they'd touched mine months prior in the darkness of a hotel room.

When I regretfully pulled away, it was only to reassure her that her confession would be the same as mine. "I'm pretty sure, too."

We stood there for a long moment, and I thought about how long I'd waited for a connection like the one we shared. Maybe she had too. We were two people who hadn't put ourselves first for most of our lives but were finally discovering the beauty of that together. It was like a precious secret that only we understood.

The rest of the evening was utterly domestic and somehow the perfect way to savor our official declaration. Neither of us needed fancy dates or expensive meals. That was what I'd had wrong about dating. At the end of the day, it was about acceptance, company and caring for the other person. The passion part had worked itself out naturally. We didn't have any issues there. But really, truly what I loved about Megan—and I did love her, even if I hadn't completely gone all in and told her how much—were the quiet moments at the end of the day where she was there for me as much as I was for her.

The next morning, I left her in a tangle of sheets and kissed her warm brow before meeting the guys at the gym. Leo was already on the treadmill, Jackson at the bench press and Anton strolled in five minutes after me with a swagger that only he could get away with.

We sparred, then all went to a nearby diner for breakfast. As the four of us sat there, it hit me why Anton had wanted a crew. The jabs, insults and faked annoyance were actually our way of caring. Jackson was the only one of us who'd had normal parents, and it showed with the lack of darkness in his soul. But he was fierce in other ways. He would do anything to give his son a better life, and we all respected him for that.

Leo stood and said he would pay the bill. We were all-hands-on-deck for Andy. He had an event in Queens with a massive crowd, and the parking and drop-off were going to be a bitch. My brother said goodbye to his friend Myers, and Jackson left to fetch the car.

I leaned over the table. "She's got the earrings and is going to give a pair to her sister. I honestly don't think he'll come out of hiding just like that but help an old man out and stick around the city for me today."

"Ah… so sentimental. But yeah, I get it. Samantha's away on business, anyway. Plus, I'm having lunch with Gus. Did you ever meet him?"

I hadn't, but I knew the name. He was one of Anton's mother's original crew members. Rumor had it he had been madly in love with Sophia Myers and would have followed her to hell and back, no questions asked. I knew the feeling.

As we loaded in the SUV and headed to fetch Andy, it happened. The false sense of security that my father had always warned me about spread over me. The problem was, I didn't know what it was until it was too late.

Chapter Thirty-Four

Megan

Freedom smelled like exhaust and foul garbage, but I didn't care. I could have danced in the streets. After almost a week of being confined to Frankie's apartment, the stank of the city was welcome.

Even the horns and shouting from taxi drivers made me smile. Yes, I was looking over my shoulder, but I could no longer let Billy dictate my happiness — and neither could Ruby. I'd get her out of the center and either find her some school or a job. I could tell that Frankie didn't want her in the guestroom, which was fair. I was already taking a lot of space in his previous bachelor pad.

I'd decided to walk, which would take me a while, but the air and electricity of the city gave me all the energy I needed. I couldn't help but dawdle a little. There were so many interesting shops and cafés.

There was the little store with trendy onesies that I typed into my phone as a reminder to pick something up for the twins and a restaurant not far from there boasted of French and Thai fusion. I snapped a picture of its menu from the window. The occasional parks were full of dogs, people and small stands with used books. A Hare Krishna even offered me a copy of the *Bhagavad Gita*. The diversity had me drunk.

When I finally got to the center, I signed in and sat in one of the beige plastic chairs in the small waiting room. It seemed odd to text my location to Frankie. All he had to do was either track my phone or now my earrings, but I liked communicating with him. The days I'd spent at his apartment—I was still having a hard time calling it 'home'—there'd been nothing to write. So I sent off a little text, hoping it wouldn't annoy him or distract him from his work. There was some big sporting event they were all at. He'd left early, and I'd kinda missed making him breakfast and sipping coffee in one of his shirts while he ate it.

I thought back to the restaurant that I'd passed. There was no way I was going to tackle cooking Italian food. The Riccis all had that field covered. But I could try a fusion meal.

"Hey." A nervousness in Ruby's voice surprised me.

I stood and hugged her. "Hey, yourself."

She fiddled with her hands and looked past me. "I don't have much time. Group in ten minutes. What are you doing here on a Thursday, anyway? Did you change your days off?"

"Oh. Right." I'd purposely not told Ruby I'd lost my job—or quit, which would have been worse in her eyes. I was trying to build our future. "I needed to bring you these." I fished the small box out of my bag and handed it to her. She opened it then stared at me blankly.

I pointed to my ear. "Look... I have basically the same. There's a tracking device in them. Better than a phone. So if anything ever happens..."

"Why would anything ever happen?" Ruby gestured around to the concrete walls. "I can barely leave this place. And you didn't answer my question." Her brow formed a V.

"I'm in between jobs," I confessed, "but not for long. And I'm still going to get you a place to live...hopefully in two weeks."

"Wait. You're not working as a live-in nanny anymore? Where are you living then?" The realization washed over her face and she scoffed. "With *him*?"

I cringed. What was about to follow was exactly why I'd kept my status from her.

Predictably and exactly as I'd imagined it, she said, "So I'm here, living basically behind bars, and you're out there having a love affair with an older man who is obviously loaded. By the way, I saw his watch. Jesus, Meg. We had a plan. It was *your* plan!"

"I'm sorry." I didn't even know why or if I really was. But I didn't know what else to say. Then I went into scramble mode. "Nothing has changed, just because I have a boyfriend—"

"You have no job. You know, I didn't even want to come to New York. That was all you. I hate it here. And right now, I'm pretty sure I hate you."

"Don't say that." I reached for her arm, but she swatted me away. "Two weeks. I swear."

She raked her eyes over me. "That's all new. You're spending money on new clothes and I'm rotting away in here. I can't believe how selfish you are. I have to go.

Don't bother calling me at eight. I won't answer." She shoved the box into my hands. "And you can stick these where the sun don't shine."

"Ruby!"

She turned on a heel and marched away. I stared down the empty hall for a long time, trying to gather my thoughts. On the bright side, she'd grown a backbone in the previous months. I just never thought I'd be the one she'd show it to.

I left the shelter, defeated and embarrassed. Without the energy I had earlier in the day, I decided to take the train back to Frankie's. But I wasn't ready to go back to an empty apartment, as beautiful as it was.

Instead, once I was downtown, I found an outdoor café and scrolled through the job postings for teachers in the city. The pay was miserable, but if Ruby got a part-time job at minimum wage and Frankie would be kind enough to co-sign a lease, I could manage rent for a studio apartment, and she would hopefully have enough income to eat.

It was late in the afternoon and the music overhead changed to more energetic. A sandwich board at the entrance of the café boasted margaritas half price during happy hour, and I realized that was exactly what was happening. Young people migrated to the tables and the place filled with a lively buzz. It was just the change I needed and I flagged over my waitress.

"I'll have a frozen Margarita, please."

"Sure. I just need a credit card. Happy hour rules. But you can settle in cash if you want."

I dug my old card out of my bag and handed it to her without a second thought. It had been a minute since I'd been day-drunk, but why not? What else did I have to do? Frankie had said he wouldn't be home in time for dinner, and I had literally nowhere to be. The waitress brought over the drink with a smile and her small act of kindness gave me a glimmer of hope for my future. I could make it all work, I had too.

The cold, sour liquid made me pucker my cheeks and shiver. But then, with every sip through the paper straw, it warmed me. I was lulled into the gentle arms of a hard alcohol I'd never drank. Tequila. I said the word over and over in my head, and it even sounded inviting.

Yeah. I liked te-quiiiiii-la.

An easy smile voluntarily tugged at my cheeks and my shoulders released all the tension from the fight with Ruby. The months away from my sister had made me forget how much she'd never appreciated what I did for us.

So what if New York was my idea? What was she going to do? Stay in Iowa and pop out countless Johnston babies between blows to the head? No. I'd saved her from a tragic life. One day she would thank me.

"Is this seat taken?" a blue-eyed man with a pointy nose asked, gesturing to the chair opposite me. He reminded me of someone, but I just couldn't place it.

But I couldn't figure out his tone. Did he want to sit there or take it to join another table? Either way the answer was the same.

"Nope."

To my surprise, he actually slid in and offered his hand. "Hi. I'm Cal. And you look very lost in your thoughts."

In the spirit of nicknames, I offered mine with my hand. "Meg. You come over to help me find my way out?"

"No. I came over because you have the prettiest green eyes I've ever seen."

A giggle bubbled out of me, and I slapped my hand a little too hard over my mouth. "I should warn you. I have a lethal boyfriend."

"Yikes. Lethal, huh?" He raised his eyebrows. They were a darker blond than his hair, which had natural sun highlights in all the right spots.

"Yup." I sipped the last of my drink and the straw made a gurgling sound.

"I have a little confession." Cal winced. "I've been stood up. Do you mind if I sit here and have a drink? Seems like a waste just to leave."

Frankie would not approve of my small talk, but I had clearly stated I was taken. Heck, I'd even thrown in a warning. The stranger in front of me knew nothing of my problems and was surely better company than the walls at the apartment.

"You can sit. Besides, it's the only free chair in the place."

Cal motioned to my empty glass. "Can I get you another?"

The list of why I should say no ran through my head like a fast-paced teleprompter. 'I was buzzed' being at the top. But I was so damn tired of doing the right thing all the time. It was the entire reason I was with Frankie. That little part of me that liked adventure and was itching to put herself first.

"I'd love another."

Cal winked before heading to the bar. I dug my phone out of my bag. The battery had been depleted from all my scrolling and picture taking earlier in the day. I sent a text to Frankie saying as much and that I'd stopped at a café on my way home. When Cal came back with fresh drinks, I put my phone away and mindlessly touched my earrings. Yes, I was tipsy, but I was enjoying the random company of a stranger. That hadn't happened in ages. Besides, I would leave after the second drink and go straight home. Maybe I would even take a cab.

"You send a text to that lethal boyfriend telling him you've found someone else?" Cal's smile was more of a confident smirk. If he only knew...

"Hardly. It would take a lot more than a drink. Sorry."

"Wishful thinkin', I guess." A little twang came out in his voice that I hadn't noticed before.

"Where are you from?" It definitely wasn't New York.

"Tennessee. Came to the big city to be an actor."

I slid my drink a little closer, and the sweat from the glass cooled my fingers. "Exciting. I could never get up in front of people like that. Have you been in anything I've seen? Oh, wait." My eyes bulged out. "Are you already famous and I just don't recognize you?" That might have been why he seemed familiar. I was such a fool — and well on my way to getting drunk. The second Margarita was more bitter than the first. *Probably a different bartender.*

He laughed. "I wish. No. No luck so far. Just a crap job at a chain food restaurant in Midtown."

"Well, I wish you much success. Maybe someday I'll say, 'Hey! He bought me a drink!'"

We clinked our glasses and each of us took a sip. Cal had taken out his straw and laid it on the round table between us.

"What about you?" he asked and narrowed his eyes. "You have a neutral accent so... Midwest. Nebraska?"

I jerked back. "I'm insulted."

He chuckled. "Then you're definitely from Iowa."

Oh, he was good. It was true that there was some kind of rivalry between the two states that no one really understood but everyone went along with. I'd heard it was about college football from before I was born, but I honestly didn't know.

"Guilty." I took another long sip, not sure where to steer the conversation after that. I didn't want to talk about Iowa and why I'd left.

Somehow, Cal took the hint and changed the subject. "So what do you do?"

Nothing.

"Early education. Still job hunting."

"Well, good luck to you, Meg." Cal checked his watch. "I need to make a call. Save my spot?"

I nodded and he left the enclosure of the café and stood under a parking sign at the curb with his phone to his ear. His empty seat made me uncomfortably aware that I was alone. The chatter around me hadn't seemed so loud when I'd been adding to it. I took more sips of my drink, wondering if maybe it wasn't somehow stronger than the previous. When my gaze went a little fuzzy, I knew I'd had too much. It wasn't that I was some kind of lightweight. I just didn't have tons of experience with the hard stuff.

I stood, promptly wobbled, then sat back down. *Crap.* I blinked several times trying to stop the double vision and remembering I hadn't eaten lunch.

Cab. Home. Bed.

Just as I was getting a little clarity in my head, Cal was back.

"Sorry about that."

"No problem. And my turn to apologize. I've got to go. Thanks for the drink." I stood and the rush to my head made me stumble. "I didn't have lunch, probably shouldn't have had that second drink."

Cal scrunched his face. "Shit. That was a double, too. God, I feel horrible. Let me call you a car."

It was unlike me to take help from a stranger. It was also unlike me to be drunk before dinner. But if he was ready to find me a way home, I was more than willing to take his random act of kindness.

"Thanks," I muttered, wishing I had some water and noticing that my lids were growing heavy.

Cal texted into his phone and sent me a reassuring smile. I reached for my own, but it had gone dead. I hadn't taken the second phone I used for Ruby, since I was going to see her.

But the earrings! Frankie would know where I was. It was almost as good as having him by my side. Also, he'd previously proven he would check up on me. Heck, he might be on his way to get me. My boyfriend was dreamy like that—a dark knight in shining armor.

Cal laughed. "You have a perma-grin. You really are drunk. Sorry, Meg. I feel horrible. Five minutes for your car."

"I really...'preciate..." The day, my failure as a sister, getting day-drunk with a stranger... It all spun in my head like a tornado. All I could think about was how I needed Frankie. I sniffed and realized I was on the verge of tears. What a mess. Not only was I a lightweight, but I was going to be a pathetic drunk.

"I'm sorry."

"Let's get you out of here." Cal offered me his hand and a hiccup escaped my mouth as I stood. I leaned into him, my eyes focused on the ground and putting one foot in front of the other.

In the blur, a lightning bolt hit. It wasn't the color of the blue eyes that I recognized, it was the shape. I tried to wiggle out of Cal's arms, but he gripped my shoulders hard and led me to the curb, where a car was waiting with its back door open.

"No, no. I'm good." Even then I had a shred of hope I was wrong. But Cal pushed me into the car, and I was met with the same eyes but a different shade of blue.

"I'm going to ask nice, for old time's sake." Billy's tone was condescending. I hated condescending men. "Where's my Ruby?"

There were two, maybe three foggy versions of Billy Johnston, and they all moved in unison with my swaying head.

I smiled, and after a couple of heavy blinks, I said what I always did and would. "I don't know what you're talkin' 'bout."

Thwack!

The sting only lasted a fraction of a second before everything went black.

Chapter Thirty-Five

Frankie

There was one thing I hated about Queens more than its depressing landscape and endless graffiti...traffic. The sporting event we'd taken Andy to had finished, and we were in a gridlock to get back to the city. Jackson was at the wheel. When it was all-hands-on-deck, he always drove and I'd lost a bet with Leo, so he was riding shotgun.

I closed my eyes and folded my arms. Maybe a quick nap would help pass the time. Small talk with the womanizing client next to me was definitely not how I was going to pass the rest of the ride back into the city.

Megan and I had fallen into a comfortable routine. I would have never thought waking up to the same person every day would be so invigorating, but when her kind, green eyes blinked open next to me in the mornings, I was sure we'd chosen the right thing in being together. She'd memorized how I liked my coffee, and even though she had no reason to get out of bed early, every morning when I was in the shower she rose and made me breakfast. Maybe she thought I was spoiling her with clothes and an easy lifestyle, but she was pampering me right back.

I'd always considered myself more of a rugged loner, but the nice things I'd acquired over the years told a different story. Maybe I could see if Anton's wife, Samantha, had some school connections that could get Megan a job teaching. I selfishly didn't want her to work. I liked the thought of her waiting for me at home, but I knew that was old-fashioned and would never fly. She wanted her own path, her own money — not that she was going to keep any of it. She'd pour it into her sister like she'd explained she'd basically always done.

I probably needed to fully confess that I loved her, that I was pretty sure I couldn't live without her, that being with her made me want to be an even better man than I was trying to be and that I didn't deserve her — but I would never let her go. But it couldn't be just over dinner or in the wee hours of the night when we were the most open. She needed to know it during the day. Maybe I should buy her some jewelry.

The jolt of the car made me open my eyes. Traffic broke. *Fucking finally*. I flipped my wrist and checked my watch. The delay had cost us an extra hour. I should let Megan know I'd be later than expected.

No way I was going to talk to my girlfriend in front of my employees or client. I shot her off a message and waited for her reply. The second little check indicating the message was read didn't come. She'd stopped off for a drink, which was unlike her. Maybe something had happened with Ruby. She'd mentioned that her sister was feeling restless.

Her last message had said that she was low on battery, but she should have been home and recharged. I called her—fuck not talking to her in front of the boys. No answer.

"Jackson, can you make up for lost time, please."

"You got it."

Never had I been more thankful for the professional racing lessons we'd offered Jackson two years prior for his birthday. We whizzed in and out of the cars like a stunt car in a movie. The problem was, the faster he drove, the more my heart raced. Something was wrong, and the Ricci instincts were blaring sirens in my head.

"Whoa. What the fuck?" Andy swerved and held on to the roof of the car while I opened the tracking device on my phone.

Leo turned around and narrowed his eyes.

"Not answering." I held his gaze for a long second before looking back at my screen. The green dot that was Megan's earrings pulsated north on the West Side Highway.

"Fuck." I worked my jaw. It had been ages since I'd been afraid. Was that what was causing my thumb to tap uncontrollably? Or was it that I'd known he'd come for her, and I'd set up my own justification for killing him. I couldn't deny that I'd wanted to ever since I'd first seen him, especially when I'd been under the impression that he'd been her boyfriend. If he laid a hand on her…

What? I'd kill him twice?

"Hey." Leo had turned around again.

"This doesn't concern you," I bit back.

His jaw dropped. "Excuse me?"

Anton had been right. I didn't want Leo or Jackson to have any part of what I was going to do to Billy

Johnston, but I did need his help. I searched 'Fuckwad' in my contacts and pressed call.

"Talk to me," Myers said from the other end of the phone.

"You, me and Gus. Manhattan side of the Midtown tunnel in fifteen. Bring everything." I ended the call and went back to staring at the application that tracked Megan.

"Uh…" Leo turned around with his eyebrows as high as the Empire State Building.

But I shot him a glare that dared him to stop me. He shook his head slowly, the disapproval seeping out of him. If I'd had the time to worry about it, I might have wondered if he were pouting. Me choosing Anton over him must have stung on some level, but it was for his own good, and if he gave it some real thought, he would probably thank me later. I was the only reason on earth he would jeopardize his wife and kids, and I would never ask him for such a favor.

"Anyone want to fill me in, here?" Andy tried to catch our eye but we all just ignored him, even after his dramatic sigh.

Twenty minutes later and I was still staring at my screen. Megan was in New Jersey and hadn't stopped moving. We were going to have to break every speed limit to catch her, and the only thought keeping me sane was that Billy probably wouldn't kill her. It took a special kind of evil to pull the trigger and end a life, and I wasn't so sure he had that in him. Besides, he was searching for Ruby, and Megan wasn't going to tell him where to find her sister.

Jackson threw the car in park and nodded in my direction. He had even less of a clue as to what was happening than Leo, but he was offering me his support in nothing but a gesture. Leo, on the other hand, got out of the car at the same time I did.

When the doors were shut, he said, "I accept you don't want me there. It's stupid, but I get it. Here's the thing, though." He put his arm around my shoulder and tugged me close. "This is different. This is doing it for selfish reasons. This" — his voice had gone down to a haunted whisper — "is what you said you would never do."

There was never a good time for a lecture from my little brother, even though I knew he was right.

"I haven't done anything." I ducked out of his grasp and walked over to the waiting SUV. Anton — dressed in black cargo pants and a tight, black hoodie — got out of the passenger side and Leo went over to him and whispered something in his ear. I climbed into the back and offered my hand to Gus, who shook it once without making eye contact.

Anton slid in as Leo stared at us with dark eyes and a concerned frown. "Where we headed?"

I handed him my phone. "Follow the green dot. It looks like it stopped, but it could have been traffic."

Gus put the car in drive and headed west across town.

"I figured you'd want a change of clothes," Anton thumbed over his shoulder to the folded pile next to me. "Vests are in the back. You want a power bar?"

Food was the farthest thing from my mind, but he was right to offer. If we were in for a fight, we would need energy. Anton held the bar over his shoulder, and between bites, I shuffled out of my suit and into the tactical gear.

A quality I'd never fully appreciated in Anton was his disinterest in small talk. Maybe he'd learned it from

Gus, because his lips were also sealed. We rode up the highway and into Jersey without another word. There was only a hint of the sun left when we were a mile away from the green dot.

"Five bucks on a run-down farmhouse." Anton finally broke the silence.

Gus tilted his head and blocked my view of the screen we'd all been watching for the previous two hours. "Meh. Could be a shed." He thumbed to a dirt road to our left. "Let's park here. We're better off on foot."

We got out of the car, all careful not to slam any doors. It didn't matter that we were still out of earshot, the hunt had officially begun. In the back, laid out and beautiful, were three vests, six guns and three knives.

Gus shrugged an apology and whispered, "Short notice." But what would have been a normal lack of gear didn't matter. It was who was holding the weapons who did. No amount of police academy training or a lifetime of hunting would compare to what Billy was up against. He was as good as dead, and we hadn't even laid eyes on him.

Slowly — and that was the part that was killing me — we walked and stalked toward a small shack. How Billy had found the perfect spot for murder so far away from home made me wonder if he'd had help. I raised my hand and the three of us came to a simultaneous halt.

"He's not alone," I whispered.

"Goodie." Anton's eyes twinkled, reflecting the rising moon.

We edged closer until we ran out of cover from the trees. I motioned for Gus to stay in hiding and he nodded then pulled the silencer out of his side pocket and attached it to the gun that had been on his hip.

I dropped to the ground and Anton followed as we crawled closer and closer to the shack. We'd come from the back, so if someone was standing guard, they were doing a piss-poor job of controlling the perimeter.

A faint whimper caught my ear. *Megan.* My heart stopped. Never once on a job had I been more on edge. Anton tapped my shoulder and raised his eyebrows. With his right hand flat, he signaled a steady line. *Right. Keep my shit together.*

A scream pierced our ears then ripped my heart in two before transforming into a pounding in my temples, an evil war drum calling out every ounce of anger inside me. He was hurting her, possibly torturing her. And he would see no mercy from me. My father's face scolded me from the dead, but I'd stopped trying to make that man proud. The only thing that mattered was her and the vengeance I would unleash on Billy Johnston.

Again, Anton tapped me. He pointed to himself and showed the number one then to me and two fingers. It was the right thing to do.

Much slower than I wanted to move, I came to standing. Anton nodded once then swiftly walked to the corner of the shed and disappeared around it.

Clack-clack.

I loved that he was shooting to kill. I jogged to meet him, a body of a young man at his feet, the door to the shack still closed. This time, I pointed to myself and showed the number one. After a step back, I raised my leg and kicked open the door.

The sight in front of me was too horrid for even my imagination. There was smeared blood on the scratched wooden floor of the shack. The only part of me that recognized the woman I loved was my heart, which shattered into a million pieces.

"What the — ?"

Clack-clack.

Billy dropped to the ground with a bullet to his head as a naked Megan whimpered in a chair next to him. Her eyes were swollen shut from trauma and tears, and her hands were zip-tied behind her. But worse, far fucking worse, were the cuts all over her body. A can of pepper spray caught my eye on a rusted-out wood burning stove.

"Jesus fucking Christ," Anton whispered behind me and left.

Finally, my instincts kicked in. I flipped open my knife and moved behind Megan to free her hands then scooped her up in my arms. She shivered and trembled then started to sob.

"I'm gonna get you out of here. I'm so sorry I wasn't here sooner." Never had I spoken truer words. And never had so much emotion swelled in my chest to the point I couldn't swallow. We had been too late. I should have never let her go out.

Gus jogged toward me. "Anton went to get the car. I'll call a friend, and we'll take care of this."

Megan mumbled something about not knowing what I was talking about, and I tried to comfort her with a shush and a peck on her matted hair. The gravity of what Billy had put her through started to swell inside me as the warmth of her blood soaked into my clothes. She was literally going to be scarred for life…

I hadn't even had the pleasure of killing the bastard. Anton had taken that away from me. I had let her down. Her cold and bloody body went limp in my arms.

"Megan!" I shook her, which caused a gash on her leg to leak fresh blood.

Tires squealed in the distance, meaning Anton had already reached the car and was on his way back. Gus hurried over and checked her pulse.

"She's in shock. She just passed out." Those were both things I knew, but their recollection gave me zero comfort. How could I have let this happen to her? She'd said she felt safe with me. *Hardly*.

The minutes it took for Anton to slam on the breaks and jump out of the driver's seat passed like lifetimes. We wrapped her in a blanket then got her into the back and I climbed in next to her without even a second thought or goodbye to Gus. He knew what to do, and we both trusted him to do it.

When we finally hit the highway, Anton spoke. "I still have one of my mom's studios in Midtown. Samantha doesn't even know about it."

A hospital was out of the question. What were we going to say? We'd found her on the side of the road? In tactical gear? Then there would be more questions. Who had done this to her? It wouldn't take a lot of digging into her past to point to Billy. He'd be called in as missing sooner rather than later, so there was no need to tie Megan to him any more than she already was.

No, we needed a private doctor who did house calls and not to either of our houses. As much as I was dying to get to the closest place that would take her, there was more to think about than her surface wounds.

"Sounds good." That was ironic. Taking the woman I loved to a secret doctor at a hidden location didn't sound fucking good at all. I stroked her hair. Her face was mangled. Even in the dark of the car, it was easy to tell she had a broken nose. *I should have known better.*

"My doctor or yours?" Anton asked.

"Yours."

I'd forgotten how much of a leader Anton Myers actually was. In truth, I was grateful for his quick actions. Everything he'd done had been perfect. It had been me who'd hesitated, who'd let Megan roam the streets without protection.

Anton dialed his doctor and spoke to him on speaker phone. He informed him of the cuts, the eyes and the state of shock.

After he hung up, he said, "You know what I never understood? Why the fuck anyone would want to take a beautiful woman and beat her fucking face in." He scoffed. "One time I actually heard my father scream that he loved my mother before he threw her into a wall. What the fuck kind of love is that?"

I had no idea. But if I loved Megan and yet I'd let this happen on my watch, I wasn't any better.

Chapter Thirty-Six

Megan

The distinct scent that was my Frankie wrapped around me. Home, I must have been home, though I had no recollection of how I'd gotten there. My head throbbed. How much tequila had I drunk? I reached out for my boyfriend but only found an empty bed. The sheets weren't soft and cold...

Random images flashed in a fog, like remembering bits of a nightmare. I tried to open my eyes, but something was in the way. My muscles strained as I touched my head and I let out a small groan.

"Hey." Frankie's voice was quiet. There was something in it I'd never heard before. *Worry.*

The bed dipped to my left and he ran a gentle hand over my hair. The realization hit me like a hurricane. I'd been beaten, tortured. I was mutilated. A sob rolled out of me before I could stop it. Was I blind, too?

"Shh…" Frankie cradled me. "It's gonna be okay. I promise."

Somehow, probably just knowing I was in his arms, I managed to calm a bit. Frankie hummed and I was aware of another presence in the room.

A warm female voice said, "Megan, I'm Josie. I'm here to take care of you. Can you tell me about your pain level?"

I scanned through my body. My eyes burned, my head was a time bomb waiting to explode and the smallest movements tore at my skin. Even my bones were screaming in pain.

"We lightened the meds to get you to wake up," Frankie whispered. "God, I'm so fucking glad you did." He sniffed and let out a quiet curse. If he was upset enough to cry, I was worse than I'd thought.

"Everything…" My voice was scratchy, weak and my throat was dry. I coughed, which sent a shrill of pain to my chest.

"Okay, sweetheart, I'll give you something for the pain through the IV and we'll change your dressings after." Josie's words only worried me more. Other than my eyes, how many other 'dressings' did I have? Then I remembered the cutting… Another sob came, followed by Frankie's sweet reassurances. I barely heard Josie busying herself around the room. But it didn't smell sterile like a hospital. I was somewhere private, just not at Frankie's.

A warm haze washed through my veins and started numbing my aches. Frankie laid me back down, and without the pain of every limb screaming at me, I realized I needed to pee…urgently.

"Toilet."

"Oh!" Josie, who smelled like a faint rose, bumped into the side of the bed. "I'm afraid you'll have an audience. If you carry her, I'll do the rest, Mr. Ricci."

Funny, how quickly one loses all humility when one is utterly helpless. I emptied my bladder and didn't even care that poor Josie was probably holding my IV bag above my head.

"Do you need—?"

"I think I can manage." I held out my hand and accepted the wad of toilet paper.

"She's all done."

Frankie carried me back to the bed, and with the drugs in full effect, I tried to cut through their haze and ask him some questions.

"Where are we?"

"At a friend's place."

I gathered the small amount of courage I had left. "Am I blind?"

"No, no, sweetheart," Josie said. "The bandage was just to keep you from touching your eyes while you rested. I can take it off now."

Her stomach brushed against my shoulder as she unwound the gauze from around my head. "Slowly now."

The last layer tickled my nose as she swept it away. I took a deep breath, swallowed and fluttered my eyes open.

It was evening, and the room had a warm glow. Frankie slid in next to me with an overwhelming sadness. "I love you," he mouthed for only me to see.

The tears stung in my eyes. How had he saved me? What had happened to Billy? And what about Ruby? No, if I was with Frankie, she was safe. Besides, I couldn't think about her, I could barely register what was happening to me.

"Now. Let's start on the right, shall we?" Josie guided my foot toward her, and I finally looked at my legs. A line of bandages ran the length of both of them.

Josie removed dressing after dressing, the black scabs making my legs look like a zebra. I wiped away the stream of tears. My body was mangled.

"Hey," he said, but I couldn't bear to look at him. A man like Frankie wouldn't want to be with a scarred woman like me. "I know it looks bad now, but you're going to heal."

My lip trembled and I nodded, pretending to believe him. I closed my eyes as Josie tended to the other side. When she finished, she said something about soup, but I was drowsy and more emotionally exhausted than I'd ever thought possible. I drifted away, trying to imagine my life moving forward as a broken woman.

Days blurred together, marked only by Frankie leaving my side in the mornings to go home and shower. I didn't even think he'd been training at the gym, which he probably needed and missed. Slowly, the physical pain was easing but the emotional damage intensified each time I looked at my body. I would be reminded of Billy's revenge for as long as I lived.

The night that he'd taken me only came back in bits and pieces—the guy at the bar, the cabin in the woods, him screaming for me to tell him where Ruby was. My small triumph was that I hadn't. But there was no memory of how Frankie had gotten me out, how he'd found me Of one thing, I was sure. Billy was dead, and I never wanted to speak his name again.

Chapter Thirty-Seven

Frankie

Leo sat on a leather sofa in my lobby, texting into his phone. He stood when he saw me then crossed to meet me at the elevator bay.

"We miss you at the gym." His hair was still a little wet from his shower. "And Andy's threatening to fire us if you don't come back. Apparently, you're his good luck charm or some bullshit."

It was the first time I'd seen him since I'd frozen at the sight of Megan and was unable to put a bullet into Billy Johnston's head. I punched the button on the wall then glared at my brother. His smug grin only made my blood boil hotter.

When the door to my apartment was safely shut, I finally said, "You know how bad I wanted to kill that fucker?"

"Yep."

"He put fucking scars all over her body—marked her for life." Finally being able to let out my anger honestly had the words pouring out of me, the desperation clear in my raising voice. "Not a fucking day will go by when she isn't forced to think about him!" Yelling was completely out of character for me, but if I was going to show my rage to anyone, the safest person was him. Leo wasn't afraid of me. I dropped my head back and calmed. "I promised to keep her safe. What the fuck good am I to her? How will she ever forgive me? You know I told her I love her? Me." I pointed to myself as if there was a question about who.

Leo twisted his lips then winced. "So…you're not going to like what I'm about to say, but I don't want any secrets between us."

I unbuttoned my sleeves and grumbled. His preamble wasn't exactly reassuring, and I was already in a shit mood. Plus, I wanted to get back to Megan. Her stitches were coming out and I needed to be by her side, feeding her lies about how we would barely see the marks in a few weeks.

"I told Myers to do it. I told him to take the shot." Leo stood his ground, crossing his arms.

What the ever-living fuck?

"You did *what*?" I spat out my words and stopped myself from taking a step toward him.

"I'm sorry." He lifted his hands in surrender. "I know you wanted to add that fucker's name to whatever list of shit you have but hear me out."

Even then, as betrayed as I was feeling, I couldn't be mad at Leo. He'd been my everything for far too long. I wouldn't lose him while I was seeing Megan slip away from me.

I let out a long breath. "This had better be good."

Leo walked around the island in the kitchen and sat on a stool. "It was impossible to know how you were going to find her. But the end result was always going to be the same. He would be dead."

"No shit."

"So if Megan had been conscious, you were going to show her a side of you that you've done a lot of fucking work to stay hidden. Once you see the devil that lives in us, it can't be unseen. Also, you've never *wanted* to kill anyone. You've been neutral. You never gave a fuck about those jobs."

"You killed Mac." I noted the hypocrisy but wanted to hear his reasoning.

"Yeah." He nodded slowly. "Exactly. I didn't want that for you."

"What?"

He glanced up then to me, his confident expression replaced by a sadness in his dark eyes. "The pleasure, Frankie. The evil, the…the warped fucking glee of taking a life. It's not the same feeling. It's like a high that, no matter what you do to chase it, can't be replaced. It haunts you — constantly there every time someone pisses you off. It reminds you how good it feels, how easy it is." He paused and stared me in the eyes for a long beat. "How we were born to do it."

He wasn't wrong. Back in the days that I'd been a gun for hire, there had never been emotions attached to my kills. I'd planned them in detail — but *wanting* the person dead wasn't a part of it. I'd wanted Billy dead since day one — fantasized about how I could cut him, hurt him. It *was* different. But that also meant that Leo had been suffering after Mac.

"And here I thought you had all your shit together. Why didn't you talk to me?"

He stood and tapped the counter. "Come back to the gym. It's the only thing that helps."

Apparently, I'd gotten all the sharing out of Leo for the day, but I wouldn't forget what he'd told me.

"I can't leave her alone."

"You're smothering the shit out of her. Get her home then give her space. Fi can come talk to her. She needs therapy, friends and no pressure from you. Got it?"

I rubbed my temples. I'd had a headache for over a week and sleep hadn't been very abundant. Maybe I needed my own space. "When did you get so smart?" I faked a disgusted frown.

"I pay attention. Plus I have three kids. Gym, tomorrow."

Leo was almost out of the door when I said, "Tell Andy we're not renewing his contract at the end of the month. We're all taking paid vacations."

"Finally."

The door clicked shut as he left, and I stood in my kitchen mulling over what he'd said. All I wanted was to bring Megan home and care for her. But Leo was right. I was the last thing she needed.

I dug out my phone and dialed Myers. "I need a two-bedroom in one of your safest buildings."

"Just that? And here I thought we were all even on favors." There was a teasing sass to his voice. I didn't care for it but what choice did I have? "Furnished, I imagine."

"You can give me the keys tomorrow morning."

There was a small pause while he understood that I was coming back to the gym, that—just like when his mother was ill—it had been our place to heal in our own fucked-up ways. And because I hadn't denied him in his time of need, after me hating him for so long, he would do everything in his power to make my request happen.

"Looking forward to it, old man." Anton ended the call, and I was oddly grateful for the insult. It meant there was no pity for how he'd seen me choke when we'd found Megan. In fact, he'd only followed my brother's wishes. *Holy shit.* We might have become friends.

That afternoon, I held Megan's hand as the private doctor removed the stitches from her arms, legs and torso. Apparently, Billy had been saving her head for last and Anton had managed to kill him before he'd sliced her there as well. At least she had that.

The swelling on her face had gone down, and the bruises were waning into the light purple phase. She could easily go out in public with a bit of makeup, which I knew she wanted to do. Ten days in the studio apartment with Josie and me fussing about had given her a strong case of cabin fever.

When the doctor had left and Josie was making herself a tea, I cleared my throat and confessed my plan.

"So I got a place for you and Ruby."

Hurt flashed in her eyes. "What? Why?"

A tightness clenched my throat. *Fucking emotions.* "Because we did it all wrong, and now we have to start again. Trust me... I hate this idea. I don't want you out of my sight. But—"

"Then no. I want to stay with you. I feel safe with you. No." She shook her head, but I knew Leo was right. And just like he'd listened to me about Fiona, I had to do the same for Megan. My wants, needs? None of them mattered. I had to finally put her first, for real.

"You need time to heal without pressure from me."

"You don't pressure me."

But she was wrong. I was overbearing and always got my way. I let out a small chuckle, hoping to cut the tension. "I had you living with me, ready not to have a job and make my coffee every morning. It's not an intentional pressure, but it's there."

She let the words hang in the air as she stared out of the window. "I haven't told Ruby...everything. She doesn't know about..." Megan gestured to her legs and the healing cuts.

"You should tell her. She's going to see anyway. Maybe it will scare the shit out of her—make sure she knows how far a man like Billy is willing to go. Hopefully she never meets one like him again." I wanted to reassure her about my love and our future, but that was going to have to be on her terms. Besides, Leo was right. I had been smothering her.

"I've tried to protect her for so long. But hiding facts from her only got me here." Megan let out a puffed breath through her mouth then turned to me. "You're not leaving me, are you? Backing out because the sight of me is terrifying?"

"Not a chance." I kissed the back of her hand, not sure what level of intimacy she was ready for. "But I am going to give you space to heal."

"I don't like this."

"Me neither—which probably means we're doing the right thing."

Chapter Thirty-Eight

Megan

Ruby huffed and plopped down on our couch. "It's so weird going from the coffee shop to the lap of luxury. My co-workers would never believe I live here."

The apartment Frankie had gotten us was wildly beyond our means. The two-bedroom loft overlooked the Hudson River, had a doorman and valet underground parking — not that we used that part. But yeah, I wondered what our neighbors thought when Ruby rode the mirrored elevators with her green polo, khaki work pants and visor. We definitely didn't fit in, but we were trying.

I still had a lot of guilt that ate at me. It was what my therapist and I spent the bulk of our time talking about — guilt that we were living off of Frankie, guilt that I'd somehow managed to become a victim. There was a flip side to it as well. The small resentment I had for Frankie whom—after digging pretty damn deep—I'd discovered that I was holding responsible for not keeping me safe.

Not that those emotions had kept me from talking to him almost every night since he'd said goodbye two months prior. There was no way I was ready to lose my connection to him. He knew and understood me in a way no one else ever had or probably would.

He'd gone to Florida to meet Chezzie's boyfriend then kept moving south to Costa Rica, Peru and Brazil. In a way, we were both finding ourselves without ever letting go of each other.

Normally, I penny-pinched the money Frankie transferred to the bank account he'd insisted upon opening for me. That guilt that I didn't deserve it stabbed at me each time I punched in my pin code. But knowing that I was going to see him, for a date in a public restaurant, I'd spent money on my hair and clothes. My justification was him deserving as beautiful as I could get had made it slightly easier to add new shoes to the outfit.

I was most comfortable in pants and long sleeves, and the warm fall lent itself to a tapered, silk jumpsuit. The flashy pattern was out of my comfort zone, but the material was too comfortable, and it covered every single scar. That was important to me.

Ruby grinned over at me and checked me out from head to toe. "You look beautiful. I'm borrowing that outfit if I ever get a date."

"You'll get a date. Actually, Fiona's been wanting a girl's night out. I'll set it up." I smiled and headed back to my bedroom for one last look at myself. With all that Fiona Ricci had on her plate, that woman had been a staple on my path to recovery. She'd shared her story, her own tragedy, and had given me a lot of hope that I could come out on the other end a better, stronger person—her and Carla, who had turned out to be my version of Fiona's Kimberly.

The nerves fluttered in my stomach as I checked my face in the mirror. Even though Frankie and I had stayed in touch, seeing him, having him close enough to touch would be completely different.

Eager and nervous, I was early...too early. The bartender was still preparing for her shift when I walked in the restaurant downtown. I ordered a glass of wine and sent an unsure face emoji to Ruby, who sent back an eggplant and a doughnut. *Subtle.*

The almost-empty glass hadn't done much to calm me, but when a warmth blanketed over me, I didn't need to turn around to know the man I loved had walked in the door. Thirty seconds later, that wonderful smell of his cologne brought a wide smile to my face. *So much for playing it cool.*

I turned on my stool and there he was, just as talk, dark and gorgeous as ever. He had on a tailored blue suit with a crisp white shirt open at the collar underneath. He steepled his hands and tilted his head to the side. He'd shaved his beard and was noticeably tanner than when he'd left.

"How did you get more beautiful?"

I wished that were true, but the ugly parts were just hidden. Frankie caught my hesitancy to accept the compliment but didn't understand the reason.

"Sorry. That was cheesy. Can I just say how good it is to see you? Come on. Let's get our table."

We were seated next to the window, which took away any intimacy from the date. Once we ordered, the initial nerves disappeared, and we were back to chatting like we had over the phone the previous months. But it was so much better. I'd forgotten how much he talked with his hands and how expressive his dark eyes were.

At the end of the meal, when the plates were cleared away, he interlaced our hands and kissed my knuckles. "I really, really didn't want to leave you."

I'd gone over it with Fiona, Ruby and Carla. Him giving me space had been essential for my recovery. "But it was good that you did."

"So what do we do now?"

The same question had played on repeat in my mind over the previous two weeks after I knew I was going to see him again. The answer was something neither of us would like, but I said it anyway. "Go slow, date, *talk* about things."

He cringed, but it was fake. "Sounds terrible."

"Especially the talking part, right?" I teased.

He let go of my hands and sat back in his chair then looked at me with a tight face. "There are some things I can't say, some moments of my life I won't relive."

Fiona had hinted that Leo and Frankie had a dark past, and from talking with Ruby, I knew that there were some moments of abuse that were better forgotten. I may have had scars all over my body, but Frankie's were on his soul. I wasn't sure there was anything that would heal that part of him.

"But you'll try, right?"

He grinned. "It has become blatantly obvious that I will do anything for you — so yes."

With the distance, I'd forgotten how heavy his presence was. Not that I minded it, but he was intense. It was why I'd easily fallen into his arms and let him take care of me. There wasn't much of a choice. With a man like Francis Ricci, it was all in or not. But if he was willing to take some baby steps, I was willing to let him consume me — just not in one big bite like the last time.

The waiter came with the bill and Frankie quickly paid.

"Anxious for the goodnight kiss?" I stood and tucked my little purse under my arm.

"Do I get one?" He waited for me to pass, and I was glad he couldn't see I was grinning from ear to ear.

"We'll see."

Out on the street, the air had turned cool, and the streetlights glowed above our heads. Frankie hung back, keeping his gentlemanly distance and biting his bottom lip. Resisting him was going to be the hardest thing I'd ever done.

I walked over to him and said, "Thank you for a lovely evening," then kissed him on the cheek. There was a small hint of stubble, and I decided I liked him without the beard.

As I turned to leave, he tugged me back to him with a mischief in his eyes. "Megan."

"Frankie?"

"You may have forgotten, but I am a very patient man. Don't think this will be difficult for me." His threat sent the best kind of zing through my nerves. I may have even let out a whimper. No, I certainly did, because his cocky grin was staring right at me.

I let out a small huff and said, "Goodnight."

At the corner, I hailed a cab, and when I looked over my shoulder, he was exactly where I'd left him, the same smirk on his handsome face. *Crap.*

Epilogue

Megan
Six months later…

My plan to make Frankie take it slow had completely backfired. Turned out, he had more willpower than any man in the history of men. He'd made zero first moves, and if it hadn't been for the occasional bulge in his pants, I would have wondered if he was still attracted to me at all.

It had gotten to the point that I was actually thankful for my scars. They were the only thing holding me back from ripping off my clothes and reminding him how good we were together.

We'd gone from dinner once a week in restaurants with simple kisses goodnight to watching movies at his apartment with heavy make-out sessions on the couch.

And despite his initial reluctance, we'd talked about some hard facts. I'd told him about my nightmares and waking up in cold sweats. I'd shared my massive fear of knives, and the next time I'd come over, he'd hidden all his. Maybe he'd felt obligated to tell me some of his story after I'd shared so much of mine, but slowly he was letting me in. He talked about camping trips that sounded more like '*Survivor* for kids' than a family weekend and how he'd hated the helplessness he'd experienced when his father beat his mother in front of him and Leo. It was probably the tip of the iceberg, that the darkness in him was deeper but he was sharing more than I'd ever expected.

Being with Frankie was not only wonderful, but it was also inevitable. No one would ever love me like he did, the proof in everything he did for me. He was a lot, for sure, but I was pretty sure I was ready to go all in. And for me, that meant more than having sex. It was showing him my body. Carla had suggested little by little, but I was more of a Band-Aid ripper.

I fidgeted with my hands all the way up the elevator then shook them out before knocking on his door.

He opened it with a big smile in a T-shirt and track pants.

"You're casual." I walked down the hall and dropped my bag on a barstool. His flatscreen was muted, and there was a baseball game playing on it.

"Sorry. Game went into extra innings, and I have money on it with Leo. Do you mind if I order a pizza? I didn't like the way the fish looked at the market and never got to a Plan B."

I narrowed my eyes. He was practically normal. "I'm up for a ball game and a slice."

"You're the best." He pecked me on the cheek and grabbed his phone before settling in on his couch and unmuting the sound. By the time the pizza arrived, the game had finished, and we sat on the floor and ate it around his coffee table. There was a lightness to Frankie that I'd never noticed before, and I couldn't help but selfishly wonder if it had something to do with me.

Whatever the cause, I liked it, and when I'd finished with my slice, I climbed into his lap.

"Hello." His easy grin was my happy place.

I draped my arms over his shoulders as my heart nervously pitter-pattered. "I'm ready."

"For what?" There was an easy tease in his words, but I wouldn't get sucked into his game.

"To show you everything." I swallowed over the massive lump in my throat as his regard went from playful to serious.

"You don't—"

"I need to. I don't want to spend my life hiding what we both know is there." I searched for courage in his pretty eyes.

Frankie stroked my cheek and said, "I don't need this from you."

"That's part of the reason I'm okay to do it." I stood and Frankie scooted onto the couch, his gaze never leaving my own. I threaded my arms out of my light-blue turtleneck and slowly pulled it over my head. My arms were feathered with scars, and Frankie was the first person to see them other than Ruby, my doctor and Carla. He studied them, his lips twisting with emotion. With trembling fingers, I reached for the button and zipper of my jeans then stepped out of them until I was in my socks and underwear.

My legs were the worst. The cuts had been deeper and longer on my thighs. The raised white lines of my skin made me look like an albino zebra. The emotion clogged in my throat, and after all the pain I'd been through, it was somehow worse.

"Does it hurt?" The small crack in his voice released the tear that had been threatening to fall since the jeans had fallen to the floor.

I shook my head, my hair brushing my shoulders. "Not anymore."

"Thank you for trusting me with this. I know it has taken time." He reached out to touch then stopped. "May I?"

I nodded once then wiped the tear from my cheek. His touch had never been so gentle. He ran his hand down my left thigh, and I was so happy I didn't flinch. The truth was, I was dying for him to touch me, skin to skin.

"I can't believe I let this happen to you. I'm so sorry." Frankie bowed his head into my stomach.

There had been days I'd blamed him, screamed to Carla that he'd promised to keep me safe, but rational me knew that if it hadn't been for him, I would be worse or dead.

Frankie dropped to his knees in front of me and kissed the scar below my hip. He looked up, searching for permission to continue. I nodded, and one by one, he placed a gentle peck on each scar, pausing between as if asking forgiveness. In an odd way, it was like he was claiming them, trying to wipe away any bit of Billy by making them his own, giving them new meanings.

Once he'd worked his way to both my arms, he stood in front of me, his eyelids heavy. The air between us was thick with meaning. We both knew what it had taken for me to show him my body.

"Forgive me," he whispered into my lips.

"There's nothing to forgive." I closed my eyes and nuzzled into him.

"Then marry me." He dropped to one knee. "Please."

My heart swelled. I'd known we were working our way down the path of forever, but I didn't expect him to ask so spur of the moment.

"Frankie, I'm standing in your living room in my underwear."

"Trust me. I'm two seconds away from doing something about that. But an answer would be nice."

I shrugged a shoulder. "I'll think about it."

Frankie stumbled backward with his hand to his heart. "Oh, oh, oh. She'll think about it?" He came back to standing and waggled his eyebrows. "I'm going to give you a lot to think about in that case."

Before I could stop him, Frankie had me over his shoulder, and he smacked my ass. I giggled the entire way down the hall, and it was his ability to flip our serious moment into something fun that made me feel normal for the first time in months.

He tossed me on the bed and whipped off his T-shirt. "I have been a very patient man, Miss Megan. That ends *now*."

And just like that, he flipped another switch from playful to intimate. As he crawled on the bed, his gaze pinned me in place and pierced my heart.

"I love you," I said once he was hovering over me.

"Then you'd better marry me." His kiss started tender with gentle pecks on my lips. As he explored my body, I forgot about the scars and the trauma. I was just a woman making love to the man she loved. He'd done that, given me the space to forget. Not every man would have stuck around after what had happened to me. But there was a force in Frankie that would not just lift me up, but it would hold me there.

After he'd given me plenty to think about, I snuggled into him like I'd done so many nights prior to my abduction and let out a long breath.

"Can it be a winter wedding?" That way I could wear long sleeves. I didn't want any hint of my scars showing on the most important day of my life.

"Is that a yes?" He shifted to look me in the eyes.

I smiled. "It's an 'absolutely'."

Want to see more from this author? Here's a taster for you to enjoy!

Luca's Lessons
Deana Birch & Amelia Foster

Excerpt

A silver foil wrapper tumbled down the stone walkway along the Limmat River, and Luca stepped to the side, his arms crossed. A giggling young couple with too many piercings for his personal preference hurried by, unaware of the menacing, forgotten paper. In his dark suit, crisp white shirt and matching silk navy tie, he waited.

The improperly disposed-of litter flopped one more time, trapped itself at the edge of the stone wall and, away from the light breeze, rested. Satisfied by his small conquest—surely it was his will that had brought its journey to an end—Luca smirked. He walked over, picked it up and secured its fate in a wire bin. A pestering thought of germs poked at his side, but he brushed his hands together at a job well done and continued on his path to the private bank.

While the inconvenience had been a distraction, it had been welcomed. Early and eager were two qualities he admired, but not in himself. He reached for the door of the gray, historic building at exactly seven minutes past his scheduled appointment. *Perfetto.*

After a brief check through security, including a confirmation of his identity, he climbed the two flights of stairs to the private bank of Steinmetz and Favre.

The heavy wooden doors of the suite opened to sleek metal-and-cream marble that created a stark contrast to the building's dated exterior. But the interior did not surprise Luca. He'd already seen the clean, powerful reception in the magazine article about the youngest woman entrepreneur in the history of private banking.

And it was no mistake he'd sought out Claire Favre. Young, driven and on-the-rise was exactly the kind of mind he wanted handling his soon-to-be-acquired secret business. The piece about her and her partner in the weekly publication inserted into the Sunday paper had done more than pique his interest. Fortunately, Luca's reputation and family history had provided enough of a motivation that he'd obtained an appointment without too much delay.

He gave his name to the young, just-above-cheap-suited man behind the massive desk and took a seat in the black leather club chair. Magazines in four different languages were fanned on the iron table next to him. He aligned the one on top to sync with the others and the rhythmed echo of high heels ricocheting off the hallowed walls made him look up.

Madonna mia.

The picture had done her no justice. Claire Favre's sharp hip bones pointed behind the fabric of her tight black skirt and they swayed in a hypnotizing motion as she drew nearer. The formfitting blazer matched the skirt, and a pink silk blouse formed a deep V below. Different from the photo, where her blonde locks had been loose and casual as she'd smiled, her hair was now pulled back into a low, tight bun and her lips remained firmly locked together.

Luca stood, happy his height put him at an advantage, and buttoned his jacket at the waist. The momentary shock of her in-person beauty sank into his gut. It had no business in his throat or chest.

"Herr Bernardi." She extended her small, manicured hand but barely smiled.

"English, please." Luca ignored the slight jump in his heart rate as they touched.

"As you wish." Her light shrug remained formal.

Surely a coincidence.

He narrowed his eyes.

Ms. Favre's smile grew tighter and she spun around. "My office is just down the hall."

Luca followed the banker and stared at the back of her exposed neck. He would not check out her ass, not in a professional setting where the woman deserved respect. He would not.

He did. He most certainly did. And damn it all to hell and back if his palm didn't twitch with desire.

When the penance of being a gentleman and walking behind a woman to whom he owed respect — not ogling — had finished, he squared his shoulders at the threshold of her office and renewed his purpose — business.

Ms. Favre ushered him to a cubed leather chair opposite her desk and he reached for the button of his jacket while she floated to the other side of the impressive oak plank.

A quick glance of her surroundings revealed nothing — no framed photos of her and the late husband the article had referred to or children it had not hinted at. Truly nothing. This woman was clean, uncomplicated and professional—everything Luca desired in a banker...and perhaps other things.

"Please," she said and motioned to the seat behind him. With a quick brush on the back of her skirt—*is hand jealousy a thing?*—she gracefully sat. "Tell me what brings you here, Mr. Bernardi."

Where to begin? The long and challenging path of fully respecting and refining one's own needs? The obvious motivation of a man-made success? Best to start with the not-so-shocking. One never knows.

In the warmest, most casual tone he could muster he said, "I am in negotiations to buy a business. A private club, actually. And I was hoping to keep said investment separate from my others."

Her blue-gray gaze pierced him and she drew her light, thin eyebrows together. "You have a business you'd like to hide, and you want to use my bank to do so?"

"No." Convincing her was going to take some massaging, especially since the bulk of his wealth would not be coming along for the ride. "I have a business I'd like to keep to myself, but I'd like you to handle investing and growing the worth of the account."

Claire crossed her fingers on the desk and circled a thumb slowly into the opposite palm.

"Is it an illegal business?" she asked.

"No, but it is private, much like your bank." Luca flattened his lips and fought a smile. The woman calmed herself with touch. He admired and recognized the gesture. In a cold room full of stark decorations, her softness slammed into him.

He blinked. Business. And the need to hide his new project.

"And what is this soon-to-be-acquired opportunity?" She creased her pink lips.

There was the catch. The hitch. The hard-sell.

He stared into her eyes. "A private club."

She stilled her hands and cocked an eyebrow. "A misogynistic group of racist old men smoking cigars and plotting world domination?"

Interesting choice of words.

"No." This time he allowed the smile to shine. Her spunk and terseness must have helped her along the way.

But what way? According to the magazine article, she was barely thirty years old, and her private schooling, with winters in Gstaad and springs outside of Geneva, had assured her enough wealthy contacts for life. Her path and its perks had been easy — a silver spoon and a glass slipper.

"Are women welcome in your club, Mr. Bernardi?"

Her chest rose then fell slowly.

"Very much so." He dipped his chin.

She'd mentioned it twice now. Maybe empowering women was her motive.

Luca continued, "I welcome all to my club, Ms. Favre. The members and I pride ourselves on acceptance."

This brought a slight tilt to her head and what Luca hoped was a glimmer in her hazy eyes.

"All? That doesn't sound too private."

Her objection was welcomed with fervor, the familiar heat Luca longed for in a challenge. That, and her 'As you wish' comment from reception, braided into a perfect rope of feisty and submissive — not that the powerful woman before him would ever admit to wanting to surrender herself to the will of another.

But, contrary to what were probably her beliefs, she had all the signs. Her manners were impeccable. Her attention to detail…perfection. And that softness… The gentle side of her that Luca would bet his portfolio she didn't think people saw—but he did. He knew exactly the kind of woman who sat in front of him.

"I assure you that the membership fee secures the privacy," he said with a quick nod.

"And what is the membership fee? If I may ask?"

You may. Such lovely manners.

"Fifty thousand euros initially, plus another fifty thousand a year. On top of that, there are certain benefits that members may or may not choose to acquire. But, essentially, ten million would be my earnings in the first year."

She smiled curtly. The minimum balance to open most private banks in Switzerland was usually around a million francs. With a promise of more, maybe the risk of taking on what appeared to be a seedy client would dissolve.

"What exactly transpires at your club, Mr. Bernardi?" Her business etiquette remained flawless.

Well, that would depend entirely on which room one would peep into. But there was no reason to beat around the bush.

"Exploration of one's boundaries, Ms. Favre." Luca met her stare with heavy eyes.

"Sex. You plan to run a high society sex club." Her tone was flat, almost bored.

How could she hold his gaze? He was certain she was more a bottom than a top.

"I'm interested in continuing the initial goal of the founder, who provides a safe environment for all genders to escape without worries or hassles. It has been a tradition for years that every member sign a confidentiality agreement. It covers everything done and witnessed behind the closed, or sometimes open" —he tilted his head—"doors of the club."

Claire Favre appeared to remain unfazed. Is she?

She looked past Luca and he studied the pale, sweet skin exposed from her neck to her chest. From the lack of freckles and spots, it hadn't seen much sun over the summer. He knew its shade well, the perfect cream that would flush pink with proper stimulation.

Luca lifted his gaze. He would not be caught dreaming about bunching up her skirt and examining the most sensitive areas of her body. *Business*, he reminded himself.

"Might I ask why you thought I would be the right banker for your secret investment?"

Luca was still very much denying the answer himself. The woman had intrigued more than his financial affairs when he'd seen her in the photo.

"Empowerment, Ms. Favre. We're in the same business. You want to empower—"

She raised a hand and scoffed. He'd finally rattled her.

"I fail to see how tying up women and spanking them with riding crops is empowering." Her expression must have been attempting to scold him.

Hilarious.

Ah, the misconceptions. The fantasized, glorified, utter wrongness in the perception of the lifestyle... Luca had hoped a woman of Claire's status would have been better read than what popular opinion had painted as the BDSM culture. But alas, stereotypes were indeed festering wounds.

Luca curled his index finger around his mouth and tucked the opposite hand under his elbow.

She sat behind her desk, eyes slightly narrowed and waiting, oh so patiently with her hint of challenge, for his response. The blend was intoxicating.

Before the stirrings of his under-thoughts could bubble to the surface, he said, "I'd like to prove you wrong. The best way to do that I think would be to show you."

Her eyelids fluttered and the rosy flush he'd been trying to deny he craved crept up her neck. Claire swallowed hard.

Sorry, Ms. Favre. Flexing my mental muscle is an unbreakable yet delicious habit.

"Excuse me?" she managed.

Luca cleared his throat. "There are, perhaps, images you have about what goes on in a private setting such as my future club—images that, while they may scratch at the surface of truth, do only that…scratch."

Her skin returned to its cream natural state and Luca grieved the departure of the pink.

He continued, "Why don't you visit? Take a tour. I'm sure you'll find that it's just as much a legitimate business as the pesticides that kill millions of bees every year. Hopefully, more. I assure you that no one gets hurt unless they want to." Another man might have winked, but Luca only shifted his jaw instead.

She stiffened her posture. "You want me to come to a club and watch people get spanked and have sex?"

He grinned. "You seem rather fixated on the spanking part."

She rolled her eyes.

That would never do.

"I'm not fixated on anything. I'm just wondering… If your business is so much on the up and up, why would you want to hide it in my bank, because it doesn't seem like any of your other sources of income are shifting into my vaults with it? And secondly, why then, would I take a risk on you, a stranger to me, for a venture that you would like to brush under the rug?"

Luca crossed his foot over the opposite knee and adjusted in his chair.

"To answer your questions..." He twisted the platinum watch below his starched cuff. "For starters, perhaps I am interested in having some privacy on this matter and wish to not mix it with the accounts that have been in my family for decades. I am well aware of the labels that accompany my lifestyle. I still have a sweet, aging grandmother, and I have no intention of killing her with rumors of my sex life."

Claire's hands folded once again, but this time she rolled her shoulders back and shivered.

"And secondly, I read about you. I know you are a perfect balance of risk-taker and security. Much like anyone, I'd like to see my money grow. As I have no friends who are clients of yours, I feel the risk is mutual."

She sat back and tapped her delicate thumbs together three times.

Stalemate.

Her gaze ran the length of Luca and when it met his, she gave a slight purse of her mouth. "When?"

He wet his lips.

"Friday or Saturday night. You'll need to sign a non-disclosure agreement and you won't be able to visit the higher floors. But you will get a sense that the members are as normal as you and me." He paused at the brief fantasy of her in his private suite. "And you will see the respect and consent of a tight community."

Her eyes raked over him again. A good sign? He couldn't tell.

"I'll think about it."

She rose, as did he, and he followed her to the door.

"I'll see myself out." Luca nodded. There was no way he could follow that ass down the hall after he'd discovered how her skin could blush with just a few words.

"As you wish," she said.

Despite the brakes halting in his mind, Luca exited her office.

How had she known? How could she have possibly known the symphony of music those words were to his ears?

About the Author

Deana Birch was named after her father's first love, who just so happened not to be her mother. Born and raised in the Midwest, she made stops in Los Angeles and New York before settling in Europe, where she lives with her own blue-eyed Happily Ever After. Her days are spent teaching yoga, playing tennis, ruining her children's French homework, cleaning up dog vomit, writing her next book or reading someone else's.

Deana loves to hear from readers. You can find her contact information, website details and author profile page at https://www.totallybound.com

Home of Erotic Romance

Sign up for our newsletter and find out about all our romance book releases, eBook sales and promotions, sneak peeks and FREE romance books!